Merry Christmas
to Carlyle
from "Grandma C"

AT THE SEVEN STARS

At THE SEVEN STARS

by John and Patricia Beatty

WITH HOGARTH PRINTS
AND LINE DRAWINGS
BY DOUGLAS GORSLINE

The Macmillan Company, New York
Collier-Macmillan Ltd., London
1963

Library of Congress catalog card number: 62-17330

First Printing

Designed by Ursula Suess

The Macmillan Company, New York
Collier-Macmillan Canada, Ltd., Galt, Ontario
Divisions of The Crowell-Collier Publishing Company

PRINTED IN THE UNITED STATES OF AMERICA

For
Frank and Joan Belcher
Charlie and Rose Craig
well-remembered friends in England

Contents

Designed & Engraved by W Hogarth

The
Plate

Published as the Act Directs
Sept 7 1762

mes

Foreword

THIS story could easily be true.

There could have been a Richard Larkin from Pennsylvania Colony and a Betsy Lewes from London, just as there was a real Samuel Johnson, William Hogarth and David Garrick. Prince Charles Edward Stuart, or "Bonnie Prince Charlie," really lived in the eighteenth century as did the Earl of Burlington, Henry Pelham and the Duke of Newcastle. The Elibank Plot of 1752 is history, not fiction. Lady Primrose, Alexander Murray and even Alastair Ruadh Macdonnell are names to be found in histories dealing with the Jacobite movement.

For that matter, in the middle of the eighteenth century, there actually was a tavern called the Seven Stars just off Fleet Street. Jeremy Belcher could have owned it and the group of plotters who called themselves the Society of the Stars might have met there.

William Hogarth's little brick house still stands in Chiswick, a suburb of modern metropolitan London. His home is only a few minutes' walk from the Earl of Burlington's Italian villa, known today, as in 1752, as Chiswick House. Perhaps William Craig was once the gravedigger at old St. Nicholas church where Hogarth, the painter, and his family now lie buried.

The speech of the characters in this book has been re-created from eighteenth-century literature and documents. Samuel Johnson, Hogarth, Garrick and the others, including the London cockney characters, actually would have spoken in this manner and used the words we have given them.

JOHN AND PATRICIA BEATTY

CHAPTER I

The Seven Stars

THE great lumbering hulk of a man roared out of the dark alley close by the Saracen's Head, flailing about him with his stick and kicking at the robbers with his large feet. "Get you gone, you devils, or you'll feel more of the weight of Samuel Johnson's stick. Leave poor children alone!" he bellowed. Beating at one of the robbers mercilessly, he held him off the ground by the collar and finally flung the man off to slink away after his companions. Then the big man knelt down and very gently helped a boy up from the cobblestones and stood for a long moment staring down at him. "Are you well?" he rumbled.

"Yes," said the boy, "I'm all right, sir, and thank you."

"What has England come to when brutes attack and rob infants!" the man thundered. "And just now I put a penny in the hand of a sleeping baby girl on the steps of the church, where heaven grant that she'll be safe."

"Thank you for that, too," said the boy. "Come sit down with us on the church steps, sir. The little girl, Abigail, is in my charge."

Never in his life had Richard Larkin seen a person half so strange and ugly as his huge rescuer, who obligingly sat down with him now on the steps of St. Sepulchre's Church.

"I am but of a whimsical and melancholy temper at this hour of the night, my boy," rumbled Samuel Johnson, "and it is only because I have too much good nature that I do not steel my constitution to send you and that slumbering creature off and out of my life." He pointed a trembling pudgy finger at Abigail, asleep in Richard's coat, her yellow-white head on Richard's knee.

"Sir," stated Richard humbly, "I'd like to ask your advice as well as thank you for saving me from being robbed just now."

"That is easily given. Whatever besets you, put a good face on the matter and recruit your spirits." Johnson's deep voice had a satisfied tone. "And now lad, advice given, I must find my bed before I am out of humor with you and your sister." He lurched to his feet.

"Wait," cried Richard, reaching up to catch the man's brown cloth coat. "If you walk around London putting pennies in the hands of children and protecting others from footpads, I think you might give more advice."

"Sure, I am distracted," replied Johnson with a sigh. "My compassionate temper forces me to remain to hear you out although nothing, sir, is so costly as advice or so little appreciated."

Richard shifted slightly and Abigail's head fell forward. Samuel Johnson put out a great paw of a hand and gently touched her hair and then with another sigh pulled Richard's coat higher up over her shoulders.

"Tell me, lad," he asked quietly, "what do you think an ill-looking fellow like myself could give you other than a penny for the child's morning food? I have little enough myself for my labors among the sordid animals of this London. Tell me, don't you think me the most perfectly well-made gentleman you've ever met?"

Richard drew back as Johnson leaned toward him. The man was tall and heavy, his stomach out-thrust in ill-fitting brown rug clothing. His great body constantly twitched, swayed and jerked as if it were possessed. He pushed his huge head, with its badly powdered wig slipping over one ear, into Richard's face. The lips were thick, the eyes shortsighted, and the deep pits of smallpox marked his broad, heavy face. Indeed, he was the ugliest, strangest figure Richard had ever seen.

"Nay, do not blush, lad, to tell me of my beauty. Mark my polished cheeks and stateliness of behavior. I possess uncommon marks of distinction," the man roared with laughter. Richard remained silent, glancing down at Abigail uncomfortably while Johnson laughed and at last became quiet again. "Do not pay too much account to my harshness, boy," he went on in a voice that held less roughness. "Melancholy does not always make me so riotous. When I am caught up by one of my attacks, I try to walk it away and so I wander about London alone night after night. I hold many odd conversations in the midnight hour." Johnson paused. "And now I would like to hear your speech. Look'ee, boy, forgive me my early temper."

"Are you an officer of the parish?" Richard peered fearfully at either end of Snow Hill, where there was nothing to be seen but the occasional weak glow from the lanterns, only half-filled with oil by the thieving lamplighters.

"By Gemini, no," protested Johnson. "I am no more a parish personage than I am a Hanover rat."

"You wouldn't take Abby away from me?" Richard whispered.

"Take your sister from you? Fie, sir, I would not."

"She isn't my sister, but she is my charge. Just after I left Fleet Prison I found her crying in the yard of St. Paul's where she'd been abandoned. When you gave her the penny, I had already seen the robbers coming and had gone to try and lead them away from her."

Johnson twitched and stared hard at Richard. "You are a debtor?" he marveled. "But you are no more than seventeen surely? Confound these evil times that send babies to the Fleet."

In spite of himself and in spite of the fear he felt at the awesome man next to him, Richard had to laugh. "I'm fifteen," he answered, "and I'm not a debtor, and, sir, I'm not a Londoner and no Englishman either."

"No Englishman!" cried Samuel Johnson in surprise, "but you are well spoken for a boy, and I know you are brave, so you must be an Englishman."

"I'm from Pennsylvania Colony and was sent here by my mother's family to live with her only brother when she died of fever. They thought my uncle was a rich London merchant." Richard's voice faltered.

"You have no father?" asked Johnson.

"He was killed by the Delawares ten years back."

"The Delawares? And what, pray, are they?"

"Indians," answered Richard, amazed at Johnson's question.

"Ah," mused the large man enchanted at the name, "the impudent, naked, painted savages that infest the American wilds."

Richard ignored the man's eloquence. "My mother's family sent me to London, but when I tried to find my uncle, I was ordered away from his house. His creditors had seized it weeks before. I learned from them that he'd been put in the two-penny common ward of the Fleet to rot until he paid his debts." Richard's voice rose, trembling with rage. "And how can anyone pay his debts when he's in prison? Tell me that, sir!"

Samuel Johnson snorted loudly. "There is a proper riddle, lad. I am often chapfallen at the prospects of my visiting the two-penny common ward of the Fleet, myself, for I am as poor as a rat."

"Well, my uncle isn't poor now," Richard added bitterly, and Abigail stirred at the hardness in his voice. "He died last night of gaol fever. They told me when I went to look for him today, and they asked me if I had the money to bury him."

"And, I take it, you do not?" Johnson blew out his breath and leaned back against the gray stone of St. Sepulchre's, his hands knitted together.

"No, I don't," replied Richard. "I arrived in London with only ten pennies left from my passage money."

"And I and Davy Garrick came down to London from Lichfield with two pennies and a ha'penny some years back," mused Johnson, and then he pointed at Abigail, "but I did not pick up stray babies in the highroad or the yard of St. Paul's."

"A ragged woman, who might have been her mother, told me she had to leave the little girl there, so the parish people could pick her up as a parish child, and she asked then if I wouldn't take her with me." Richard paused. "The woman said it was hard and cruel to be a parish child."

"What is the child's age?" asked Johnson.

"She tells me she's three."

"If she went in the parish cart to wherever she came from, she would never live to be four," the large man added morosely. "My melancholy grows upon me at the thought of a child in the workhouse."

"No, she won't go," Richard declared. "There isn't any parish in England that can claim me as a vagabond and as long as I can look out for Abby, I'm going to do it."

"A good Samaritan," rumbled Johnson, crowing like a rusty iron weathercock. "I do love the young people, but take care, my lad, that you do not buy trouble, for London is up to the brim with it and evil. But if you can be a good Samaritan, can I do less?"

Richard looked at him hopefully in the flickering light.

"What is your name, boy, and what do you call the poppet here? Abby, did you say?"

"My name's Richard Larkin, sir, and the child is called Abigail, or at least that's what I think she says."

Samuel Johnson shifted his position and leaned on the black polished wooden doors of the church. "I am weary now," he stated, "and my melancholy begins to wax again, so I must leave you soon. Go to a tavern called the Seven Stars, off Fleet Street, Richard Larkin, and take the poppet with you. You will find the host and his wife tenderhearted fools as I am. They could use a strong well-made lad like you to work for them, and Jeremy Belcher's wife is kind and fond of children. There will be a place in a corner of the kitchen for two vagabonds, I am sure." With an effort Johnson lurched to his feet and stood there swaying. "Tell 'em Samuel Johnson sent you. They know me well. And if you need me, lad, look for my house in Gough Square, off Wine Court Alley and Fleet Street. They all know me there. Every ale drawer on the Street marks Samuel Johnson's handsome face. Go to it, lad."

"They all know me there. Every ale-drawer on the Street marks Samuel Johnson's handsome face."

"Thank you for your kindness." Richard smiled and gently placed Abby's sleepy head on the steps. "I am your humble servant, sir." As Richard got up, he noticed Johnson's shoes. They were patched, the buckles missing, and the sole gaping enough to show the stocking.

"Please, sir," Richard ventured, "I don't really need the penny you gave to Abigail just now. I have some pennies of my own and perhaps you need it." Richard glanced at the man's shoes again.

Johnson began to twitch violently and to Richard's horror he raised his strong stick. After a long moment he let it fall, muttering, "Vanity, vanity. All is vanity, and I would delude myself once more." He turned and went, bobbing and jerking down the street.

Richard stared after him in wonder, then sat down again, his head in his hands. What could he do but go to the Fleet Street tavern? There was nothing else for him in London. He had been to the wharves as soon as he learned of his uncle's death. He'd asked of every ship bound for America if they would let a boy work his passage home, but no ship would take him under those conditions. He had no passage money of his own and he refused to indenture himself and spend the next seven years of his life as a bond servant to a stranger.

Abby moaned in her sleep and Richard frowned down at her. Why had he taken the responsibility for her, and why had the woman come up to him as he rested from his long walk from the ships to St. Paul's churchyard? He had stopped only to look at the wailing child when the woman began pleading with him to save the little girl from the parish. She had said that he had a kind face and was surely marked for great favor, judging by the fine quality of his dress.

It was true his breeches and coat were of good dark blue

cloth and of a decent but somber cut. His mother had set great pride in dressing him well, and the clothes he wore were all from her needle. Only his black three-cornered hat and his stout pewter-buckled shoes had come from a Philadelphia shop.

As for his kind face, Richard thought, no one had ever commented on such a thing before although, by London standards, it was not a face often seen. To Richard himself it was a very ordinary sort of face, square and sun-browned, for he had spent most of his life out-of-doors. His teeth were white and good, and his hair dark gold, the color of the tobacco leaves that he'd seen once in a Philadelphia shop. His eyes, beneath dark straight brows, were a steady, quiet gray-blue. His nose was straight and to his mind a satisfactory sort of nose, for no one ever seemed to notice it. Only his mouth, which was almost full and, as his mother had once said, pretty enough to be a girl's, could have given the woman the impression that he was softhearted.

In any event, he had taken the poppet to save her from the parish, for it was clear to Richard that this was a fate to be dreaded. He was glad that there was no English parish to claim him or force him into an apprenticeship he did not want.

Richard lifted his head and yawned. No matter what happened, he was determined to go back to the Colonies. In one day he had sampled enough of London. He would earn his passage money and find a good home for Abigail, just as he would for any helpless stray thing, and then he would leave this city of disappointment and cruelty as soon as possible.

Abby stirred as Richard yawned again. She opened her hand, and Samuel Johnson's penny glinted in the faint light and fell clattering onto the steps of the church.

Richard frowned. Who was this vast, palsied hulk of a man calling himself Samuel Johnson? The only thing about him that seemed real was his penny. Richard leaned over, picked it up and stuffed it into the little leather purse with his other pennies. Carefully he put the purse back inside his shirt, away from the clever hands of the pickpockets. He had watched them working, even in St. Paul's churchyard. He had worried about his purse as he carried Abigail from St. Paul's to St. Sepulchre's. But there were fewer people about here and Richard felt safer. Thanks to good fortune and summer weather, it would be a warm night for sleeping out-of-doors. Tomorrow morning he would find out if there really was a Seven Stars off Fleet Street, as Samuel Johnson had said.

Richard's sleepy eyes took in the dim tall pointed windows of St. Sepulchre's and the black bell tower high above him. Remembering where he was, he mumbled a prayer and fell asleep, his back against the stones and his hand over his chest where his pennies lay.

Several times during the night the men of the watch passed the sleeping children. Torches were held up to Richard's face, and the feeble old men shook their heads as the reddish light fell on Abby, who had crept over and laid her head again on Richard's knee.

Not long past the hour of midnight, with much rattling of doors, the bellman of St. Sepulchre's wandered out onto the church porch for a breath of pure air. He had just come up from the stifling black underground passage between St. Sepulchre's and Newgate Prison. He had rung his handbell the required twelve strokes outside the cells of the prisoners condemned to hang the following morning. With the twelve strokes he called upon them to repent their sins before they were executed. The bellman stared for a second or two at the children huddled on the church steps, then yawned and went inside. Stray, homeless children sleeping in the dangerous streets were as common a sight to him as were the terrified wretches in the condemned cells of Newgate.

Very late, some wine drinkers from the Saracen's Head tavern stumbled out into the night. Linkboys preceded them with torches to light their way. The richly dressed men did not notice the children though they passed close by, calling to each other and clapping one another on the back. While in the narrow alleys, within the very sight of Newgate, robbers waited, signaling to each other when best to attack the gay party from the tavern.

But Richard Larkin and Abigail slept on undisturbed, and morning came to St. Sepulchre's with the loud clatter of horses' hooves toiling up Snow Hill along the way to Holborn. Then came the milk girls from the countryside carrying their pails and crying out their wares before each house.

Richard was awakened by Abigail, pulling at his shirt sleeve. "Want milk," she said. "Milk! Wake up! Wake up!"

Richard called sleepily to one of the milk girls, who came over to them, and for a farthing gave both Abigail and Richard a drink of warm milk from a deep metal dipper. The milk already had specks of dust and grime in it, and it was all Richard could do to choke it down. But Abby was pleased and demanded more. The milk girl generously gave her another cup without asking for a second farthing, then she hurried down Snow Hill with her yoke and pails. Richard watched her go, touched by her kindness.

"Get up, Abby," said Richard. "We're going to go now. Take my hand."

Abigail was an obedient child. As soon as Richard put on his coat, she stood up in her ragged little brown dress and shawl and broken shoes and did as he asked. Richard sighed and felt for his purse inside his shirt. He ran his fingers through Abigail's fine, almost white hair, which was a mass of tangles, and then smoothed down his own. There was no sense brushing his coat or his shoes or in retying the club at the back of his neck, he decided. The black hair ribbon was so old and frayed that it couldn't be made to look better and it mattered little to him anyway. He was no beau or fine spark, and moreover he had no comb or brush. Despite his dishevelment, he was, though unaware of it, uncommonly good-looking, and the milk girl had blushed, gazing shyly at him when she gave Abby the second cup of milk.

Together, Richard and Abby left St. Sepulchre's, passed St. Sepulchre's Acre, went up Snow Hill past the little street of Hart Row, and on into Newgate Street. They walked by the solemn brick bulk of Newgate Prison, where the miserable prisoners called to them from small holes in the prison wall. Their voices cracked and whined as they begged or tried to sell some pitiful thing they had made in their cells. Richard shuddered. The glimpse he had had of Fleet Prison where his uncle had died had been enough for him, and the knowledge that the debtors were supposed to pay for their food if they were to survive had horrified him. To his mind, London seemed full of nothing but dark sinister streets, prisons, pick-pockets, footpads, petty thieves, and quarrelsome persons.

"Keep close by me now, Abby," he ordered as they turned down Newgate to Great Old Bailey Street, where stood the court of London justice, another grim, frowning, brick building.

London was fully awake by now. Great Old Bailey Street was thronged with people shouting and crying. The noise was deafening. Irish chairmen, their sedan chairs empty at this early hour, were bound for the west end of the city to find passengers. Burly porters carried great bales of goods on their heads and backs. Abby laughed and stepped into the street as a flock of white geese came hissing and flapping by on their way to Smithfield market. They were driven along by a perspiring, cursing country boy with red cheeks, a blue smock and a long stick. Richard had all he could do to drag her back before an elegantly dressed rider on a fine horse rode her down without so much as a look. After this Abby clung to the skirts of Richard's coat. They walked along, past the gin shops and the cellar eating houses, where the rancid smell of the food almost sickened Richard. Beggars darted about everywhere, eyeing his good cloth coat and breeches and the pewter buckles on his shoes.

Pale-faced, tousle-haired apprentices, boys of Richard's own age, stood yawning on the pavement taking down the shutters of their masters' shops and shouting curses at people to get out of their way or beckoning at them to come in and "Buy, buy, buy!" More than once Richard pulled Abigail clear of fights—dog fights among the prowling, starving curs that roamed everywhere, or fights between sailors and apprentices. They found it hard to get out of the circles of bettors and wagerers that formed as soon as a fight began.

There were few people of quality about so early. That was plain to see. Most of the people Richard saw were working-men, pock-marked, gray-complexioned, with no teeth or black stumps of teeth, stringy hair, dirty, ill-clad in rags and often barefoot. The occasional countryman on his way to market with his vegetables, eggs, live hogs, cows or ducks was at once identifiable by his fresh face and clear eyes and by the hordes of beggars and thieves following close behind him.

As they neared the end of Great Old Bailey Street, Richard

noticed slow-moving, dignified men dressed in heavy dark clothing with steel or pewter buttons and shoes with cut steel shoe buckles. He rightly judged them as important London merchants, about on business earlier in the day than usual. He didn't fear these men so much, so he stopped one of them. "Please, sir," he said, "can you tell me where I can find the Seven Stars off Fleet Street?"

"Bless me," said the man. He was red-faced and fat, with steel-rimmed spectacles, very like the great Benjamin Franklin, whom Richard had often seen walking about Philadelphia with his crowd of admirers. "Are you a hock drinker, my boy, or a notorious Tory for one so young?"

"I don't drink strong spirits, and I don't even know what a Tory is," replied Richard seriously while the man chuckled, "but there really is a Seven Stars, then?"

"Indeed there is, my lad," stated the fat merchant. "Just you go onto Fleet Street down Ludgate Hill from St. Paul's, and you will find it exactly where it's been these hundred years or thereabouts."

"I am your humble servant, sir," said Richard, sweeping off his hat and making the bow his mother had taught him. At that moment he was nearly knocked off his feet by a gang of howling, yelling apprentices as they swept down Great Old Bailey Street kicking a ball and making Londoners leap for the walls, cursing or laughing, as the game struck their fancy.

"Impudent wretches, quite out of hand!" the merchant growled, shouldering past Richard and Abby, who had taken shelter behind him.

A second later they heard a loud cry from a window above, and jumped out of the way to escape a pail of herring bones, potato rinds and dregs of ale. The fat merchant was not so quick. The foul stinking mess caught him full on his fine laced hat. He roared with fury and shook his goldheaded stick with rage at the slatternly woman who had thrown the garbage, but she only laughed and banged the window shut.

Richard caught hold of Abigail's hand more firmly and tugged her into the center of the pavement, looking about him fearfully. London was a frantic place, far more violent and dangerous than Philadelphia had been. He could not walk in the street. It was blocked with riders on horseback, carts, fish sellers, barrows, sedan chairs and cursing chairmen, porters, cows, sheep and chickens, muffin sellers, a few carriages and ragged, wolfish people of all sorts and descriptions. They milled and surged, striking out with their fists to clear the way, swaying back and forth as if drunk, and many of them were, for the gin shops never closed. The pavement behind the row of wooden posts was just as dangerous. There, pickpockets lurked, and more than once Richard felt quick hands at his coat pockets. He'd already ducked his head to save his hat from being snatched off by a tall, white-faced apprentice.

"Hurry, Abby," Richard gasped, almost dragging her along to the end of Great Old Bailey Street. They found themselves on the slope of Ludgate Hill. St. Paul's with its dome aglow in the murky morning light loomed up in front of them. Richard glanced in dismay at the crowds rushing toward them, streaming out under Ludgate itself. They'll trample us, he thought, and not even care.

"Mommy!" Abigail cried and pointed to the cathedral. With a pang for her Richard remembered where he'd acquired the little girl.

"Don't you cry, poppet. We'll buy you a doll of your own to play with, if we're lucky at the Seven Stars." He didn't dare stop to comfort her. If he let go of her hand for an instant, they'd be swept apart by the mob that grew even thicker as they battled their way down Fleet Street.

The two children were hustled along by the jostling, jamming, ill-natured crowd. Richard hung on firmly to Abby with one hand and kept close hold of his purse with the other. One day in the great city of London had taught him things that few other boys from Pennsylvania Colony knew. By the time they were finally swirled into a narrow alley that led into a dreary-looking cobble-paved court, Richard was panting, and Abby was weeping bitterly.

"Hush, Abby," Richard warned. "It won't do any good to cry here, pretty. I'll get you some cheese as soon as I can and maybe some bread, too. What about that? Will that please you?"

Without releasing Richard's hand, Abby dug her dirty fist into her eyes. She nodded tearfully and stopped crying long enough to look up at him with a tiny smile. Richard thought for the first time what a pretty, winning, doll-like child she was with her clear pale skin, silver-gilt hair and strangely slanted bright blue eyes. Why, she's like a wild flower, he thought, and wondered how she could possibly have been given away to a passing stranger. Richard shook his head. He'd never understand London.

"We'll find the Seven Stars soon, Abby," he promised her, "and then we'll see what I can do about that cheese and bread."

As he spoke Richard was jostled aside by a red-haired freckle-faced boy who came briskly out into the courtyard. The boy was about Richard's age and carried two heavy pails of steaming water which he threw over the stone steps of a dingy building just inside the dark archway. "What'cher want 'ere?" he demanded loudly. "What'cher lookin' at? And why was she a'howlin'?" He pointed at Abby, who stared back in terror and began to sniffle again.

Richard shoved Abby behind him and stood glowering at the other boy. "I'm looking for the Seven Stars. I'm speaking to you, and she's crying because she's hungry and you yelled at her. Now is there anything else you'd like to know?"

"Tom-doodle, can't you read?" The boy jerked his thumb upward and lounged against the doorpost, grinning, his green eyes alight like a cat's in his thin face.

Richard glanced up at a painted signboard hung on gilt branches not four feet from him in front of a narrow brick house. The sign carried a device of seven golden stars on a blue background. It wasn't necessary to read the words beneath.

"The Seven Stars, poppet!" Richard said. "We're here," and he pinched Abby's cheek lightly.

"I don't know yer; go along, bob. Do yer want ter fight?" the red-haired boy began. "I'm Timothy Quayle, and I'm Irish. What'cher want 'ere?"

"I don't want to fight, unless I have to," Richard replied grimly. "But if you want to fight, I'll give you the best one you ever had. I came here to see Jeremy Belcher."

Timothy Quayle's face fell. "Oh, yer want ter see the master? Who sent yer? Are yer after me place 'ere?"

Richard hesitated and then answered, "Samuel Johnson sent me, and I don't want your job."

"The Samuel Johnson of *The Rambler*?" Timothy asked eagerly. "Ever'body who comes in 'ere talks of 'im."

"What's *The Rambler*?" Richard was curious, and surprised to learn that Samuel Johnson was so well known.

The Irish boy seemed pleased at Richard's ignorance. "'Tis a journal of much lit-e-rar-ee merit," he announced, making Richard smile, for it was plain that the boy had learned this speech by heart.

"Have you read it?" Richard asked. Abby peeked out from behind him, feeling safe now that the angry words were over.

"No," Timothy said sharply. "Come along if'n you want ter see Master Jeremy. He's not so busy this early in the mornin'." Without another word he picked up his pails and stamped inside. Richard and Abby followed.

Richard looked about him. The inn's cramped, garbage-littered courtyard, encircled by narrow, grime-stained brick houses, did not impress him.

Timothy Quayle stood aside as they entered the inn. He put the pails down in the dim, narrow hallway. "'Tis a Lunnon tavern," he announced with a good deal of pride, "and 'tis got four floors to it, too. Most houses in Lunnon are tall like this 'ere one; yer see, yer got ter build up in th' air 'cause all the ground in Westminster and the city is used up already. 'Tis not like any country inn, it isn't! Do you have fine tall houses like this 'ere one where you come from? 'Cause I can tell you isn't from Lunnon or any place in Ireland, sure."

"No," Richard replied. Never in Philadelphia had he seen buildings so narrow, though some of them did have as many floors as these. He did not really like the narrowness at all.

"Course 'twas built after the Great Fire, yer knows. A lot of Lunnon burned down then. Yer 'eard all about it, haven'-cher?"

Richard nodded, for once feeling on familiar ground. Even his mother's most ignorant neighbors in Pennsylvania spoke with awe and fear of the Great Fire of 1666, and his mother, who had been a woman of some education, told him often of the horrors of that time—how the Black Death had swept over England and how the fire had checked the plague at last.

"Come along, both of yer," Timothy ordered importantly. "Don' dally lookin' and admirin' th' tankards."

Richard and Abby followed him obediently as he led the way down the dark hallway. There was time only for a brief glance at the large common room with its sawdust-covered floors, black scarred tables and strong wooden benches. On the other side was the small taproom with its barrels on trestles, and jugs and bottles and pewter tankards. Cups and leather drinking jacks hung by their handles underneath the shelves. The shining copper and pewter made Abby gasp with pleasure and reach out toward the cups, but Richard caught her away. They hastened on, past a dim narrow stairway with worn steps leading upward and then down a small flight of steps into the great kitchen of the house.

"Over there, 'tis th' master talkin' to 'is wife and th' cook-maids," said Timothy. "Jest yer go over and talk to 'im yer-self. I've done me business by yer, I'd say."

"Thank you, Timothy," said Richard, clasping Timothy's hand. The Irish boy looked astonished.

"Where'd yer say yer came from?" he asked, his eyes nar-rowing suspiciously. "Yer don' talk like us Irish in St. Giles, and yer don' talk nor act like any'un I ever seen in Lunnon afore."

"I'm from Philadelphia in Pennsylvania Colony," answered Richard.

"'Od's blood," exclaimed Timothy. His mouth fell open. He stood there speechless, his eyes goggling, until a loud bel-low from the host of the Seven Stars made him run like a deer up the kitchen steps.

Jeremy Belcher walked slowly toward them. Although the host of the Seven Stars was a short man, something about him gave the impression that he was not to be trifled with. He had the air of an old soldier, and Richard warmed to that. Jeremy Belcher's face was small, pink, very clean, and his black bristly eyebrows above sharp hazel eyes were almost fierce. They were the only things fierce about him, however. A bright red scarf was knotted about his wigless head and a long blue apron hung down over his white lawn ruffled shirt and gray breeches. His hose and shoes were black and of good quality. In one hand he carried a great carving knife, but not even Abby was afraid of it when held by the smiling host. His eyes twinkled as he looked at the little girl.

"Your servant, sir. Samuel Johnson said you might be needing a potboy," Richard began.

"Oho, you know *the* Samuel Johnson." The landlord spoke up in a pleasant voice. "And he sent you, did he? Well, he's right this time, although I don't say that I always side with his views. I do need a lad to help young Quayle. I supply food and part of an attic room to the right boy." Richard smiled as Jeremy Belcher went on questioning him. "Have you had the smallpox? Are you a runaway apprentice or a parish workhouse boy? Where is your family?"

Richard told him that he had been inoculated against the smallpox, and the host's eyebrows shot up in surprise, for this practice, though known in the Colonies, was almost unknown in England. Richard went on, recounting the story of his debtor uncle and his meeting with Samuel Johnson. Abby impatiently pulled away from his hand and ran over to the huge table in the center of the room where the host's wife was preparing a goose for the spit.

"Who is the pretty little one?" Belcher asked, satisfied at Richard's story. Richard told him the tale of the woman he had met in St. Paul's churchyard.

"Ah, that proves that you have a good nature even if little

sense," Jeremy Belcher sighed. "But I have been accused of the same, so we can keep the poppet here with the cookmaids if you work hard enough for two."

"Oh, I'll work hard," promised Richard.

"You can commence this very day," said the host. "You will take your commands from me and Mrs. Belcher. But, first, have you had anything to eat?" he smiled and watched Abby slyly pull a small piece of cheese off the big table.

"I promised her some cheese," Richard confessed, "and I guess Abby takes what she wants, but I'm not really very hungry."

"Fie upon it, I never knew a boy of your age who didn't have an empty pit for a stomach. We'll feed you both and then we'll see how a lad from the Colonies stacks against an Irish Londoner like Timothy."

He led Richard over to the chimney seat, telling one of the cookmaids to bring him the ordinary fare for apprentices: bread, cheese and small beer. Abby, sitting on the lap of Jeremy Belcher's lace-capped, pretty wife, was already being fed pieces of cheese and apple.

With his food on a wooden platter beside him, Richard relaxed and looked about the kitchen of the tavern. It was a busy place. He inspected it with his mother's eye, approving of the huge ruddy-glowing fireplace equipped with spits, trivets and mysterious pots bubbling and steaming over the fire. One of the white-aproned cookmaids stood near a haunch of beef, basting it now and then with a large spoon, while the other maid swiftly trussed fowls. Mrs. Belcher put Abby down and began stuffing a large sole to be baked in the oven at the side of the chimney. Strings of onions and other vegetables hung from the rafters at the opposite end of the room, and not far from Richard's feet lay a huge basket of crusty brown bread. A row of fresh-baked meat pies had been placed on a bench beside him. It could not have been seven o'clock yet, but the large lantern-lit kitchen of the Seven Stars gave Richard the feeling that it was never at rest and that the hearth fires were never allowed to die.

Abby came over and snuggled up against him, grinning. "Like it here," she confided in a loud whisper, and Richard smiled at her.

The inn of the Seven Stars was the most pleasant thing he'd seen in London, he decided, even if the dinginess of the place and the silent, dark, black-tabled rooms did make him uneasy. The kitchen with its bustle of activity and its yellow lanterns was almost cheerful, if you didn't look too hard into the far corners where the black shadows lurked. But certainly there was nothing to be feared from Jeremy Belcher and his wife, he told himself, and if need be, he would even fight Timothy Quayle.

Richard bit thoughtfully into a piece of bread and then lifted Abby up on the chimney seat beside him.

CHAPTER 2

The Charles Wain

"'Tis th' finest inn in th' city," Timothy Quayle announced with great pride to Richard a week later as the boys strewed fresh sawdust over the floor of the common room. "'Tis better by far than th' King's Head, th' Horn and th' Bolt-in-Tun, and 'tis said they be th' finest ale houses in Fleet Street. And Master Belcher is fer sartain th' best and kindest man you can find to work fer anywheres."

Richard nodded, reaching for a besom broom to swirl the whitish sawdust back under a black bench. Things had turned out well for him in spite of his misgivings. Abby was content in the inn kitchen, and he'd grown fond of Timothy Quayle, although he didn't enjoy sharing the cramped hot little attic room up under the roof. Timothy had finally decided not to fight after seeing Richard move a heavy table as if it weighed next to nothing. Even so, Richard was homesick for the Philadelphia he'd left months before and for his mother's comfortable two-story wooden house. He didn't like the great surging hard-faced, foul-mouthed crowds of London, and he kept to the Seven Stars as much as possible. He even refused Timothy's polite request to visit St. Giles, where Timothy's father, mother, and five sisters lived crowded into one room. Timothy now and then disappeared into that Irish section of London and came back to the Seven Stars, always happy and smiling and ready to dance a jig to please Abby; but, too, he most often returned with a black eye, a cut hand, or a missing tooth.

"Oh, we 'ad a fine row today," he would say, and Richard was hard put to understand Timothy's ideas of pleasure, for it seemed that every Saturday night in St. Giles parish the Irish filled the streets with a struggling heaving mob of battlers and called this amusement.

The work at the Seven Stars was not really difficult, mostly cleaning up after the night's business, scouring tankards, running errands, and now and then serving food, wine or ale to the guests. Timothy, who knew London well, did most of the running. The provisions—casks of ale and beer, fish, sides of beef and plucked fowls—were brought to the tavern by tradesmen, who carried everything inside, relieving Richard and Timothy of the heavy tasks. Jeremy Belcher was kind to Abby and the boys in an absent-minded, fatherly way. He seldom raised his voice to anyone and patiently gave directions to Richard, who knew nothing at all of tavern work.

The patrons of the Seven Stars were not particularly remarkable, as far as Richard could tell. Judging from their talk, there were a few who were journalists, authors, or booksellers; but most of them were sober, quietly dressed merchants who called for ale and a pork or beef pie, ate and drank in no haste or confusion, and left the Seven Stars almost as if they had never been there at all. This, exclaimed

Timothy proudly, was the true sign of a fine tavern, where drunkenness, cursing and loud behavior were never to be found.

For several days Richard watched for Samuel Johnson, but the large man did not appear. One afternoon when Jeremy Belcher was in a talkative mood, Richard mentioned his name.

"Ah, Samuel Johnson is a fine man," stated the host of the Seven Stars as he walked about the dingy taproom rapping the ale casks to see how full they were. "He is the greatest talker in all England, unless I mistake my guess, and although he is already well known, I prophesy he will become a famous man when he finishes his work as a lexicographer."

"What would be a lexicog . . .?" stammered Timothy before Richard could ask.

"Samuel Johnson is developing a dictionary, my lads," said Belcher amiably. "A lexicographer is a man who makes up such a thing, and do you know what a dictionary is?"

"No," Richard confessed and looked at Timothy.

"'Tis too well known that I can't read a'tall, so how should I be knowin'?" Timothy shrugged unhappily.

"You would have to know how to read to use such a thing, Timothy. You see, lads, if someone uses a word, or you read a word you don't understand, all you have to do is look it up alphabet-wise in Samuel Johnson's dictionary, and there is the meaning—or so people tell me."

"You mean all the A's are together and all the words beginning with B are together?" asked Richard.

"That's it exactly," replied the host of the inn, "so you see what a great and novel thing a dictionary is."

"But what if it's a word you've heard someone use and you don't know how to spell it. How could you find it, then?"

"Bless me, Richard, you are a lad of parts. I never thought of such a thing!" exclaimed Belcher, almost dropping a tankard he'd been examining for tarnish.

"Does Samuel Johnson come here often?" asked Richard.

"Sometimes he will come here day after day if he doesn't go to the Mitre or the King's Head in Ivy Lane." Belcher shook his head and his grizzled bob wig flapped a little. "And then we don't see him for weeks on end. This is one of those times. I do believe he is a very poor man although he does not complain of this, and if I dared I would not ask him to pay. I would count his conversations the finest gold and full payment for his food and ale. He is a proud man, and I dare not broach the subject."

"Yes, I know," Richard nodded. "It must be hard to repay a man like Samuel Johnson."

"Well, he may come in at any time, my lad. Keep an eye open for him and call me at once if he comes. I love nothing more than to talk with the man known already to all the ninety-three booksellers of Fleet Street."

"Even though he talks of Hanover rats and such?" asked Richard innocently, and Timothy gasped and grinned.

"What do you know of such things, boy, coming from the American Colonies?" demanded the owner of the Seven Stars.

"Very little," answered Richard, "but Samuel Johnson did speak of Hanover rats, and the King is from the House of Hanover."

For the first time Jeremy Belcher was stern. "Do not meddle in such matters, Richard, if you can help it," he said. "If you listen closely, you will hear many political opinions here at the Seven Stars, and you must not repeat any of them. Most London taverns serve as meeting houses and clubs for men of one or another political belief. Many would call the Seven

Stars a Tory inn, for not all who come here are happy with King George and his German favorites. But you must not talk. Better yet, you had best have a short memory for what you hear, for men in London take their politics seriously." And with these warnings the host departed abruptly toward the kitchen.

Timothy pulled at Richard's shirt. "Master Belcher only warns you," he said. "He carries no affection for the kings from Hanover."

"But George the Second is the King of England," Richard insisted. "Even to us in Pennsylvania he is the King."

Timothy shook his red head. "German George isn't King at all. Not every'un in Lunnon or England favors those rats from Hanover. 'Tis like Samuel Johnson said."

"You're only fourteen, younger than I am. And you're thinking about politics and kings and such things!"

"Why not?" asked Timothy. "If there's anythin' a Lunnon man loves, 'tis politics and bettin', and I'm old enough to be tucked up by the hangman fer me idears, and if'n I'm old enough to be tucked up, I might as well 'ave me idears." Timothy grinned, drew his hand across his throat, made a whistling noise, and sang in a high soft voice:

> "Shall we basely crouch to tyrants?
> Shall we own a foreign sway?
> Shall a royal Stuart be banished
> While a stranger rules the day?"

"'Ave ye ever heard th' song before?" he asked. Richard shook his head. "'Ave ye never heard of 'Jamie the Rover'?" Richard shook his head again and Timothy stared at the ceiling of the taproom, shrugged his shoulders and flung out his hands. "Ye might as well 'ave come from th' heathen Burmans," he said despairingly.

The arrival of some guests interrupted them, and Richard dashed down the hall to get the host or his wife to greet them and make them comfortable.

By the end of his first month Richard felt quite secure in the routine of the Seven Stars and he had some pennies ahead for his passage, too. He had to admit that he had found no solution for the problem of Abby. But it would take him some time to earn the rest of his passage money, and by then something might turn up for her. The Belchers might even decide to keep Abigail, favorite as she was in the kitchen. Every time he entered, it seemed she was plumped like a fat little mushroom on Mrs. Belcher's lap.

One evening, a few days later, Jeremy Belcher called him in from cleaning the steps of the Seven Stars. "We are having guests tonight in the Charles Wain and you will be required," the host said, referring to one of the private chambers upstairs. It was the English custom to name the private apartments of an inn with names like the Peacock, the Dove, the Apollo, the Tudor Rose and such, and Jeremy Belcher, as a man who appreciated literature and knew what was fitting to his inn, the Seven Stars, had named his private chambers after constellations. Richard had learned that Charles Wain was the English name for The Big Dipper. It was the largest, finest apartment, while the others, Andromeda, Pegasus and Hercules, were small rooms for patrons who might come in to settle some affairs of business or seal a bargain over a few pints of Jeremy Belcher's best ale.

"These are men of quality, and they must be treated with care," the host warned Timothy and Richard. "We do not often have men of such parts here, so the Seven Stars must show them all of its hospitality, for I value their patronage," he added significantly.

"Will they be wantin' their dinner?" asked Timothy. "Who are they, and at what time will they be a'comin', sir?"

"They are members of a new gentlemen's club, and they have a fancy to follow in everything that this tavern suggests. It is their whim to call themselves the Society of the Stars, and I do believe they plan to call each other by the names of stars, too. We shall not know their real names. The gentleman who came to me to make the appointment said they would arrive at seven."

Richard was intrigued. Timothy had told him a little of such clubs, and it amazed him to realize that grown men played at such things. Yet, Timothy had told him with some envy, feeling that the Seven Stars had been slighted when Samuel Johnson founded his famous literary group, the Ivy Lane Club, at the King's Head in Ivy Lane, instead of the Seven Stars.

"Sir," Richard asked, "will this become a club like the Ivy Lane Club? Will Samuel Johnson come? Is he to be one of the stars, sir?"

Belcher shot Richard a strange glance and shook his head. "No, lad, I somewhat doubt if Samuel Johnson will come tonight and to my knowledge, which is faint, this is not a club of that sort. These are not literary men, but highly placed gentlemen." He stooped down and wiped his hands on his apron, his voice came up muffled. "Remember what I told you a little while ago about not seeing what goes on and hearing less."

Seven o'clock came, and in spite of his curiosity, Richard was not there, for he had been sent to get ale for an old man who sat just inside the door of the common room. The man was heavy and tall, with a faintly hooked nose, hawk-lidded blue eyes and a drooping lower lip. On his head was a small grizzled bob wig, not too far from the plain style of Jeremy Belcher's, and he wore a bright blue coat above buff-colored breeches and black stockings. What most took Richard's eye was his pocket watch, an enormous silver one. The man placed the watch on the table and looked at it intently.

At a few minutes past seven, he called to Richard to bring more ale and leaned backward to stare over his shoulder up the steps that led to the private apartments of the Seven Stars. "You are having a meeting here tonight, boy?" He had a high wheezing voice that did not fit his great bulk. He held out his empty pewter tankard, his eyes sharp on Richard's face.

"I don't know," Richard replied, recalling the host's warnings. The stranger only smiled and Richard had the uncomfortable feeling that the man knew he had lied.

Richard hurried to the casks of ale and found Timothy, his eyes popping with wonder and excitement. "Did ye see the quality comin' in?" he asked. "Five of 'em 'ave a'ready come in, all wrapped up to th' ears in black cloaks and black hats, and one of 'em is Irish, I can tell ye."

"How can you tell?" asked Richard, drawing off the foaming ale and twisting the wooden spigot tight again.

"Well, I'm Irish meself, and I 'eard 'im askin' th' way to th' Charles Wain."

Richard shook his head. This was something he couldn't do, even if he could read. The many sounds and dialects of London baffled him; it seemed that everyone who lived in England could be identified or recognized by the way he talked. In a few seconds Timothy or Jeremy Belcher could identify a man from York, Devon, Cumberland, Lincoln or Lancaster. They could even tell what part of London a man came from.

"So, he's an Irishman." Richard straightened up with the tankard of ale and was confronted by a fat, important-looking man, puffing out his pink cheeks, and holding his black cloak closely about him.

"The way to the Charles Wain at once!" The man acted as if he were accustomed to ordering people about.

Timothy sprang forward with a low bow. "You are welcome, your Lordship, and 'tis my pleasure to show yer to th' Charles Wain. You shall be served immediately. Pray, follow me, sir."

Having recited the speech Jeremy Belcher had taught him, Timothy bounded upstairs followed by the important man. Richard looked after them, impressed by the rich purple satin of the gentleman's breeches and his scarlet stockings.

A moment later Timothy bounced down again, his eyes alight with wonder. "Ah, ye should be seein' th' fine raree show of velvets and silks up there," he said. "They'll be wantin' their dinner late, and now they're a'callin' for canary wine."

"Was that a real lord?" asked Richard, still standing with the tankard of ale.

"Who knows?" Timothy danced a little jig. "But they are

fine folk, I do believe, and there may be somethin' silver in it for th' two of us, Dick." Timothy paused and looked at Richard, grinning. "'Tis a strange thing, though. They all called for canary and then they asked fer a big punch bowl of water."

"Maybe they're going to mix the wine and the water."

"Not likely they'd water wine even if canary is strong stuff," Timothy said archly, winking, and then getting down a punch bowl from the shelf. "I'll fill this'n with water, jest as they say. It pays us ter humor fine gentlemen. Then, I'll call the master ter serve 'em the wine."

"I'd better be taking this ale to the common room." Richard turned around and stared across the narrow hall. The man in the blue coat was glowering at him impatiently.

Frightened, Richard started across, when a second man flung inside the inn and collided with him. The ale spilled down over his black mantle. The man muttered a curse, picked Richard up by the collar and hurled him into the hallway without another word. Richard caught the gleam of black eyes under a black hat. There was a flash of dark red and the gleam of a gilt sword scabbard as the man ran up the steps three at a time.

Timothy rushed to help Richard up, ale-stained and shaken.

"What did I tell ye about th' quality?" he asked, almost proudly. "They don' suffer anythin' from anybody, and they don' even see th' likes of you and me."

"It was an accident." Richard wiped his face where he had cut it on the stair rails. "Why did he do that?"

"Ah, 'tis a proud gentleman," went on Timothy, "and yer did spill ale on 'is fine black cloak."

"I didn't mean to. He must know that."

"I been tryin' ter tell ye, Dick. I said 'e was a fine gentleman and 'e didn' even notice ye." Timothy dabbed at the corner of Richard's mouth, which was bleeding a little. "'E may well be one of th' finest men in England."

"I'm no Englishman, then . . ." Richard stopped suddenly as the large man in the bright blue coat came out into the taproom.

"Where in the name of Beelzebub is my ale?" he thundered.

"'Twill be right along, sir," promised Timothy, turning as white as his apron. The large man looked terrible in his anger. Timothy swiftly drew a second tankard of ale and took it to the man, who grunted at him and went back to his seat.

"Rest a bit, Dick," Timothy ordered. "I'll go after th' master ter serve the canary and I'll carry th' water up before we 'ave troubles from upstairs, too. Then yer can go up ter serve later on."

Richard nodded and sat down on a stool in the taproom. He didn't want to go up to the Charles Wain now, but he knew that he would have to, if Jeremy Belcher ordered it.

Just then the host came hurrying back down the steps with two empty wine bottles in his hands and Richard stood up, resigned to his tasks.

"Go up and see to the gentlemen, Dick. Timothy will be down shortly to draw ale for the common room. And Dick, take two more bottles of canary with you. The eight gentlemen will be wanting more while Mrs. Belcher dresses their dinner."

"Eight?" asked Richard. "I thought there'd be only seven."

"Well, eight it is, and all fine folk, too," Belcher shoved a silver tray with two open bottles on it into Richard's hands. "Up with you, boy, and remember how I told you to serve the wine. These gentlemen will notice and take kindly to the Seven Stars if you do well."

Slowly Richard climbed the dim, winding stairs and even more slowly moved along the black passageway that led to the Charles Wain. Even at that distance he could hear the voices of the club members. They sounded as if they were quarreling.

Reluctantly he opened the heavy door of the apartment and went in. The Charles Wain was brilliantly lit with a dozen of Jeremy Belcher's best wax candles set in silver candelabras. Richard wanted to cry out at the array of colors before him, the gleam of gold, silver and jewels. The dark wood-paneled room glowed as it never had before and a grand fire crackled red on the hearth.

Richard moved across the apartment and placed his tray on the sideboard where Timothy Quayle stood, his hands folded before him, a look of great satisfaction on his face.

"A fine lot, aren' they?" Timothy commented quietly. "Take a good look at 'em, Dick. They won' be noticin' th' likes of us. I filled their glasses not a minute past."

Richard looked about him with interest. Seven men were standing in Jeremy Belcher's finest apartment, all elegant and all talking loudly.

Three men stood at the far end of the room, grouped in front of the fireplace. They were strangely assorted. One was a tall, thin individual wearing a wrinkled cream-colored, gold-embroidered coat, white satin breeches, white stockings and shoes with diamond buckles. Strangely enough, his coat was covered with dark wine stains and his lace was brown with dirt, snuff and London grime. His wig was unpowdered, uncombed and slipping, and as he raised his glass, drained it and ran his pale tongue around the inside, Richard noticed a great red stone gleaming on one clawlike dirty hand. Suddenly aware of Richard's interest, the man glared at the boy with small, angry eyes. His face was long and melancholy and so covered with pockmarks that Richard shuddered.

The voice came thick and harsh over the other conversation. "The potboy marks me out, it seems. The insolence of the city scum these days. A potboy thinks he is as good as a lord."

A man in bottle-green leaned forward. "Pay the boy no heed, Capella. What does it mean if a tavern boy stares?" There was a note of warning in the speaker's voice and he shot a hard glance at Richard.

Richard turned quickly and pretended to look elsewhere, watching the men out of the corner of his eye.

The man in bottle-green was still quite young. He wore a plain cloth coat, a black stock, sober black breeches and stockings. He was not tall but he carried himself erect and Richard approved of his dress, for he wore no wig. His reddish hair was caught at the nape of his neck by a thin black bow, and his face was pug-nosed, good-humored and open. The most distinctive thing about him was his pinned-up coat sleeve. He had but one arm.

Strangely enough, the expensively dressed Capella obeyed his one-armed companion. He mumbled something indistinct, which seemed almost like an apology, and Richard caught the name "Betelgeuse."

So, the one-armed man was called Betelgeuse. Capella and Betelgeuse . . . little as Richard knew of astronomy, he recognized these as the names of stars.

The third man was not at all like the other two. He was tiny, garbed like a beau all in black brocade, his thin shanks resplendent in scarlet stockings. He wore a huge powdered wig, far too large for his small face, and the wig's large black bow at the end of his queue was too big for his scrawny neck.

With his rabbitlike face it made him slightly ridiculous. His reddish eyes blinked and the tip of his pointed nose was pink with nervousness. Despite the richness of his frock coat and the fine white lace at his skinny throat and wrists, he looked ill at ease, although whether he was more uneasy or angry, Richard could not tell. Of the three, he alone held no wine glass and as Capella grumbled to Betelgeuse, the little rabbit-like man flicked open a small silver box and took a pinch of snuff. At once he sneezed and Capella boomed, laughing, and hit him hard on the back. The man in black was almost felled.

"Don't do that," he squeaked. "Aren't things bad enough?"

Timothy hissed into Richard's ear. "See th' fine sparks by th' table, Dick. Have ye ever seen such a raree show in th' Colonies?"

Richard shook his head. "No, Timothy, I haven't," he whispered. "Do you know any of them?"

"Naw, but I think they are important."

"Well, if they aren't important, they certainly act as if they were." Richard recognized two of the other men at once. He had seen both of them downstairs. One was the fat man who had asked the way to the Charles Wain; the other was the stranger who had so rudely thrown him aside to get up the stairs.

The fat man, like the others, had taken off his black cloak. His purple satin coat and breeches shone rich in the candle-light. His fine coat, its silver lace aglow, was almost too tight, showing a prodigious amount of gold thread waistcoat over his large belly. Although he wore a smart well-powdered Spencer wig, he reminded Richard of a hog stuffed in satin, for his pink face was almost snouted.

He clapped one plump hand across his stomach and laughed heartily. "Ah, good Sirius, tell us the rest of the tale. What did our King say then?"

"Nothing, Arcturus. He only smiled and said that his audience with us was at an end."

Sirius turned and Richard got a good look at the man who had shoved him. He was tall and reminded Richard almost instantly of an Indian. He had seen the same expression on captive Delaware braves and the same burning insolent grace in their gestures. The man's dark red velvet coat was rich and the deep color suited him. He must have known it, for that was the only color he wore except for the snow-white lace at his wrists and throat. He had a long hard face, brick-red, with heavy curved black brows above piercing dark eyes. His wig was immaculate and gave an additional hard stonelike line to his head. Yes, he's like a Delaware, Richard decided silently. Here was no man of peace and gentleness, even if he was a great nobleman and knew the King.

"It is possible, Arcturus, that the King may have been speechless. But what of the Prince?" A fairhaired man to the left of Sirius broke in. He was unusual-looking, young, full-faced, with eyebrows so pale that they almost did not exist and eyes of such a light blue that in the bright candlelight they were nearly opaque. His mouth was crooked in a waxy white face and his expression was cold and fishlike. Richard didn't like the looks of him despite his handsome athletic figure, his airy gestures and his elegant green and silver brocade coat and breeches and fine laces and ruffles. A popinjay, thought Richard, as the young man delicately waved a scented handkerchief in the air.

"Yes, did the Prince have no comment at all, Sirius?" Fat

Arcturus clapped his hand on the shoulder of the elegant young man in green and silver. "Antares, here, has the right of it. Surely, the Prince said something."

Sirius turned to a tall thin man, who stood protectively at his elbow. "Spica will bear me out. He saw the comedy, too. The Prince said only one thing."

"What was that?" asked the elegant Antares. "Did he call for wine, Spica, and let the matter pass?"

The tall thin Spica did not answer. He only nodded. Richard found his appearance chilling. Unlike the other three standing by the oval table, Spica was severely dressed. He wore a scarlet cloth coat, a black military stock, a military bob wig and buff-colored buckskin breeches and halfboots. Like Jeremy Belcher, there was the look of the soldier about him. Perhaps it was the scarlet coat, so often worn by soldiers. His face was sharp-planed and dark-featured. His mouth was a slit, his teeth sharp and white as he smiled quickly, agreeing with Sirius. Then the smile vanished and his cold dark eyes darted around the Charles Wain as if searching for something. They rested for a long moment on the rabbity little man in black and then flicked back at last to the group of four by the table.

Richard recited the names and laughed to himself. Capella and Betelgeuse, wine stains and one-arm; rabbity-face with no name; Arcturus, hog in satin; Sirius, Indian in dark red velvet; Antares, silver-green popinjay; and finally, Spica. Richard shuddered. Now, he knew what had struck him most about the last man. He reminded Richard of a snake, and a deadly one at that. But that was still only seven. Richard counted to himself. Jeremy Belcher had said that there were to be eight guests.

Suddenly fat Arcturus called out loudly to the others,

"Come to the table, sirs. Let us forget our differences and drink again to the King."

"Without Rigel?" Antares simpered. "He may not be pleased."

"He's late," said Sirius. "He knew the time appointed."

Then Betelgeuse approached Sirius and whispered into his ear.

"Ah," said Sirius, nodding agreement. "It seems we are to go ahead." He snapped his fingers at Timothy Quayle. "Fill our glasses, laddie."

Timothy bolted away from the sideboard with one of the bottles of canary wine in his hand. His red hair afire in the candles' glow, he hastily refilled the wine glasses. The guests took their places at the oval table, each man standing at his chair. Richard stood back, out of the way. Timothy knew better than he what to do. He marveled at Timothy's proper expressions of regret, teasing and hurt when the little man in black refused the wine.

Between Betelgeuse, the one-armed, and foppish Antares there was a vacant chair. The little man in black brocade tried to sit in it, but in firm fashion Sirius took his arm and led him to a place between himself and the snake-eyed Spica.

Once more Arcturus proposed a toast to the King. Sirius replied, calling out. "Aye. *Slaint an rey*. Over the water!" and six of the men passed their glasses reverently over the bowl of water before drinking.

Timothy brushed by Richard as the men drained their wine. He winked knowingly and whispered, "They aren' drinkin' th' health of any of th' Hanover breed. I got ter see ter th' common room, Dick," and before Richard could answer, Timothy was gone, leaving a bewildered Richard to serve the Society of the Stars all by himself.

The seven gentlemen had just seated themselves with a great crashing of chairs when a man appeared from the dark hall. He, too, was dressed in a long black cloak and a black three-cornered hat. As he entered, Sirius, Betelgeuse and Antares rose to greet him. "Come in, Rigel."

Richard looked at him closely. So this was the eighth guest. Obviously, he was a person of some importance.

"Pray, sit down, sirs," the newcomer said in a deep voice as he removed his hat and cloak.

Richard took an extra glass from the sideboard and filled it, placing it uncertainly at the empty seat. The man smiled wearily at the boy, sighed, and sipped his wine.

Rigel was not a young man. He wore a long wig, the sort of wig older dignified Londoners sometimes wore. His coat was sky-blue with plain silver buttons. His eyes were a steady bright blue, his mouth sad and compressed in a square frank face. Rigel had the air of a large but well-bred dog, Richard decided. The long wig added the final touch, spaniel's ears.

Slowly Rigel seated himself. He nodded to each man in turn and reached out to grip the one arm of Betelgeuse, who grinned at him in affectionate welcome.

"Did you have a rough passage?" Betelgeuse asked in concern.

Rigel shrugged. "The usual weather. I expected it." He turned his head and nodded to the little rabbitlike man. "Ah, sir, it is good to see you here. I am glad you are of our society."

The little man in black spoke sadly. "I would rather not have to tell this to you, sir. But I do not favor the scheme."

"Now, sir, do you take our characters for a jest?" Antares leaned casually on one elbow, waving his lace-edged handkerchief.

The little man grew angry. "Yours, sir, I do. I take it for a jest as should all who know you."

Antares was not offended. He only giggled and fluttered his handkerchief again. "Come away now, sir. Join us. Make Rigel and Betelgeuse happy. They have come from far away to be with us tonight. Shall we find a suitable name for our little friend here who appears dressed as a black corbie at our feast?" The blond young man crooked his finger gaily at Richard. "Boy, do come fill our glasses. Let us drink now to our association and its success."

Richard was afraid among such powerful and somehow sinister men, but he circled the table and filled the glasses without spilling a drop of the pale yellow wine. The man in black put his hand over his glass again refusing to drink. Richard noticed that his thin violet-veined hand trembled.

There was tension in the air of the Charles Wain, and hatred. Richard could feel it, could almost smell it. He felt himself holding his breath as he watched the little man try to make himself as small and inconspicuous as possible in his heavy wooden chair.

Sirius spoke up in a deep musical voice. "Now, Antares, put away that silly handkerchief of yours. Act the man. Do not quarrel with our good old friend. Give him a name. He'll change his mind and be one of us." Sirius stroked his red velvet arm. With the last words his voice had gone hard and metallic.

Antares carelessly stuffed his handkerchief into the pocket of his silvery coat and a strong scent wafted across the table to Richard. He arose daintily and inclined his fair head. But his tone had changed; his voice was accented now, soft, slurred and dangerous. "Oh, come, sir," he cajoled. "You must join our society and take the name of a star as we do. Some of these fine gentlemen you may already know. Others are strangers to you, I believe. If you know their true names, you are honored." Antares snickered and Betelgeuse, Rigel and Sirius looked up angrily. But Antares went on smoothly, pointing to Sirius. "In red velvet, our society's founder and London leader. He has taken the fitting name of Sirius, the dog star, the brightest star in the firmament. On the other side of you is a brave man, who still wears his scarlet soldier's coat. We call him Spica although some do say Procyon, the little dog, would suit him better."

The little man in black interrupted. "Save me your drunken prattle, sir. I know Spica's sort well enough. I daresay I know every inch about the blackguard of a fellow."

Spica let out his breath and started to get to his feet; Sirius rumbled a warning at him and Spica leaned back, smiling, never taking his eyes from the little man who had insulted him.

Antares cocked a white eyebrow at Spica and went on in an oily voice. "Across the table we have Capella with the usual wine stains on his coat. Him surely you mark well enough, for he is of this city, too. Then we have our fine but fat Arcturus, who should find a new tailor, I suggest, for his purple coat is rather tight and his waistcoat is of last year's pattern." Arcturus blinked at Antares, his mouth quivered angrily. "Next to Arcturus is our affable and handsome Betelgeuse in bottle-green, although he is no lover of the bottle, like others I could mention. And finally in a befitting sky-blue, wise Rigel. As for me, I have chosen the name of Antares the Red." He swept a low bow. "Sir, you must remember our names, I fear, for we do not put out the transactions of our society in ink, for reasons you well know. You must remember us by these introductions."

For a moment Antares stood swaying a bit, a puzzled look on his face. He scratched his head with an elegant white finger. "Demn, I do forget some. The heavens are positively full of us these days. I forget Polaris and Deneb, who ride soon to the north. There's great Regulus in France, the hope today of our cause. The lady Vega and lords Mercury, Aldebaran and Fomalhaut are here in London but not of our company tonight." He paused for a long moment, then he began to tick names off on his fingers and a diamond winked on his left hand. "Ah, there's Altair and Castor and Pollux in Prussia, and we must not forget our friend and benefactor there, Mars himself, who supports us. But best of all for our purpose, there is the Sun in France! So, you see, sir, we are a goodly company already and there are thousands ready to join us."

"Keep your tongue in your head, you fool," warned Sirius. He leaned forward, gripping the arms of his chair. "You talk too much."

"But what does it matter?" Antares sat down with a flourish. "Our reluctant friend here knows of the affair set for the tenth of November. You told him yourself, my dear Sirius. Surely, he can guess it all. Any child could do that. But as yet, we still have no name for our little friend. There is always Procyon, the little dog, not yet adopted by anyone." He looked at Sirius in mock concern.

"Damn your eyes, you whey-faced jackanapes," thundered Sirius, "and damn your blood, you endanger our cause by your loose talk. Sober yourself." Sirius reached across the little man, picked up the punch bowl of water, and threw it over

Antares, who sputtered and shook his head, sprinkling drops of water in all directions.

With cold dignity Antares got up, drew his handkerchief from his coat pocket and daintily mopped the soaked shoulders of his fine silver-green coat. Richard, standing to one side of him, watched as a scrap of paper fell out of his pocket to the floor. Richard moved quickly, picked it up and stuffed it into his own pocket with the thought to return it later. Perhaps Antares would reward him well for retrieving it. Richard felt in his pocket and heard the crunch of good paper. It might be a note from a great lady.

Antares' eyes jumped at Richard's quick movements, but he turned back to the group with angry composure and spoke slowly. "I shall, of course, require the services of a second, for I fully intend to call out my friend and beloved countryman for this insult. Who will act as my second? You are all witnesses to a just cause for a duel. My honor demands it."

"You will find no seconds here, you young ape," Rigel cried out frankly. "There are things far more important at stake than the honor of a hotheaded fool. Regulus and the Sun require better service from you than this, and if you must spill blood, spill it for them. Sit down. Sirius did rightly and I trust you are sober now. He is your leader. Obey him."

"Sirius will rue tonight, nevertheless," Antares muttered. With his hand on his sword, he reseated himself and glared at Sirius, who only laughed at his words, throwing his head back until his white wig touched the deep red velvet of his coat.

The little man in black drummed nervously on the table with his fingers. "Sirius will regret many things soon, I'll warrant." He blinked his eyes rapidly.

"Enough of this. Send the boy to see what has happened to

our dinner," Arcturus patted his stomach. "Good food goes a long way to soothe ruffled feathers." He glanced at the man in black brocade and sighed; then he mopped his pink forehead with a handkerchief.

But the little man was not to be put off so easily. "I can see the block and ax on Tower Hill looming before you all. Or have you forgotten the heads that rotted on the spikes of Temple Bar a few years back?"

Rigel beckoned to Richard. "See to our dinner, lad," he said kindly.

As Richard hurried out, he could hear Rigel's deep voice speaking slowly and deliberately. "Our martyred lords, Kilmarnock, Balmerino, Derwentwater and Lovat. How shall we forget such men? I can vow to you that the Sun does not forget."

"Ah, but our Regulus, the prince of stars, does forget," Antares said acidly. "Often he forgets those who have suffered for the cause."

Richard shut the door as a babble of voices answered Antares. He dashed down the steps and into the kitchen. "The gentlemen upstairs are calling for their dinner." Mrs. Belcher nodded, and cried to the cookmaids to hurry with the dishes.

Jeremy Belcher hastened in. There was no time to talk. He plunked a large joint of roast beef, pink and juicy, onto a great silver plate and passed it to Richard. "Wait a moment, lad," he ordered. "I shall bring the leg of mutton with caper sauce, and Mrs. Belcher will carry the roast pike with fennel. Then the maids can bring up the rear with the plates, cutlery and napkins. My wife and I shall serve the gentlemen, and you and the maids can come down again and bring up the roast dumplings, the cheeses, the bread, the cabbage and carrots and the syllabub. Once you've taken the joint in, you can bring four more bottles of wine, two claret and two Portugal. I trust that Timothy can take care of the common room until the guests in the Wain are served."

They flew about the kitchen and at last all was ready. The little procession climbed the stairs, past the common room. Richard looked in, wondering if the large old man with the silver watch was still there. He couldn't see him, but there were other customers and Timothy was running from table to table as if he were in Bedlam madhouse, his freckled face red with the effort.

They went on up the stairs and into the Charles Wain. All but three of the guests greeted Jeremy Belcher's fine dinner with loud cries of pleasure and fell to their food with enthusiasm. These three sat in a row, the candlelight splendid on their scarlet, black, and silvery-green coats. Spica was watchful; the little man in black was clearly frightened, and elegant Antares sulked moodily.

Richard and the two cookmaids put down their burdens and ran back down the steps almost stumbling in their haste. There wasn't even time to speak to Abigail, who sat sleepily in one corner of the warm kitchen, chewing on a leg of duck. She should be in bed, Richard thought with a sigh.

They picked up their second load and up they marched again. Richard refilled fresh glasses with the heady dark red wine. Then he moved close by the door where he could see all of the guests clearly. Except for the three, the gentlemen ate quickly and with good appetite, wiping their sharp knives on their napkins and speaking little. In no time at all, they were finished. Arcturus, Capella and Rigel pushed their chairs back away from the table, called for live coals from the hearth and for the host's finest white clay pipes. Jeremy Belcher proudly took them down from a rack above the fireplace.

The host, his wife and the maids cleared away the remains of the dinner, pleased with themselves and with the heavy purse Sirius tossed to Belcher. All had gone well. Before they left, Jeremy Belcher nodded at Richard and pointed, making it clear to the boy that he was to stay behind and serve the guests should they need anything else.

All was quiet for a few minutes after their departure, then the little man in black stood up. His voice quavered, "Do not trouble yourselves, sirs, to find a proper name for me. I convey my apologies to your worthy Rigel and Betelgeuse and they will always have my respect. Perhaps I shall meet them again someday under happier circumstances." Rigel looked mournfully down at his pipe and puffed thoughtfully. The little man blinked and went on, "As for Capella and Arcturus, I believe these gentlemen to be misguided. Your Spica knows in what little esteem I hold him. As for you, Sirius, you aim too high without the qualifications for it. You are not the man for this perilous business. And as for you, Antares, I do not quite know what to make of you. Indeed, you are a jest. Does any man, or more to the point, woman, know what to make of you? No! I cannot espouse your cause. I do not find it wholly detestable, as you have occasion to know of my cooperation in the past. But upon sober reflection I am convinced that the cause has grown cool. It cannot succeed. There was hope in 1745. Today, 1752, there is none. I shall take my leave of your society while I may, sirs. I do not hold with regicide!"

Antares cried out first, his voice thick with anger and a new accent. "So, ye'll depart to blaze the thing all over London, will ye, and have us taken up? Aye, ye'll clype soon enough."

The rabbity little man trembled visibly. His voice shook.

"That is a gross and scandalous lie, you young coxcomb. I shed my blood for our rightful King not seven years past. There is no slur upon my loyalty as there is upon others I could name of this company. Make yourself easy on that head."

"Leave him be, Antares," Sirius ordered. "He cannot steel his constitution to the task before us. He has grown chicken-hearted in his counting house. He should have given his life on Culloden field before he came to this end. The contemptible wretch is of no use to us or our cause now. We cannot trust him."

"Oh, Antares is right," mumbled Capella, through his long melancholy face. "He will blaze our plan all over England even if he says otherwise." The others nodded in agreement and Capella reached for more wine, pouring a red flood of it over his satin breeches.

"Who is not for us is against us in this matter," Arcturus shouted. A shine of perspiration broke out on his fat pink face, and he banged a fist on his purple satin knee.

Sirius spoke in an unfamiliar, harsh language. Betelgeuse shook his head violently in protest as Spica nodded and began to rise. The little man in black cowered, his mouth fell open in horror, and he raised his trembling hands protectively.

Richard felt a cold breath of fear in the room. Capella, Rigel and Arcturus did not seem to understand the words their Indian-faced leader had spoken, but Antares did. For he laughed strangely.

"Ah, no, my friend Spica," he said softly in English, "not with a claymore!" and he clucked his tongue in disapproval. "This has been in my family for such business for many years." He reached inside his silvery coat and passed something under the table to the other man. Richard saw the glint of a strangely shaped knife.

In one deadly movement Spica turned and plunged Antares' dagger deep into the throat of the little man in black. It was finished in a second. There was no struggle at all. A fountain of blood spurted over the table. Spica jerked out the red-stained dagger and with a cold smile stabbed it into Jeremy Belcher's fine table.

The shocked silence was broken as Spica's eyes fell upon Richard. "Catch that boy! He saw!" he roared.

Antares snatched up his dirk from the table top and Richard leaped forward and tore open the door. The dirk thudded into the door jamb as Richard dashed headlong into the hall with Spica and Antares only steps behind. As he ran, Richard heard the slither of a sword leaving its scabbard.

Cut off from the stairs by Spica and Antares, there was only one way to go—along the black corridor to the other apartments. If he could lose them there in the inky dark, he could make his way to the roof by way of a hidden stairway. Richard ran. His heart beat violently. With a surge of hope he spied a candlelight; the door of the Pegasus apartment was opening. The light went out abruptly and his coat was caught by a very strong hand. Richard was tossed head over heels into the blackness of the Pegasus. He lay there on the floor panting as the pounding feet in the corridor slid to a sudden stop.

Richard heard the faint click of the door, then the murmur of several voices, and the rumbling, wheezing words. "No, I've seen no thieving boy. Though someone ran on down past here just a minute ago. Look'ee, curse your livers. I don't lie to you."

The footsteps departed, and Richard sat up, shaking with

fear. The door to the Pegasus creaked open and closed quietly as someone slipped back into the room. "Boy," came a hoarse whisper, "stay here until it is safe for you to leave. They'll be sure to post a guard at the top of the stairs. Is there another way out?"

"Yes," said Richard. The man's voice sounded strangely familiar. "I can get to the attic from this room. There's a staircase behind a wall hanging, sir."

The stranger was satisfied. "So, heaven will provide for you after all?"

"Don't go. You saved my life, and I don't even know who you are," Richard whispered.

"Call me Saturn," the man chuckled in a strange, soft way. "The name is doubly fitting. I call myself that to fit this tavern's name and its politics."

"Are you one of the Society of the Stars, then?" Richard's heart pounded. His eyes hurt from straining to see in the darkness. He was certain now that he had heard that voice before.

"Not I, but I know much of that worthy club. Say, rather, lad, that I may tuck them up. That's what the planet Saturn does. It's the planet of death and outworn things. Yes, I'll tuck them up."

"You must be the hangman!" Richard gasped. He knew well enough from Timothy's gruesome tales what "tucked up" meant.

"Not quite, but some have called me that. Now, hide yourself, for they will surely kill you as they have killed others before."

"Did you know the man they just murdered, then? He was a nervous little man in black."

"Ah, yes, I knew him well. I saw him enter that room tonight," the rasping voice held little surprise. "He was an insignificant fool, and do not be one yourself, boy. These are weighty matters, for the game is deep. Take the advice of one who knows. Leave this tavern at once and forget what you have seen and heard."

"But, the watch! Won't they be called because of the murder?"

Saturn's voice was contemptuous. "Not until it suits the purpose of certain men and very likely not even then. It does not suit my purpose either to call those fumbling old fools into this matter. Your little man in black will be found somewhere far from this tavern, if he is found at all, which I doubt."

"But they'll get away with it! They'll get away with murder!"

"That they will not. That I can promise you, or I am not Saturn, who takes or 'tucks them up,' whatever you please to say."

With these words the door to the Pegasus apartment closed without a sound, and Richard listened to slow, heavy footsteps going away toward the stairs.

CHAPTER 3

To Chiswick

I SHOULD have asked him why he saved me, thought Richard as he squatted on the roof above the attic room he shared with Timothy Quayle. And who is Saturn anyway, and who are the men who name themselves after stars? What is the cause they speak of, and the affair set for November? Was Jeremy Belcher in on the plot? He frowned and bit at his knuckles.

Above all, what was to become of him and Abby now?

He leaned against one of the tall brick chimneys and looked out over the thousands of London rooftops, spread before him, black shapes in the late summer's night. It seemed like hours that he had crouched there waiting for Timothy. At last he twisted his head and saw a candlelight come into their room. He scrambled down and over to the window where a round-eyed face stared back at him as if he were a ghost.

"I thought ye'd be 'alf-way to Dover by now," stammered Timothy, as he let him in. "And if I was yer, Dick, I'd be 'alf-way there. Th' gentlemen were that angry with yer. I never knowed yer ter be a thief."

"I'm not a thief," Richard hestitated at the edge of the room. "I saw a murder. That's why I ran. The murderer was chasing me."

"'A murder!" cried Timothy with a gasp. "Master Belcher was more full of spleen than I'd ever seed 'im. They said ye'd tried to prig a gentleman's gold snuffbox and run off with it."

"Well, I didn't steal anything and I did see a murder. Did the watch come here, Timothy?"

"Oh, yes, they come a'right, and the fat gentleman in purple told 'em all about yer stealin' of 'is snuffbox. 'E's an alderman of th' city, I 'ear."

"Wasn't there a body? A little man in black?" Richard sat down on the edge of his bed.

"Naw, there wasn't any body 'ere, Dick. I tells yer how it happened. First of all, I 'eard all this runnin' upstairs and then one of 'em, the Irishman with one arm, 'e come down and called Master Belcher upstairs to th' Charles Wain. Master was up there a good long time and 'e come down with th' strangest look on 'is face and sent me right away fer th' watch and asked me where ye'd gone ter. Then, I fetched th' watch, and they all went upstairs, but all th' other gentlemen 'ad gone away 'ceptin' the alderman, who talked to 'em."

"Did Jeremy Belcher tell them my name?"

"No, I think not, Dick. I 'eard 'im explainin' to the fat alderman that ye'd been 'ere a short time and that he 'ad little time to learn the particulars of his potboys. I think the master was tryin' ter 'elp yer, Dick." Timothy seated himself on the other pallet. He put the candle into an old wine bottle that sat on a rickety chair between the beds.

"So 't 'were th' little one, that took no wine that got it?" said Timothy cautiously.

Richard nodded.

"I want ter know no more about it, Dick. 'Tis a danger in these times. But I believes yer, and I'll 'elp yer." Timothy looked frightened and embarrassed.

"Thanks, Timothy, I understand. You're already taking a big enough risk." Richard's eyes questioned Timothy's troubled face and finally he asked, "Timothy, who are the men who call themselves the Society of the Stars, and what does it mean to drink to the King over a bowl of water?"

"They be Jacobites. I knew it when they drank over th' water I fetched 'em," said the Irish boy calmly.

"What are Jacobites?"

"Yer don' know much, do yer, in Pennsylvania?" said Timothy almost scornfully, but his voice softened as he saw the look of distress on Richard's face. "Jacobites want ter see th' House o' Stuart returned as kings of England and Scotland. Yer know, don' yer, that James Stuart, the 'Old Pretender,' lies over the water in France until the Hanover rats are driven back to Hanover. There are thousands of good Englishmen, Irishmen and Scots who'd like nothin' better than ter see th' rightful Stuart kings come back."

"What is 'regicide'?" Richard leaned forward.

"I don' know. Never 'eard the word afore, though it sounds fearsome. I'm a'thinkin' ye'd best get away from 'ere in th' mornin', and take Abby with yer. I'll 'elp yer. Somethin' is goin' on 'ere in th' Seven Stars, and 'tis bigger'n a stolen snuffbox, I reckon. If'n yer gets caught, 'tis Newgate Prison fer yer and maybe Tyburn gallows where they'll tuck yer up, and 'twill be th' parish for Abby, right and proper."

"I've heard that advice before," said Richard, "and I'm going to take it, too. But where can I go? I don't know any place."

Timothy thought for a long moment and then his mouth

broke into a wide grin. "Bet ye've never heard of Captain Coram and his Foundlin' 'Ospital, 'ave yer? They takes in waifs all the time. 'Tis the finest place in London for that sorta thing, and a good number of the waifs even makes it alive ter be apprenticed." Timothy paused and looked thoughtfully at his friend. "But ye've got too old for that and ye've got nobody ter pay yer 'prentice fees." Timothy frowned and then smiled again. "Ye'd best go out to Chiswick to William 'Ogarth's house. 'E 'elps th' 'ospital out and takes in foundlin's 'imself, they tells me."

"Why not Samuel Johnson?" asked Richard.

"Poor as a churchmouse," Timothy replied cheerfully. "'E can't 'elp yer out 'ceptin' with pennies and advice, not that 'e wouldn' 'elp more if'n 'e could, mind yer."

"Who is William Hogarth?"

"'E's a painter—yer should see th' prints of 'is pitchers. Does 'e know old Lunnon, does 'e? 'Is 'Rake's Progress' is in every print-seller's winder in th' city, and 'e's got a tender 'eart."

"Do you know him?"

"I seen 'im once or twicet, and I 'eard 'im talkin' one night 'ere to David Garrick, that actor friend of his'n. I 'aven't seen as much of 'im as I 'ave of Samuel Johnson."

"I'll go there, Timothy, if you say so. How far is Chiswick?"

"Not far, only a couple leagues. I'll give yer th' way in th' mornin' and yer can leave just at cockcrow. Th' watch won' be lookin' for yer then. Now, I'll bolt th' door and if'n anyone comes, yer hop out th' window quick."

With these words Timothy got up, bolted the door and came back to blow out the candle with one puff. Richard heard the rustle of pallet straw as his friend crawled into bed. "Oh, Dick," came his soft voice from the darkness. "Wotever 'appens, if'n they catch yer, yer won' say nothin' 'bout Master Belcher, will yer? 'E's a good man."

"No," promised Richard. "I won't say a word about him ever again. But, Timothy, you tell him for me that I'm not a thief."

"I knows yer no prigger of snuffboxes," came the reply.

Richard did not sleep well that night. He awoke early as a pale sun came in at the small grimy panes of the attic window. Timothy was not in his bed, and Richard sat up with a start. Had Timothy gone to tell the host that he was still in the tavern? But, no, Timothy wouldn't do that.

Richard waited, and presently he heard quiet pattering footsteps on the stairs and Timothy entered, holding Abby by the hand.

"There's nobody up yet, but there's not much time, Dick, afore the cookmaids stir up the fire and take up Master Belcher's mornin' possett," he said in a whisper. "I found th' poppet walking about in the 'all outside th' cookmaids' room. I think she had it in 'er mind ter go climb into Mrs. Belcher's bed, so I jest brought 'er along with me."

"Thank you, Timothy," said Richard. "That was a lucky thing, finding Abby as easy as that." He bent over and spoke to the little girl, who leaned sleepily on Timothy. "Come on, pretty. We have to leave now."

Abigail nodded drowsily and held up her arms. Richard sighed and picked her up. They might as well go. There was nothing to keep them. He and Abby had no other clothing and his pennies, grown to fifteen now with Belcher's pay, were still safe in the leather bag under his shirt.

He picked up Abby, and held her high on his shoulder. Her head and one arm drooped sleepily. Then he and Timothy crept silently down the three flights of steps to the door.

At the door Timothy stopped them. "I could'n get yer anythin' ter eat in th' kitchen, Dick. I wanted ter, but yer know what would've 'appened if'n I got caught."

"Thank you again, Timothy. You'd better get back upstairs now, but first tell me the way to Chiswick."

"Yer 'aven't got the' money to go ter Wapping stairs and get a waterman ter row yer up the Thames, so ye'll 'ave ter walk it. Go up past St. Sepulchre's and Holborn Hill and get onter Tyburn Turnpike. Anybody can tell yer th' way from there. That's as far as I've ever gone, meself."

"Goodbye, Timothy, and God bless you." Richard flushed as his voice broke a little.

"May th' saints give yer good luck and presarve yer both, an' call on Tim Quayle if'n yer ever need me." Tears came into Timothy's green eyes.

"I'll send you a message if I can." Richard, about to cry himself, squeezed by Timothy quickly and went out into the deserted, littered courtyard.

His feet were heavy as he retraced the steps that had led them to the Seven Stars. What lay ahead for them now? There was no one about except drunken men, laid out in rows on the pavement sobering up in front of each of the Fleet Street taverns. Richard held Abby tight and stepped carefully over and around them. It was too early even for the milk girls and the muffin sellers or for any of the other street criers. Richard looked back; it was clear he was not being followed. The Society of the Stars must have decided that he had made a clean escape. Still Richard was wary, staring into each garbage-choked alley for the snake-eyed Spica in his scarlet coat.

He passed St. Sepulchre's where he had met Samuel Johnson and looked wistfully for him again, but, of course, he was not there. Gently, Richard put Abigail down and held her by the hand as they descended Snow Hill, passed by Cock Lane and over Holborn Bridge. The steep climb from the bridge along Holborn Hill was almost too much for Abby. She sat down crying and whimpering. Richard had to promise her a cup of milk and a muffin from the first vender they met before she would go on. It was easier going as they passed the Bishop of Ely's palace and gardens, and by now the city was coming alive again.

Two little boys, much younger than Richard, in ragged coats and breeches black with filth, stood with their soot-covered faces pressed against the iron railings of the Bishop's gardens. They stared hopelessly inside at the roses blooming just out of reach.

"Shall us nim them gerjus things?" asked one of the other.

"Naw," said the second boy, "fer sartain we'd be took und tucked up. I makes it them's th' Bishop's rosies."

"Please," asked Richard, "can you tell me if this is Tyburn Turnpike and what is the way to Chiswick?"

The ragged children turned around and stared at him with red-rimmed watery eyes.

"'E wants ter know if this be th' Tyburn Turnpike?" said one to the other in disbelief.

"'E ain't never seen nobody tucked up, chicken," added the second child, "or 'e wouldn' 'ave asked."

"This 'ere is th' Tyburn Turnpike. Yer oughter see it on a 'angin' day. It's so smart wi' swabs and muckworms and Newgate birds yer'd give a yaller boy jest ter see th' like of it."

"A yellow boy?" asked Richard.

"A guinea, a Jacobus—yer knows—brass," explained the first boy scornfully.

Abby looked at them and said loudly, "They're black."

The boys were not angry, in fact they smiled with pride.

One spoke up. "Ain't we jest though? I'd like fer ter know what else sweeps'd be?"

"You clean chimneys, then?" asked Richard, for Timothy had told him more than once of the dreadful lives the apprentices to the chimney sweeps led. They spent all day climbing up and down cleaning the narrow soot-filled chimneys of London. Their knees and elbows grew thick pads of skin that protected them from the sharp bricks. Most lived short wretched lives, half-starved, frequently beaten, and only a few survived to become masters of their trade.

"What is the way to Chiswick, please?" Richard repeated.

One boy gestured, his sleeve rags flapping wide. "Jest yer go 'long th' Turnpike til yer see Tyburn Tree where they tucks up th' clippers and th' strolers and get west 'long to Turnham Green. Then, yer oughter go inter a rum-dropper und ask."

"'Ware of clippers at th' Green," said the other one, laughing. "Yer look a tom-doodle ter me, yer does."

"Clippers?" asked Richard. "And tom-doodle?"

"Gents of th' road and loobies," was the reply.

These Richard knew were highwaymen and fools. Hastily he thanked the sweeps and walked off, dragging Abby along. He heard the children jeering at him and his ignorance as he left, and then they moved on their way calling, "Swep- swep-we-er, swep."

Tyburn Turnpike was wide, wide enough for six carriages. It began to fill up with market carts, flower girls, vegetable sellers with baskets on their heads, and all kinds of people coming into London.

Richard and Abby trudged out along the dusty road into the countryside. Abby could not walk fast on her short little legs, and their progress was slow.

Richard marveled at the fine still-shuttered shops and at the great houses of the proud and wealthy springing up on either side of Tyburn Turnpike. Truly, London was a magnificent city compared to Philadelphia, but there were many things about it that he could not accept, and he felt sick with disgust as he compared the fine houses of Mayfair with his own poverty and that of the two little sweeps.

Richard spent a few farthings on milk and an apple for Abby. They were only a few steps away from the Tyburn gallows, a black, grim contrast to the pink morning sky and meadowlike fields below, where Tyburn Tree looked out over the green beauty of Hyde Park.

They left Tyburn Tree and went on westward, walking slowly. Although Hyde Park was green and fresh in the early morning, the same could not be said for the area just outside it. Here, great piles of cinders grew to the skies and the reek of garbage filled the air. London's scavengers used its outskirts as a refuse heap where they emptied their stinking carts. Richard pulled out his handkerchief and put it over Abby's nose to keep out the stench. As he did so, his hand touched a scrap of paper. It was the paper Antares had dropped the night before. Richard shuddered at the memory of what he'd seen. At least, he thought grimly, Antares won't get his paper back.

Richard took a deep breath and picked Abby up to hurry on past the foul dumping place, wondering to himself where all the filth came from. He had never seen anything so dirty as the streets of London, city scavengers and all.

Just past the dumps, cows grazed at the edges of the refuse heaps. Tardy milk girls with pails and yokes hurried about, milking the cows, for they must hasten into the city if they were to make a day's profit.

Richard and Abby moved on through fields and small

country villages and Richard asked the way of an old woman, who trudged along with a large basket of fresh lavender under each arm. She was decently dressed in a white pinner cap and clean apron and had a pleasant look about her.

"Turnham Green," she queried, "would ye be goin' there? Well, keep onter this way, laddie, and ye'll find it soon enough, I warrant." She peered at Abby and then pinched her cheek. "Now, that's a pretty poppet. Ye twist her arms behind her for a spell until they withers, laddie, and then yer takes her into the city to St. Paul's steps. She'll fetch ye many a copper from the chicken-hearted quality. They pays poppet clapperdudgeons well if they got a pretty face."

"She's not going to be maimed and she's not going to beg," cried Richard. He hauled Abby away in horror.

The old woman chuckled and nodded her head, her toothless purple mouth agape. "Oh, ye'll change yer tune, laddie. There's things worse'n beggin', I tell yer."

Grabbing Abigail up, Richard ran away from the horrible crone.

They crossed Stamford Brook in a few strides. A scattering of houses up ahead meant another village. Richard spied a large painted sign on the side of the road. It swung on wooden posts, creaking back and forth in the morning breeze. A picture of the crowned head of a man and the name "The King of Bohemia" were painted on it.

Richard remembered the advice of the sweep "to find a rum-dropper and ask the way." He knew that the tall old wooden building was surely a tavern, not only from the sign, but from the lathered saddled horse hitched outside.

"You stay here, Abby. I'll go in and ask the way and buy us some cheese and bread." He seated the tired child on a soft tussock of grass alongside the road. "Now, Abby, don't talk to anyone at all, you understand, and if anyone bothers you, you come to me as fast as you can." Abby jerked her head several times to show she understood. Then she stuck all the fingers of one hand in her mouth and sucked at them vigorously.

Richard stepped into the common room of the King of Bohemia. It was an oak-paneled room of the seventeenth century, old and grimy. The tavern, as befitted such an early hour, was nearly deserted but for a tall ginger-haired man in a patched dusty cloak and frayed tricorne hat, who stood in the center of the room, a pewter cup in his hand. Another tall man listened intently, as the red-haired man spoke to the landlord.

Richard caught the words and froze. "Lord Lovat lived here in this house we know, and you are a true man to the cause. The great lairds have concerted last night in the city, so I am bid to tell all of the friends of the Sun that shines in France that the time is at hand."

"For better things to come, eh?" added the host of the King of Bohemia.

"Aye, for better times, lad, and have ye no water handy for a proper toast?" asked the first man, with a jab of his elbow at the other's ribs.

Richard didn't wait to hear more. The men were too involved in their own matters to notice him as he slipped outside and swiftly routed Abby from the grass. He wanted only to get away from the Seven Stars and the terrible thing he'd witnessed. It seemed that by strange coincidence he was to be part of it wherever he went.

"Hungry!" wailed Abby as they hastened on. "Bread and cheese. Want bread and cheese!"

"You'll get it, Abby," he promised her as she popped her fingers into her mouth again. "We've got to get to Chiswick."

"Hungry!" she cried. "You said bread and cheese!" and she pulled back on his hand, kicking at the dust in the road.

"Come along, Abby," Richard pleaded in desperation, while people walking along stared at him and smiled. Abby dug her heels into the dirt and refused to move.

"Hungry!" she roared.

Suddenly a girl of about Richard's own age came running up to them. She had a long hazel switch in her hand and there was an angry, upset look on her face. She stopped near Richard and looked at Abby. Abby stared at the switch and stopped her wailing. "Have you seen a little white dog with a pushed-in face and brown ears?" the girl demanded.

"No," said Richard, "I haven't."

"That miserable animal," the girl sighed. "Master Hogarth will be full of anger if I go back without his dog again."

"You know William Hogarth?" Richard asked in surprise. "Then I must be in Chiswick."

"Well, near enough. This is Turnham Green here, where the Packhorse and Saddle, the King of Bohemia, and that little forge are. But what do the likes of you have to do with Master Hogarth?" Her sharp brown eyes glared under winged black eyebrows.

"We've been sent to see him." The girl's eyes made Richard uneasy. "I am Richard Larkin and your servant," he added, bowing and taking off his hat.

"Oh, foundlings, I suppose, more foundlings," the girl frowned. "Though your manners are fine enough, I must say. And who sent you, pray?"

"Nobody really sent us," Richard lied, thinking it best not to mention Timothy's name.

The girl sighed and swished the stick through the grass at the side of the road. "Well, the truth does come out at last.

And I tell you that I am a foundling, too. If you help me find Master Hogarth's little dog, I'll take you to his house down by the Mall, near the river. He'll see you anyhow. He has a good humor, never fear, but you can't take advantage of the master, no, you can't. They call me Betsy Lewes."

Richard stared at the girl. She didn't look like any foundling to him. Her gown was of a good gray cloth and her apron and cap were clean and white, but most important, her shoes were pewter-buckled and of good stout black leather, as good as Richard's own. She caught his appraisal of her and sniffed, tossing her head and frowning, while wisps of dark brown hair fell over her square tanned forehead and along her pink cheeks. Betsy Lewes was not pretty, Richard decided, but she had a solid, no-nonsense look about her, and in spite of her sharp ways he approved of her. With her honesty and forthrightness she seemed more like a boy than a girl. A wide mouth with white wide-spaced teeth and a short nose did not improve her beauty, though they did please Richard. She reminded him of boys he'd known in Philadelphia, but he did not tell her this. He knew that she would not be pleased.

He grinned at her. "Let's go find Master Hogarth's dog," he said, and was rewarded by a quick smile and a merry laugh.

It wasn't hard to find the little dog Trump. They had walked only a few yards past the Turnham Green forge, the blacksmith's shop, when they heard a frantic barking and, sure enough, there he was, shoulder deep in high meadow grass, yapping his head off at a herd of goats. As they approached and looked over the fence, an old nanny goat lowered her head to make a run at him.

"Oh, dear!" Betsy cried out in horror. "What will Master Hogarth say if anything happens to Trump? What shall I do?"

Richard laughed and skinned under the fence. Scooping up

the little dog, he handed him, squirming and struggling, to Betsy.

"I'd better put something around his neck," she said, and took some cord from her apron pocket, "or he'll run away again." She knelt and put the cord around Trump's neck.

"Going to go now?" asked Abigail, pulling at Richard's coat.

"Who's the poppet?" Betsy Lewes turned and gestured to Richard to walk alongside her. "What's her name?"

"Abigail, or so she says," replied Richard. "She's a foundling, too. A ragged woman dumped her off on me."

"She's not your sister, then?"

"No," said Richard, and he told Betsy of the woman in St. Paul's churchyard. It shocked him that Betsy did not seem surprised or even bothered by his story.

"Yes, that happens all the time," she said calmly. "Master Hogarth has told me about the Foundling Hospital. It has hundreds of foundling babies brought there from all over London every year. It's better than the workhouses by far, you know, for more babies survive there than on the parish. Where do you come from, Richard Larkin? I can tell you aren't a Londoner."

Richard told her his story, except for the days at the Seven Stars. And though her eyes widened in interest at the name of Pennsylvania, the rest of the tale did not affect her much.

"I've always wanted to see the New World," Betsy confessed. "If I was a boy and free to go anywhere I wanted, I'd go there right away, I would, but I don't want to be a bonded servant."

"And so would I, if I had the passage money. And I'd take Abby with me, too," Richard vowed, suddenly deciding that Abigail should go back to the Colonies with him.

Betsy laughed self-consciously. "It's terrible hard for foundlings like us to get money ahead, but if you ever do go, take me along, too."

"I will, Betsy. I will remember." Richard made the promise in great seriousness and Betsy looked sideways at him with a tiny mocking smile on her lips.

"Well, let's get along the Turnpike," she said, "and take this silly dog of a Trump to Master Hogarth before he misses him. We'll cross the cow pastures and go around Lord Burlington's fancy place and by the bowling green."

It was an easy matter to go through the meadows that lay south of Turnham Green Lane, for few of them were fenced and there were almost no houses to block their way and no streets at all. Soon they came to a red brick wall, and Betsy, to Richard's surprise and amusement, stuck out her tongue. They skirted the wall and came finally to a broad grassy expanse which Betsy said was called the bowling green. They decided to rest here for awhile because Abby was tired.

"Why did you stick out your tongue at the brick wall back there?" Richard asked as he sprawled out on the grass.

Betsy sat down with a thud and clasped her knees with her hands, still keeping a tight hold on Trump's cord. Abby crawled over to play with the gentle white dog, as she'd been longing to do. "Chiswick is one of the nicest places outside London," Betsy began. "It has pure air and a healthy climate, they say. And the quality come to Chiswick during the summer to get away from the fevers and fits of London. People have been coming here for over a hundred years, I've heard tell, for the good clean air. There's been some great folk living here, like some of the Walpole family, beautiful Barbara Villiers, the Duke of Bedford's family and lots of others. They lived nice and quiet in their fine houses along the river on the Mall. But then that Earl of Burlington comes along, and is the house he already had good enough for his lordship? Oh, no, what does he do but build that ugly, silly Italian villa of his to give his routs in and hang his Italian pictures in! That's what Master Hogarth says and nobody knows more about art than he does. Look'ee, do you know his prints?" Betsy turned to Richard, her face aglow with pleasure.

"No," answered Richard, "but I've heard about them."

"Well, you wait until you see 'em. Nobody in the whole world knows what London is like the way my master does." She laughed a sharp hard laugh again. "That's why he takes in us foundlings, I reckon."

"Do you think he'll take Abby and me?" asked Richard anxiously.

"Oh, he'll grumble about more mouths to feed, but he's the pleasantest gentleman in England, I know. He'll take you right enough, but you'll have to do a day's work. Nobody bubbles Master Hogarth," Betsy warned.

"I'll work," stated Richard, "I'm used to working hard. How did you happen to come to Chiswick, Betsy? Were you born here?"

"La, no, I said I am a foundling, like yourself, but it isn't quite true. I've been to dame school and I can read, even if I don't write well, and foundlings don't often do that, you know. There was an old woman who said she was my granddam who had me stay with her. But I ran away from that old devil who, as far as I know, still lives in Marylebone Parish. She just wanted me as her servant to push her about London in her bathchair. She said she couldn't walk although I heard her walking about spry as you please at night. It was dreadful hard getting that chair through the streets and if I got her stuck or didn't move fast enough, she hit me with the stick she always carried. So I ran off to Leicester Fields and Mistress Hogarth found me, sitting on the doorstep of their London house. They took me in and brought me to Chiswick. And a lucky day it was for me, too."

"But what about your grandmother? Can't she get you back?"

"No," stated Betsy, her cheeks flushed with anger. "Master Hogarth found out that she wasn't any real kin to me at all. She's just said she was to get the little bit of money my father left to me before he went into sea service and then she spent it all."

"Is your father a sailor, then?"

"He was." Betsy saddened. "His ship was an East India merchantman, but it's months overdue in Bombay now, so Master Hogarth tells me that he is probably drowned or taken by Barbary pirates, and my mother died when I was born. So that is that!"

Shc jumped to her feet, tugging Trump away from Abby, who wailed in disappointment. "Come along, you two," Betsy commanded, "we've got to get this dog back before Mistress Hogarth sends out old Matt to find me. He's so feeble that he can barely stumble out to the Black Lion and back for Master Hogarth's ale without spilling every drop." She glanced at Richard. "You'll probably do most of old Matt's chores," she added. "He's served Mistress Hogarth's family for many years, and they think he deserves a seat in the chimney corner from now on. You came at a good time, I think, Dick."

Richard was pleased at Betsy's words and happy that she had called him Dick. With high spirits he followed her along.

The village of Chiswick changed as they approached the river. Before isolated red brick houses had dotted the fields here and there, but now as they turned into a little cobbled lane Richard spied the gray Thames ahead of him and a cluster of chimneys thrust up among the green branches of the tall trees.

"That's Chiswick Mall and a fine place it is, too," Betsy pointed. "You'll find the Burlington Arms and old St. Nicholas Church down Church Lane. You'll see plenty of both places, for the Hogarths like their servants to go to church and the master keeps a good cellar of wines and ales. We turn left next, and then we're almost there. Come along, you bad dog, before I switch you. It gets on to midday."

Betsy hauled at Trump, and as the dog tried to pull away she sighed and picked him up, tucking him firmly under her arm. "You have the very best home a dog could ever have," she scolded him, "but still you run away every chance you get."

She threw away the hazel switch and led them down a narrow lane, to stop at a high brick wall in front of an iron grill gate. "This is it," she announced. "Just you come in and wait over there under the mulberry tree. The berries are ripe now, and I know Master Hogarth wouldn't mind if you ate some. All the other village children do."

Betsy opened the gate and stepped inside, down the stone steps. Richard followed her, lifting Abby over the steps into William Hogarth's garden. It was the prettiest little place Richard had ever seen. The entire house and garden were enclosed by the high brick wall. A wall was something Richard had not often seen in Pennsylvania. He stood staring about him while Betsy took Trump into the house. Carefully tended flower beds stretched along the lane side of the wall, and in the back he spied a vegetable plot. Many of the flowers were new to Richard, but he recognized roses, hollyhocks and sweet-scented stock, and he could not mistake the neat rows of carrots and cabbages. The grass was well clipped and spotted here and there with white daisies, which Abby bent down to examine. Richard was most impressed by the mulberry tree even though there were other, much more majestic, trees in the garden. The mulberry tree was bushy and small with bright green leaves. Large dark berries that looked much like blackberries grew in clusters along the branches. He picked one and popped it into his mouth and then picked several for Abby. She gobbled them up at once and smeared them all over her face. He decided that their flavor was not as good as a blackberry's, but even so they were good enough to eat.

Richard had picked some more when the front door opened and Betsy Lewes came out, shaking her head. "Don't eat them all," she hissed. "Master Hogarth's been told about you and he's coming right out. Sit down."

There was a little bench encircling the mulberry tree and Richard sat down, pulling Abby up beside him. He stared straight ahead, looking as serious as he could, to make a good impression. The house in front of him was tall, several-storied, oblong and made out of red brick and tile. There was a low brick wing to the right. Richard idly counted the many white-framed windows. It was obvious from the number of them that Master Hogarth was not a poor man, for glass was costly and windows heavily taxed. Richard admired the elegance of the hanging bay window and the three fine chimneys. His gaze wandered over to a well-built low wooden structure that joined the brick wing, and he wondered what it was for. His speculations were interrupted as the door opened again and a small man in a red and yellow calimanco banyan dressing gown stepped out. He had a yellow handkerchief tied over his head. William Hogarth pattered up the pebble walk to Richard and Abby and stopped before them.

"Get up, Abby," Richard whispered. Abby scrambled down from the bench and to Richard's amazement dropped the man an awkward curtsy, something she'd never done before.

The man, who was not much taller than Richard, had a merry, clever face with bright blue eyes and a mouth that seemed hard put to avoid a smile. The most noticeable things about him were a deep scar over his right eyebrow and his hands, short-fingered, strong and white.

"Master Hogarth, I am your servant, sir," said Richard, bowing and taking off his hat as Abby curtsied once more. "I have just come from Philadelphia and my name is Richard Larkin."

Hogarth covered his mouth with his right hand as the corners turned upward in a smile. His voice was high and accented, very like other London voices Richard had heard on Fleet Street. "Whatever else I can say for you, you both have an artful conduct. The child is a pretty creature. I have been told that you helped find Trump and that you are waifs."

"That's true, sir," said Richard, "and we hope that you can find work for us."

"And what does the child do?" asked the painter, his eyes twinkling as he looked at Abby.

"Nothing, really," replied Richard, but he added hastily, "she amuses, that's all, sir, and she doesn't eat much."

Hogarth sat down on the bench and smiled at Abby. She came promptly to him, putting a mulberry-stained hand on his knee and looking up at him with great seriousness.

Hogarth sighed, looked at her and gently twisted her pale hair in his fingers. "I am a childless man," he said, "and I do have a vast affection for wee poppets like this one. I could take her likeness well. There's something distinctive about her face. She's a fine little cupid, I vow." He paused and turned abruptly to Richard. "And what does a great lad like you do that may be worthwhile to me, sirrah? What have you done before you came to my country box here in Chiswick to plague my tender conscience?"

Richard was not frightened. Though he was certain Master Horgarth was a man who might anger easily, there was no malice or cruelty in him. He only played at being stern, and Richard knew that he and Abby would be allowed to stay.

As Richard spoke, Abby cooed "Uppie, uppie," and climbed into Hogarth's lap where she sat happily, all four fingers of one hand popped into her mouth. "I can rake leaves, prune fruit trees, run errands, shoe a horse, skin a fox or a skunk, and care for a sick beast. I can chop firewood as well as anyone, and I can stack it more neatly than any other boy in Chiswick, I warrant. I can read and write a fair hand, so my master at my village school told me, and I have read Caesar, Virgil and part of Horace, sir—in Latin, of course. I can scrub and . . ." Here he caught himself before adding that he could draw ale and serve wine as well. He wanted no questioning about the Seven Stars.

Hogarth began to laugh and held up his hand for Richard to stop. "It will do, lad," he said. "Most of my critics would say that I was not half so talented as my new foundling boy. I shall take you as my servant because you can rake leaves and chop firewood and perhaps you can read to Dame Thornhill and Jane, my wife, as well. But do not plague me, please, with your Latin poets and warriors. If it is not English, I do not countenance a thing willingly. And, lad, there are no skunks in England to skin. Now, take the poppet to the kitchen, out behind the house, and feed her well, for I know that she is hungry."

Richard pried Abby from Hogarth's lap and led her away.

Hogarth called after them, chuckling. "Have Betsy wash the child's face, Richard Larkin. And when you've eaten, bring her to that wooden building, for I shall require her for a time. I'd like to know if what I see is pretty child or mulberry juice."

Richard and Abby went along the side of the wall to a wooden building behind the main house and rapped at the door. It opened instantly and Betsy Lewes asked, "Did the master take you both?"

"Yes," Richard replied, "and we're to come in to be fed, then Master Hogarth wants you to wash Abby's face so he can see how she really looks."

"Come in then," said Betsy, "all of the servants are in the kitchen. You can meet them right now."

She took Abby by the hand, clucking at her like a mother hen. Abby smiled and leaned against Betsy's skirts.

Abby will go far in the world, thought Richard. She knows just how to make people like her and look after her. He thought sadly of the Seven Stars and wished he had had more of Abby's charm. Now, how had she known to curtsy to William Hogarth?

The kitchen was not so large as that of the Seven Stars, but it was just as full of good cheer. A little fire burned away merrily in the large fireplace, and a middle-aged, kind-faced woman knelt before it, coaxing it along with a bellows. She glanced at Abby and Richard, and smiled as her soft blue eyes took in their dusty shoes. Then she went back to her work without a word. The fireplace was red brick with seats on each side and recesses in front for tinder and matchsticks. Iron cranes from which to suspend pots stood out from the sides while large black firedogs held the wood. Over the mantel on a rack hung spits for roast meat and trivets for the saucepans. Betsy hurried over with bacon, which she placed in the smoke chamber over the flames. A second young servant girl, also dressed in gray, joined the woman with the bellows. She pushed an iron toasting dog crowned with roasting sausages into the hot coals. As she knelt before the fireplace she grinned at Richard, her white teeth gleaming in a dark gypsylike face. Her wild hair curled back under a plain white mobcap, the same kind that Betsy Lewes wore.

"Naw, naw," warned the older woman. " 'Tis not time yet, Moll, fer th' sausages. Th' fire must catch better." She nodded her head at Richard and Betsy and then in an accent that reminded Richard faintly of the two little sweeps, she said, "Set yerself and wait."

Betsy pulled Abby over to a group of stools next to a good-sized wooden table where an old bald man with a dead complexion sat eating moodily away at a large piece of brown bread covered with butter.

"That's old Matt," Betsy explained loudly. "He can't hear a thing you say; he's that stone deaf, and he wouldn't care if he heard you say he was. Now you spread some butter on the cut bread there on the table and I'll bring you some small beer. That should do, shouldn't it? I'll fetch a cloth and wash the poppet's pretty face."

Richard nodded and put great gobs of butter on a piece of bread, which Abby quickly snatched away from him. Patiently he fixed himself another piece. He had only begun to eat it when Betsy, moving quickly and efficiently, was back with a wet linen cloth and proceeded, in spite of Abby's howls and struggles, to scrub her face.

Moll came slowly over to the table, carrying two small mugs of beer. She smiled and put the mugs down in front of Richard and Abby, but she did not speak, and Betsy said as she left, "She doesn't talk at all. She's a gypsy, you know, and I guess she speaks the gypsy tongue, but she's not at all a bad 'un, and she doesn't steal, which is more'n you can say for most of that thieving tribe. That's Hannah Charke over there with the bellows trying to get that pokey fire hot enough for Master Hogarth's morning sausages. She's a good, tender-hearted woman, Dick, but nobody can bubble Hannah, either. She's dreadful busy all the time, and Mistress Hogarth swears she's the best cook in London. You should just taste her roast swan."

"I'd like to," said Richard, nodding and drinking down his small beer. He buttered another piece of bread for Abby and himself. "What does Master Hogarth pay?" he asked.

"Two pennies a month, but he clothes us and victuals us well. You'll not do better'n Master Hogarth as long as he's here in his Chiswick villakin. And if he likes you, he'll take you back to Leicester Fields in a couple of weeks."

Richard choked. "Does he go back to the city then?"

"La, all the great folk do. I told you that. They only pass the summer months at places like Chiswick and Twickenham. When it gets colder and London gets safer for their health, they always go back to the city. The theaters open then. Nothing happens in London in the summer, Dick."

Richard shook his head. He found it hard to agree that nothing took place in London in the summer. The news that Hogarth was leaving Chiswick in late September worried him. Saturn's warning rang in his ears, and he finished his food in a silence that puzzled Betsy. She watched him unhappily.

"I'd hoped at least you'd talk to me," she said with some bitterness. "Moll and Matt never say a word and Hannah's much too busy all the time. As for Ann Hogarth, and the other ladies, they're much too grand to take notice of me."

"Oh, I'll talk with you," Richard said, "but I'd better take Abby to Master Hogarth now." He got up, and Abby and he went out the door, leaving Betsy sniffing angrily.

They went down the walk and past the iron grill to the road. The clatter of wheels on the cobbled lane made Richard look up sharply as he pulled Abigail along. A shiny black carriage with a painted coat of arms on the door rumbled toward them. Tall lackeys in green livery stood at the back of the carriage while another drove a span of dapple-gray horses. A little man in green livery rode postilion, like a monkey, on one of the horses.

Three people sat inside the carriage. The first person was a proud-profiled woman with a curled, powdered headdress. She wore a deep blue velvet cloak. The other two were men—so alike in profile and posture that they might have been brothers or, at least, of the same family. They lounged against the seats of the coach, their brick-red faces the same beneath white-cockaded hats. One man wore a fine silver-and-gray brocade frock coat. The second man sat silent, staring at Hogarth's wall as they went past. His face was hard above the rich dark red velvet, trimmed at the neck with a frill of white lace. His dark eyes were wide and vacant as they stared at Richard, who stood frozen with fear against the iron grill.

It was Sirius, the leader of the Society of the Stars.

CHAPTER 4

The Eclipse of Saturn

HORRIFIED, Richard stood transfixed as the sound of the wheels died away down the cobbled lane. He did not know if Sirius had recognized him or even seen him. There was no way to tell. At least the man had not leaped down to collar him and drag him off to Newgate, claiming that he was a thief. Richard shivered. Who would protect and stand up for him to prove that he hadn't stolen a golden snuffbox? No one except Saturn, and who was he, after all? Should he leave Chiswick and run off again? He looked at Abby and frowned. He could not keep this up forever, and the journey on foot from the Seven Stars to Chiswick had been tiring to both of them. The little money he had been able to save would not take them far.

He sighed and began to walk down the path that led to Hogarth's wooden building. Abby yawned and dragged her feet beside him. Richard tapped on the stout wooden door and stepped inside as the painter called to come in.

It was not a handsome place. Richard looked around the

room. It had an unfamiliar odor—not a pleasant one either. The room, or shed, was a low structure, with several good-sized windows that made it very clear and light. A number of copper plates were stacked against a wall, and a high table in one corner held a pile of large sheets of white paper.

Hogarth stood near another large table that held a fantastic collection of materials. There were jars of colors, brushes standing in pots, several paint-encrusted palettes, and a large number of small tied bladders. Everything lay helter-skelter.

Easels abounded in the studio, and on them rested Hogarth's paintings. Some were of biblical subjects, Richard suspected, but others were quite unfamiliar to him. They seemed to be in all stages of completion, as if the painter worked on each of them now and then.

"Stop sniffing the air, boy. That's oil paint you smell. Come put the child in that chair," Hogarth ordered. Richard hurried to lift the sleepy Abigail into a plain wooden chair a few feet beyond one easel.

"She's ready to go to sleep, sir, I think," said Richard. "She's walked a long way today."

"No mind," commented the painter, taking up a sheet of paper and a crayon. "I'll try to get some sketches of her while she dozes before I attempt a painting. It's a dear creature. Has Dame Thornhill or my wife seen her yet?"

"No, sir, we've only met the servants."

"Humpf," said Hogarth. "Do you know anything of painting, lad? Did they teach you that along with Horace and all those other Romans?"

"No," confessed Richard, "this is all strange to me, sir."

" 'Tis like any other craft. It has its tools and its tricks and its critics," Hogarth frowned, "who, by the way, call me an ingenious inventor and 'Painter Pug.' If you're to work for me, you must know a bit about my craft even if you only learn not to brush up against wet oil. Go look at the prints and tell me what you think of them."

Richard glanced at Abby. She was almost asleep, her head on her arm, her mouth open, and her cheeks flushed. He walked over to the high table to examine the prints. These were the famous engravings both Timothy and Betsy had mentioned to him. Richard was shocked at what he saw. William Hogarth did not paint pretty things—flowers, fine gardens or beautiful ladies. As Richard turned over each print, the city of London came alive. He saw the gin-drinking poor in all their misery and the fat and prosperous beer drinkers. He looked at likenesses of wicked thieving men, drunken bullies, starved children and animals, brutal sports and leering toothless faces of all kinds. As he turned over the last detailed and frightening print, he realized that Hogarth was standing beside him. The painter's shrewd blue eyes were fixed on Richard's face.

"Eh, what do you think of my pretty pictures?" he asked.

"They are a lot like London, I believe," replied Richard slowly.

"Oh, that they are. They are London as the low and vulgar William Hogarth sees it, and I hope some few learn from them. Their sale pays me well enough, when I am not cheated by thieves, who copy and pirate my prints."

"Do people really put these in their houses?" Richard asked, in spite of himself. He stared at "Gin Lane," hideous even in the black and white of the print.

With a chuckle at Richard's tactlessness the painter confessed that they did and gestured to the copper plates. "Some of them were engraved from those plates, which are worth their weight in gold, according to my friends—and, of course, according to my critics, worthless." He led Richard to the paintings on the easels. "Now I believe, myself, that the greatest style of painting is heroic, historical, or drawn from the Bible, like this one, 'Paul before Felix,' and I am writing a little book that will give my ideas on what is beautiful, too. So, you see, I do not devote myself entirely to moralizing on the evils of London."

Richard nodded as the painter quickly showed each subject to him, and to his surprise he found himself very interested. Richard had seen almost no art work in the Colonies except for a few portraits in Philadelphia shop windows. He decided he preferred Hogarth's brightly colored paintings to his fearful engravings.

Hogarth left Richard and went back to stare at Abigail, now fast asleep. He took up his crayon again. "Look'ee, lad," he said. "I am no face-painter who toadies to the rich and powerful. If a man had a tail, I would paint it. I do not flatter. Do you know what King George called my 'March to Finchley' where I showed his guards as the drunken scum they are? He called it trumpery, mind you, so I erased the dedication to him and dedicated it instead to the King of Prussia."

"Mars is in Prussia," Richard said. Without thinking, the words of Antares had popped out.

"And that he is!" commented Hogarth. "Frederick is a veritable Mars, indeed; a true warrior, I do believe." He went on, quickly sketching Abby's face. "I didn't know you were poetically inclined, boy, but many have called Frederick 'Mars' at that."

Richard had grown pale at the slip of his tongue and his hand went to his pocket where Antares' paper crackled ominously.

"I am no face-painter who toadies to the rich and powerful. If a man had a tail, I would paint it."

The painter hummed to himself and did not speak again for a time. Finally he grew angry and threw down his crayon. "Something in the child's mouth eludes me. The mouth is devilishly hard to paint, you know. Not even Leonardo da Vinci did mouths well, not that I have any love for the Italians. I detest the Italians, as you will soon learn, lad, if you serve William Hogarth. They sing and hoot in London opera houses; they paint fat pudgy cupids on English ceilings in our finest houses. They teach English girls to dance; they teach English lads fencing and their despicable foreign manners. Everywhere in London you run into the *signori.* They overrun the land worse than the French *maîtres,* and I abhor that vile breed of macaronis, too." Here Hogarth began to pace the floor in a rage. "But I find even more odious the wealthy Englishman who bows and scrapes to them and cries up to the heavens everything that is Italian. Did you know English painters cannot survive here and must go to Italy to make bad copies of Italian paintings in order to capture English gold? Our young beaux feel that their education requires the Grand Tour of Europe and what do they do but come back with their heads stuffed with nonsense. Even worse, they drag back chipped, scarred, probably yesterday-manufactured statues to prop up in their Italian-style gardens. If it is old and from some decayed Roman villa, it is art! But the worst of them all is my neighbor, that man of no taste, Burlington, who builds an Italian villa in Chiswick! An Italian villa in Italy is bad enough, I would think, but in Chiswick, it is abominable, boy. It is monstrous, hideous and horrible!"

"I haven't seen it yet, Master Hogarth," Richard remarked uncomfortably. It was embarrassing to see his master so overwrought.

"Ah, I have used you ill," Hogarth mused, and calmed down. "I should not treat you as a target for my rage, but I value only what is English. The English noble sirs, who corrupt our English virtues, bring out all of my spleen."

"It's all right, Master Hogarth," said Richard, but he wondered privately how the painter could produce such terrifying prints of London and say that he liked only what was English. Perhaps he hoped to point out a moral and teach a lesson.

"Do you paint pictures of people, too?" asked Richard.

"Now and then," was the answer. "I took the likeness of Captain Coram, who began the home for foundlings, and I have painted David Garrick, the actor, who, alas, was not pleased with his portrait and who is now piqued with me. He is a vain man, I fear. But I liked best the quick study I did of Simon Fraser, Lord Lovat, the Jacobite traitor and would-be regicide just before he had his wicked old head chopped off on Tower Hill six years ago."

"Lovat!" exclaimed Richard. This was a name he'd heard mentioned at the Seven Stars and also at the King of Bohemia. "Who was he, and what, sir, is a regicide?"

"Lord Lovat was a Scottish lord, one of the men who supported Prince Charles Edward Stuart, the son of the Stuart pretender to the throne of England. In 1745 the Prince marched from Scotland down to Derby with his rabble army, made up of Scottish, Irish and traitor English. But he turned back at Derby and was defeated later at the battle of Culloden. The Prince got clean away to France and saved his skin, but they caught old Lovat when King George's soldiers scoured Scotland, and he paid with his head. I thought everyone knew of Lovat. What do they teach you in the Colonies, boy?"

"But what is regicide?"

"'Ods bob, you do come up with the strange ones, don't you?" Hogarth laughed and drew the outline of Abby's face. "First, you speak of Mars in Prussia, then of Lord Lovat, and now you ask what regicide means? It means to kill a king, boy—and you claim to be a Latin scholar."

Richard felt as if someone had hit him with an ax. So the Society of the Stars was plotting to kill a king, and what king could it be but King George? The plotters were surely Jacobites if they thought of Lord Lovat as a martyr. No wonder the traitors were concerned when Richard escaped from the Charles Wain. He shivered again at the memory of having seen Sirius only minutes before.

"May I go now?" Richard asked quickly, "or will you be needing me?"

"Go on, lad, take a look at my horses and my little carriage. You'll have the care of them mostly, and look to one of the reins on the carriage harness. It seems to be wearing thin. I take it you can patch harness?" He cocked his head and was satisfied when Richard nodded. "Then go to the house and see if Mistress Hogarth or Dame Thornhill require you to run any errands for them."

Richard bowed slightly and went out, leaving Abby sound asleep in Hogarth's chair. Hogarth held out his sketch to judge it, frowning and humming once more.

The garden was deserted, as Richard walked over and stood out of sight behind the trunk of a tall tree. He fished out Antares' paper. For very good reasons he did not want anyone to see it. He unfolded the paper and his fingers shook. It was a short note, written in a round, back-slanted, childish hand. It certainly was not the sort of thing Richard had expected the sinister and elegant Antares to carry about with him.

It read:

Wednesday

Dear Grandpapa,

Your dutiful grandson sends you his thanks for your gift to him and wishes you to know that he is grateful and will do anything more he can to please you and merit your rewards. He sends his warmest affection and inquires after your health and that of Mr. Kenady, and he faithfully promises that he will write you again as soon as he sees his dear Miss Philips and brings her to a meeting with you and Mr. Kenady. She should be arriving about 10th November bringing some very dear friends of hers that I know you would like to see.

Your devoted and loving,
Alec Guthry

Richard was puzzled. Antares was a young man—much too young to be a grandfather, so the letter could not have been written to him. That meant, probably, that Antares had written it himself. Antares' real name must be Alec Guthry. Or was it? The note seemed innocently simple, but it could have been in code. He had read of such things, but except for the mention of the tenth of November there was nothing to connect it with a plot against the throne. The spaces between the lines were not large enough to contain secret writing, and there was no wide margin or free space at the top or bottom. He sighed and refolded the letter. As he did so his eye fell on the brick wall a few feet from him. A yellowish brick stuck out loosely from among the common red ones. Quickly, Richard pulled it out, stuffed the paper in, and replaced it. He looked around cautiously, put his hands in his pockets, and walked back to the house and into the kitchen, quite forgetting to go to the stables and attend to the harness.

Betsy came toward him with a sulky look on her face. "You

are bid to meet the master's lady," she said in cool tones. "They are just now in the small front parlor having their morning chocolate, late as it is." Betsy stared at him critically and took down a brush and cloth which hung on pegs beside the door. "Tidy your coat and wipe off your shoes. Mistress Hogarth does not favor ragamuffins."

"I'm not a ragamuffin," Richard flared, but he did what Betsy ordered.

Betsy flounced ahead of him to a door next to the fireplace, tapped upon it, and went in. Richard followed at Betsy's heels. Inside, three fashionably dressed ladies sat around a small table, drinking from tiny painted cups. The dog Trump lolled on the seat of a gilt and brocade chair.

Betsy dropped a quick curtsy to a woman with a long pink-cheeked face, a smiling mouth, and shining dark eyes. Her gown was of deep garnet-red satin with lace at the square-cut neck and elbows, and about her throat she wore a black ribbon. On her dark hair was a white lace pinner cap. "This is Richard Larkin, my lady," said Betsy, curtsying again, and hurrying back to the kitchen. Richard made the finest bow he could.

"Richard," said the lady in a soft voice. "I am Mistress Hogarth, and these ladies are Dame Thornhill, my mother," she nodded to an old lady, dressed all in fine black silk, who had the same long face and dark, wise eyes. "And across from me is Mistress Ann Hogarth, the master's sister." Richard turned toward a little woman dressed in striped blue and violet satin some years younger than the painter. She had the same clever blue eyes and smiling lips. "You will take note of the wishes of us all when you are not serving Master Hogarth," said Mistress Hogarth. "But chiefly you will serve him. Do you understand?"

"Yes, my lady."

"Well, that is clear. You may go, Richard."

Richard bowed once more and was almost out the door, when Dame Thornhill called to him, her voice thin and silvery. "Betsy Lewes tells us you are from the American Colonies, boy. How do you like old England?"

Richard hesitated before replying and finally bowed to the old woman. "I like it tolerably well, my lady."

Ann Hogarth quickly brought her fan up in front of her mouth. The gesture was oddly like that of her brother's when he had tried not to smile at Abby's curtsy in the garden. Dame Thornhill only nodded and Mistress Hogarth picked up the chocolate pot and shook it, making a little face of displeasure. "Do tell Betsy to bring in another pot of chocolate at once," she commanded.

Richard took Mistress Hogarth's request to Betsy, who ran to tell Hannah Charke. The cook pulled out a saucepan from the ashes, took down a second elaborate pot from the shelf, and filled it. Betsy put it on a tray, her skirts and petticoats whirling behind her as she hurried into the parlor.

She was back almost at once and giggled at Richard, who stood awkwardly in the center of the kitchen. "La, they say you're a handsome lad, and that you could be a fine spark some day soon," she said slyly.

"Oh, Betsy, don't tease me," Richard said. "I don't know the fine ways of the London folk."

"You do well enough. The ladies exclaimed over your polished manners and your graceful deportment, not to mention your provoking eyes."

Richard blushed at this loud speech, for Hannah looked up from slicing a cabbage and grinned at him. He was amazed; he hadn't said anything more than "yes" or "no" all the time he'd been in the parlor.

"Master 'Ogarth'll be paintin' yer, too," said Hannah, putting down the knife, "'e'll mebbe get more pleasure outa that than 'e does of paintin' the likes of me or of poor old Matt here."

Old Matt was sound asleep next to the chimney, dozing as peacefully as Abby ever did. Richard looked at him in envy. He was tired, footsore, worried, and in grave danger. And, there was little he could do about it but stay in Chiswick under Hogarth's roof. It was plain to see that William Hogarth was a man of some power. But could the painter stand up against men like Sirius and Spica and Antares, men who did not hesitate to murder and who in the end were able to conceal their crime successfully?

Hannah pointed to Betsy. "Show th' lad 'ere th' 'orses and th' carriage if 'e 'asnt already seen 'em, and then yer take 'im down to th' Mall so's 'e can find th' river without askin' 'is way of th' looby country folk 'ereabouts. 'Tis too fine a day fer young folk to be cooped up when courtin' weather's on us."

Betsy laughed at the look on Richard's face. "Hannah only teases, Dick. Wouldn't you like to see the Mall? It's wonderful fine. The carriage isn't to be called for today, so come along. I have an errand to do on the Mall anyway." She grabbed Richard's hand and pulled him out the door and along the back of the house and out through the iron grill.

Richard stared fearfully up the lane, but to his relief there was no painted carriage in sight. "Do you often see fine carriages in Chiswick?"

"Oh, yes. They go back and forth all the time to Lord Burlington's great house and ours. Master Hogarth has callers who don't always come by way of the river."

They turned and walked down the lane for a time and then they entered Church Street. Richard stared at the Burlington Arms, a tavern of times long past. In spite of his fear of seeing

Sirius, he looked closely at the low building made of timber and white plaster.

"It was built either in the days of old King Henry, you know, the one with all the wives, or maybe in the days of Queen Elizabeth," explained Betsy. "It's very old and so is the church down by the water."

Richard and Betsy wandered along the narrow winding little street with its old houses and stopped before St. Nicholas Church. It was a gray stone building and looked very ancient to Richard's eyes. The green churchyard was dotted here and there by gray-white tombstones. Many of them were covered over with moss. In front of the church behind the iron railings lay flat gravestones, something Richard had never seen before.

"Do people walk on them, Betsy?" he asked, pointing.

"Of course, looby! How else are you to tell who's buried under them if you don't stand on them and read the names?"

Richard shook his head in amazement. They went on to the left down Chiswick Mall itself. He had to admit that the tall brick and stone houses along the Mall were, as Betsy Lewes had said, monstrously fine; each had its ornamental iron fence and gate and across the road its flower garden, next to the banks of the Thames.

Not more than thirty yards out in the river lay a small green island, covered with trees and swarming with hundreds of gulls, ducks and swans. Several men were rowing out to it in little boats.

"That's Chiswick Eyot," Betsy explained, "and the trees are osiers. Men who live here in Chiswick cut down the osiers and weave them into baskets. That's what those men are going to do, and that's the county of Surrey across on the other side of the river where you see all those cows grazing."

The Thames was at high tide, and Richard was impressed at the amount of activity that took place on the river. Fishermen in small boats moved back and forth spreading their nets. All manner of sailing craft were going up river away from London. Suddenly a large glittering barge with gorgeously liveried rowers came speeding down the river and Betsy pinched Richard's arm excitedly. "Oh, we are in luck, Dick! That's the Lord Mayor of London's barge. I wonder where he's been. Isn't it a fine sight, though? When the Lord Mayor doesn't want his barge, it is kept in Chiswick not far away from here at Strand-on-the-Green."

They watched the barge until it flashed out of sight. The sun picked up the glitter of red and blue livery and gold paint. The water dripping from the oars dazzled their eyes.

"You've seen what there is to see of Chiswick Mall," Betsy announced. "Do you think you can find your way back to Master Hogarth's? I have to look in on an ailing friend of Hannah's, who works here at Bedford House. I'm to find out if she wants me to go out into the fields and gather some tansy or herbs for her. That's my errand."

"I'm sure I can, Betsy." Richard smiled, as he thought of his life in Pennsylvania where he'd often gone hunting alone miles away from his home. "You've been so good to Abby and me that I want to thank you for everything." Richard looked at Betsy gratefully. "You came along when we needed a friend."

"Well, you have friends a-plenty at Hogarth House now." She waved to him and hastened away toward Bedford House.

Richard put his hands in his pockets and began to trudge along the Mall back to Church Street. He had better mend that bit of harness and see to the horses before Master Hogarth asked him about them. He quickened his steps as he reached St. Nicholas Church. There was a very big man digging a new grave not far from the iron railings of the churchyard. Richard glanced at him casually, stopped, and then came closer to the railings. The man looked familiar. He wore a rough gray workman's smock, but the hawk-nosed face and the grizzled bob wig Richard had seen before. It was surely the old man with the large silver watch who had sat in the common room of the Seven Stars only the night before.

The man looked up as Richard drew back from the railing. Amazement and then annoyance crossed his face. Hastily he threw the spade into the grave and beckoned to Richard, at the same time looking around to make sure that no one else was in the churchyard. Richard hesitated for a moment and then walked around the church, back among the gravestones, and into the yard.

The gravedigger met him with an expression of deep concern on his heavy face. "What are you doing here, you jackanapes?" he asked in a loud whisper. "I warned you to flee."

With a second shock Richard remembered the voice—the voice in the dark that had saved him—the wheezing tones of Saturn. The man in the common room and Saturn were one and the same! "I came to Chiswick because I was told it was safe, and I've found a place here in William Hogarth's house, sir," he replied as calmly as he could, without mentioning the man's identity.

"Safe!" snorted the man with contempt. "Some places in this little country village are no more safe for you, boy, than the Seven Stars is right at this moment. Sit down with me on this bench out of sight and we'll collect our wits and see what you are to do."

Richard obeyed and sat down next to him.

"Now," the man began, "what do you know of this dangerous game, you young idiot?"

"Why should I tell you?" asked Richard, angry at all the

insults. "You're Saturn, the man who helped me last night, and the man I served in the common room. But I don't know who you really are, so why should I trust you?" He shivered at the look in the hawk-lidded eyes as the man leaned over him.

"Do not trifle with me, boy. I am on the business of those who stand far above you and me. I can tell you little of my affairs, but I am no gravedigger and I labor here only to watch who comes and goes upon the river. It is perilous for you to learn much of what Saturn knows, and you are too deep into this business as it is. I did save your life and you owe me much. Tell me what you have guessed of this matter, and I can advise you further."

"There's a plot, I believe," Richard hesitated. "I guess I do owe you something for saving my life, sir; but can I really trust you?"

"You can trust me, boy," Saturn said kindly. "Go on."

"They plan to kill the King, and I believe they are Jacobites, for they spoke of Lord Lovat as a martyr and of Culloden battle. Too, one of them spoke of the King of Prussia as Mars and of many other stars, which he said were all here in London, except for a few in France. There were so many names of stars and planets, sir, that I can't remember them all."

"Did you hear the real names of these men?" asked Saturn sharply.

"One of them is an alderman of London, I think, and one of them may be called Alec Guthry. They used the names of stars, sir, in place of proper names."

Saturn shook his head. "I know no Alec Guthry." he said.

"That was the name on the letter that Antares dropped," Richard explained.

"Aha, so you have the letter. Where is it?"

"Not with me, sir. I hid it."

"That was wise of you," Saturn patted Richard on the shoulder. "You bring that note to me here in the morning. It may be important. Now, lad, do you remember any mention of the date set for this scheme? I think I know exactly what fine game is afoot, but I don't know when. You tell me and I'll get it to my friend when he comes up the river in the morning to collect my news."

"Antares spoke of the tenth of November," replied Richard, "and that date appears again in the letter."

"Good. This is great luck, boy." Saturn laughed a rumbling laugh, his hands held to his vast stomach. "The pieces of the puzzle are falling together in an admirable fashion. You bring me that letter here early in the morning, and I'll see that it gets to the right persons." He bent to look at Richard and winked heavily. "There will be a reward for this day's work, my lad, unless I miss my guess."

"Would there be enough to pay three passages back to the American Colonies?" Richard asked.

"Three?" exclaimed the mock gravedigger, his tufted brows raised. "You have friends who'll go there with you?"

Richard nodded. "I want to earn as much as I can and as quickly, sir; you see, in Master Hogarth's service I can only get a few pennies ahead each month."

"Well, boy, you work for me! You fetch me that letter and you say nothing of this affair, and there will be a few gold pieces in it for you. If you really want to earn your passage money, you could do it easily enough, I warrant, if you do not mind a bit of danger."

"What else have I known here in England?" Richard shrugged and paused. "But I don't want to hurt my friends."

"If you are suspected, they will be endangered. You will broach their safety. That is part of the deep game we play, boy. They can be used as pawns against you. You can protect them but you must have the cunning of a fox, the bravery of a dog-worried badger with a pin through his tail at Hockley Hole. But the rewards will be great and you will be doing something for England."

"I want my passage home and I'll take the risks," said Richard without hesitation. "I already know enough to have myself and my friends murdered, so why not go on? Just don't talk to me of doing something for England. England has done nothing for me."

"Ah, bitter, lad! You sound bitter. Well, I like that. You do not enter the King's service as a fool, blinded by rosy patriotic visions. The man who coolly plays at high stakes lives longest at this business."

"I'll bring my letter to you if you promise to give me a piece of gold for it," said Richard firmly.

"Well spoken," Saturn approved. "You shall have your gold. Now I believe I know all that transpires in Chiswick. I know the Chiswick men who plot with your Society of the Stars in this latest piece of Jacobite folly, and I live to trap them in a pit of their own digging. What I need to know are the names of all who take part in it."

"Didn't you know any of the men who met at the tavern last night?" Richard asked.

"I knew all of the Londoners present. Others were Scotsmen and Irishmen, who are maintained and paid by the Stuart Pretender in France or by the King of Prussia. They are mostly proscribed exiles—and by that I mean that they are not to come back to England under the pain of death or imprisonment. These exiles I did not know by sight. However," Saturn went on ponderously, "there are other Englishmen in high places in on this scheme, and I must know all of them. Master Hogarth will leave Chiswick within a few weeks to spend the winter in London, as is his custom. You must arrange to be left behind in Chiswick somehow. Then, you must take service at the Earl of Burlington's house. He has vast gardens and surely he can use a gardener's boy to rake up fallen leaves. Keep your eyes and ears open, lad, for, unknown to the good Earl, who is loyal to King George, there are Jacobites aplenty in Chiswick. Some of his fine and noble guests are surely aware of the plot, if not part of it."

"I know that there are Jacobites here, sir," said Richard, "for earlier today I was at a Turnham Green tavern, called the King of Bohemia, and I heard talk of the 'Sun in France' and of 'the time being at hand.' All from a man who wore a riding cloak and who rode a lathered horse."

Saturn broke in. "The King of Bohemia has been a hotbed of Jacobites for many years. The Sun in France is James, the 'Old Pretender,' or 'Jamie the Rover,' as some call him, and they refer to the plot of the Society of the Stars. Your rider posted fast to the west, no doubt, while his fellow horsemen galloped north to prepare the way."

"There's more, sir. I saw Sirius, the leader of the plotters, with a man who looked very like him. He went by Master Hogarth's house in a fine carriage with a lady in a blue cloak."

"Ah, yes. They were surely going to the Earl of Burlington's house to pass a secret message to the Earl's Irish steward. He's a man who has power with thousands of his countrymen, the sedan-chair carriers in St. Giles. They may well rise to support Charles Edward Stuart on behalf of his father, 'Jamie the Rover.' This steward of Lord Burlington's is the man I am chiefly set to watch. For your information, boy, the creature called Sirius, the fine gentleman who pushed you out of his way at the Seven Stars, is Alexander Murray, the man who is to lead the mobs of Westminster and who has demonstrated that ability already. This man is one of the most dangerous in all London. He fomented riots not long ago, and is so proud that he refused to go down on his knees and beg the pardon of Parliament, choosing exile first. The other man is his brother, Patrick Murray, the Scottish Lord Elibank. And the woman, I strongly suspect, is Lady Primrose, a staunch Jacobite and a devoted friend of Prince Charles Edward. She is a frequent caller at Chiswick House, where the unsuspecting Earl of Burlington bids many odd fish to see his rare statues and his costly paintings."

Richard grinned, remembering Master Hogarth's anger at the fancies of his noble neighbor, the Earl.

"Did Alexander Murray mark you?" Saturn asked.

"I don't think he did. The expression in his eyes didn't change." Richard's smile faded.

"With that man, you cannot be sure," said Saturn heavily, shifting around on the uncomfortable stone bench. "He may have cloaked his gaze as he spied you out. His Society of the Stars may well have agents here at Chiswick Mall as well as at the King of Bohemia and Lord Burlington's estate. There is much yet that I do not know. Can you remember anything else from the talk last night that you have not told me?"

Richard thought deeply for a moment and then spoke up. "I don't remember all the names of the stars or all of the places that Antares rattled off, sir, but I do recall something he said about Polaris and the north. Little as I know of astronomy, I do know that Polaris is the North Star."

"That would, of course, be the first move in their game," said Saturn, with a nod. "I must check our agents in France to see who Polaris is. Surely he is one of the proscribed exiles to be sent to raise the clans in Scotland once more to attack England and King George's government. Polaris is important. He is surely a Scot himself, for no one else could get the clans to follow him. Will the Jacobites never give up these hopes of theirs?" Saturn sighed deeply.

Richard was silent, and Saturn slumped, gazing moodily at his mud-stained shoes. His great body sagged with weariness. Finally he roused himself and fumbled in his pocket and hauled out a large silver coin. "Here's a crown for your services, my lad, and to seal a bargain. But first I give you the name I am called here if you should need to ask for me. I am known as William Craig in Chiswick, and who, sirrah, are you?"

"Richard Larkin, sir." Richard took the silver crown from the man's hand. "But one more question, sir. Who was the man they murdered last night?"

"A London merchant of some wealth, who had more than once been suspected of supplying money to the Stuart cause. Though I am not greatly concerned by the individual murderer, for in my eyes all of the plotters stand equally guilty, I am curious about who murdered him, lad."

"He was called Spica," replied Richard. "He wore a scarlet coat, and was one of the men who chased me down the hall."

Saturn nodded his head. "And who was the other with him, the one who asked me the questions about you?"

"That was Antares. He is the man who lost the note, and who may be called Alec Guthry."

"Well, that doesn't help me much," Saturn wheezed unhappily. "Unfortunately, all I could see was their backs by the light from the Charles Wain, as they returned empty-handed. I wish now that I had not so hastily blown out my candle when I heard your footsteps. I could have seen the face of this fine Antares. The name Alec Guthry means nothing to me. Very likely he is newly come from France or Italy and was in exile with the 'Old Pretender' or with Prince Charles Edward. I know that he is a Scot from his speech, even though his accent was faint."

"I think that he is as dangerous as Sirius," stated Richard gravely. "And he is as much an enemy to Sirius, or Alexander Murray, as you are. He tried to call him out for a duel, but the others stopped it."

"So conspirators fall out! That could be good news, my boy." Saturn chuckled and dug into his pocket again, bringing out another crown, which he pushed into Richard's hand. "Now go on with you, boy, before Master Hogarth sends you packing off. I shall be expecting you in the morning as we agreed." Saturn reached into his pocket, and pulled out his large silver watch. He tapped it. "Be here at six in the morning, and be prompt."

It was raining the next morning when Richard was awakened by old Matt shaking at his shoulder. He scrambled out of his narrow pallet in the little attic servant's room and into his shirt and breeches and down the winding staircase to the kitchen.

"Sleepyhead," scolded Betsy, standing at the door and

handing him a wooden pail. "It's seven o'clock, and everyone else is up and around except the master and the ladies. Fine folk always sleep late. Your Abby has already had her bread and cheese and a piece of bacon and gone out to play. Now you go find a milk girl right away. One might be in the Mall or Church Lane and if there isn't one there, go out to one of the fields where they're milking. Dick, don't be late today. You know how angry Master Hogarth was yesterday when you were gone so long."

Richard nodded and hurried out the door. He ran over to the wall, removed the brick and stuffed the note into his pocket. With the pail swinging on his arm, he ran as fast as his legs would carry him down to the Mall. Would Saturn have waited for him? He stumbled to a halt and peered through the railings of St. Nicholas Church, but there was no gravedigger in sight. He was too late after all! Richard sighed in despair. Why had he overslept this morning of all mornings? He had to stay up late last night patching the harness. That plus his fearful experiences of the night before, had exhausted him. Richard turned away and walked slowly down the Mall. How would he get in touch with Saturn again? What could he do? But perhaps his friend was only gone for a short time. He'd find the milk girl and come back to look again. Richard smiled and walked on.

Just ahead of him a group of osier cutters were clustered at the river's edge gesturing and talking loudly. Richard walked over to them. Perhaps they'd know where he could find a milk girl at this hour. "Please can you tell me . . ." he began, but choked off the words as he looked down on the pebble-strewn beach where Saturn lay, his eyes closed, his gravedigger's smock streaming with water, his shoes missing, and his face cold and set.

"'Tis th' new gravedigger—robbed and murthered," said an old osier cutter in a casual voice. "There's not a piece of siller nor a farthin' nor anythin' else on 'im."

"'Appens all th' time," commented another, grinning at Richard's shocked face. "'E'll 'ave a knife in 'is back, if I don' miss my guess." The man gestured to another to help him roll the dead man over. "Look'ee," he pointed with some pride. "Look'ee, boy."

Richard stared at the dagger that stuck out from Saturn's back, a dagger exactly like the one Antares had given Spica at the Seven Stars.

CHAPTER 5

Many Orbits

SOMEHOW Richard found a milk girl and filled the wooden pail. He stumbled back to the Hogarth house, not quite realizing he was there until he pushed open the iron grill. What could he do now? The cold fright in his stomach made him ill. The Society of the Stars had agents in Chiswick who had known of Saturn and his work. Richard was sure of that. Not for one moment did he believe what the osier cutter had said; he knew that William Craig, or Saturn, had not been murdered by robbers. Who was the other agent that Saturn had mentioned, the one who was to come up the river to take Saturn's messages? Had he seen William Craig, or had he found him murdered and quietly gone on his way to avert suspicion? But there was no help for him there. The other agent surely didn't know of Richard's existence and there was no way to contact him or give him Antares' letter.

Richard looked at the paper and hurriedly stuffed it back into its wall hiding place. He pressed his face against the cold rain-soaked bricks and thought for a moment. Danger lay all about him; for if Saturn had been marked out in the churchyard, Richard could have been seen too. There was no place to run to without money or powerful friends. He could not involve the Hogarths or their household. Something told him that William Hogarth would only laugh. It seemed to Richard that Master Hogarth found him a bit dreamy and over-fanciful. He had said harsh words the night before when he had found the harness unmended, saying that what could one expect from a lad who fancied Roman poets so much? No, he could not tell Hogarth and he would not alarm Mrs. Hogarth and Dame Thornhill with tales of a murder. That would upset their quiet, safe country life in Chiswick. He would go back to Samuel Johnson, who had helped him before and who had promised to help him again if he ever needed it.

Richard walked slowly back to the kitchen and put down the milk pail on Hannah's table. Betsy sat across the room, busily plucking a chicken over a wooden tub; white feathers flew everywhere about her.

"Betsy," said Richard, "do you think Master Hogarth would let me go into the city this morning?"

"La, you just got here and already you want to be going again." Betsy raised her eyebrows in disapproval.

"I have to go," he said. "It's very important."

"You have a lot of mystery about you, don't you, Dick? Well, if you won't tell me why you have to go, I won't help you either."

"Betsy, I'm in trouble," he said urgently. "I've got to go to London even when I don't ever want to go there again."

"And what have you done? Have you stolen something?"

She grabbed a handful of feathers and pulled with all her might.

"No, but I saw a man killed in London, and the men who did it are hunting for me."

Her eyes widened. "Do they know you're here in Chiswick?"

"I don't know, but I want to go to London and get some advice."

"Well, tell the master, Dick, and he can advise you as well as anyone can."

"No, it's not like that. I don't want to drag you and everyone else in this house in on my troubles."

"But if it's just a killing, we can't be involved, can we?"

"It's not *just* a murder, Betsy. It's a great deal more than that, and it's dangerous, too."

"La, I do believe you are teasing me, Dick Larkin," Betsy said primly. "And I think you like to try to be mysterious and different. As if being from the American Colonies isn't different enough."

"Please, Betsy," Richard pleaded, "can't you find some way to get me to London on an errand? I swear to you I'm not teasing."

Betsy stared at him, put down the chicken, and after a long moment said, "I really do believe you, Dick. Master Hogarth's busy with his painting of Abby now. I reckon he has enough colors so he won't be needing more of those," she paused for a moment. "But I did hear him say that his frame-makers were too slow with a frame he wants. Maybe he'd let you go there and hurry them up. But you'd have to be business-like and get a letter from the frame-makers explaining why they are late and all. Master Hogarth expects work to be done."

Richard nodded, remembering well the unpatched harness. Betsy got up and pointed to the chicken she had just dumped into the tub. "You go on with that, will you, Dick? It's for the master's dinner. I'll go take him his chocolate and mention the frame-maker. Then I'll tell him you could go. He'll let you take a horse, I'm sure. If not, he'll give you money for the watermen to row you to the city."

"Try to get the horse, please, Betsy." Richard sat down on the stool and picked up the half-plucked bird. He shuddered at the prospect of seeing Saturn's dead white face again down on Chiswick Mall.

Betsy Lewes came back shortly to tell him that it was all arranged. He was to take Master Hogarth's fine black horse, but he was not to ride him hard and he was to come directly back after seeing the frame-maker. "You don't know the city well, Dick. I told the master that, so if you say you got lost you'll have time to see your friend and get your advice. It isn't hard to get lost in London."

Richard nodded and went to the pegs where his coat and hat were hung. He put them on while Betsy fished in her apron pocket and handed him a slip of paper on which Hogarth had written the frame-maker's address.

"Master Hogarth wants the frame by the end of the week. So be sure you tell them that." A troubled look crossed Betsy's face. "I don't like bubbling the master, Dick, so don't dally around London."

"I don't like to deceive him any more than you do," said Richard honestly. "And I'll hurry as fast as I can. As soon as I've seen my friend and done Master Hogarth's business with the frame-maker I'll come right back here. Will you look after Abby for me?"

Betsy nodded her head. "And Dick, there's an old riding

cloak of the master's in the stable; wear that for warmth." She turned back to the chicken again, making a snowstorm of feathers. Richard shut the door and ran toward the stable.

He followed the same route he had taken two days before, and with William Hogarth's fast horse beneath him he felt that he all but flew through Turnham Green, Kensington, and into the city itself. It began to rain heavily, an icy autumn rain, as he rode through the dense crowds in Fleet Street, and he was thankful that Betsy had suggested the old black riding cloak. It was warm and it also disguised him. No one hunting a runaway potboy would expect to see him dressed in a cloak, riding a fine horse. Besides it was barely possible to see six yards ahead. Because of the cold, Londoners were burning sea-coal, and the air was thick with sooty smoke. Richard held back his horse to let a sedan chair cross Fleet Street and drops of black rain fell on his wrist, staining his skin.

He rode half the length of the street before he bent from the saddle to ask for Gough Square and Wine Office Court, as Samuel Johnson had told him to do.

A few minutes later he turned the horse into Wine Office Court and asked directions again of an insolent apprentice who demanded to know why the likes of him wanted to see Master Samuel Johnson. He ignored the question and rode on, twisting and turning until he found himself at last in Gough Square in front of the house where Samuel Johnson lived. It was a large red brick building looking like most other London houses except that it was more spacious.

A fine mulberry-colored carriage stood waiting in the rain in front of the house. Richard dismounted, after glancing at it to make sure that this carriage was not the sinister one he had seen in Chiswick. Suddenly, he heard an oddly accented voice call from inside the carriage. "Boy, would you carry a message for a lady, please, and earn a shilling?"

Richard held his horse's reins and walked over.

"Here I am," said the musical voice, and a very pretty woman with great soft dark eyes, clouds of black hair and an olive complexion looked out at him from between the leather coach curtains. "Would you take a message to dear Davy for me? He's upstairs with Samuel Johnson, and I'm so tired of waiting down here all alone." She gave Richard a dazzling smile and put out a white hand with a shilling in it.

"Yes, my lady," said Richard, bowing, taking off his hat and holding it over his breast. "I'll take a message for you if I can, but who is Davy, please?"

"Oh, la, that is fine!" she exclaimed, giggling, and her eyes sparkled. "Now, won't Davy love this piece of wit though? To think someone doesn't know him." She became serious almost at once. "Davy is David Garrick, boy, and please tell him that if he does not come down at once, Madame Garrick has every intention of letting him walk home alone in the mud."

"Yes, my lady," said Richard, grinning, for now he recalled how often he'd heard the famous actor's name. He took the shilling from the lady's hand and bowed once more.

Richard hitched his horse to an iron post in front of the house, and went up to the door, rapping with the heavy brass knocker. The door was opened by a sharp-featured disagreeable-looking old man who gave Richard a suspicious inspection and refused to let him in until Richard pointed to the waiting carriage, saying he had a message from Madame Garrick. The old man stepped back grumbling that Samuel Johnson kept strange enough company and that no good would come of it and that he would never finish his dictionary with all of these interruptions. He finally pointed the way up the stairs growling that Richard would find Johnson in the attic if he wanted to climb all that way. Richard sighed. Why was all life in London conducted in attics? He climbed wearily past floor after floor, stopped at a door at the top of the long flight of steps, and tapped at it.

"Come in," shouted a rasping voice that Richard remembered well from that night on the steps of St. Sepulchre's. Richard went in to find Samuel Johnson seated in a large old chair. He had been talking to another man whose back was turned.

The light of the day, even of this black murky day, was not kind to Samuel Johnson. He was even uglier than Richard had remembered. Richard looked away to repress a shiver and his gaze wandered over the room itself.

It was quite large and tables and chairs were everywhere. Great sheets of paper lay in wads and masses on the floor and around the table legs. On one side of the room Richard saw nothing but row upon row of books, lying all helter-skelter on rickety shelves. Two men sat at tables, scratching away with quill pens.

"Pray, sirrah, who are you? And what do you desire of me?" Samuel Johnson finally thundered. At Johnson's roar, the three men swung around. The two at the tables were elderly, plainly dressed and nondescript. The third man standing in front of Johnson was vastly different. He was small, almost dainty. He raised his very black eyebrows and twisted his face into such a ludicrous expression when he saw how Johnson's shout had affected Richard that the boy almost laughed. This must be the great David Garrick of Drury Lane Theatre. The actor had shining dark eyes, a largish nose and a wide mouth, but these things meant nothing in a face that switched expressions as quickly as the wind. His clothes were dazzling. Alongside Johnson's old brown cloth coat and breeches, Garrick's crimson cut velvet blazed like a bonfire and his elegant white silk stockings and gleaming diamond-buckled black shoes contrasted violently with Johnson's old scuffed things. Diamond buttons twinkled on his coat and his gold silk-fringed waistcoat. On his head perched a fine bob wig with curls and a large black silk bow. He leaned on a gold-headed ebony cane and cocked his head at Richard.

"Eh, what have we here, Samuel?" he asked in rolling tones. "Does the lad have some new definition for your dictionary or an article for *The Rambler*? Out of the mouth of babes, Samuel! Have you come to that?"

"Please, sir," Richard broke in before Johnson could bellow again, "if you are Master David Garrick, sir, the man who acts, your wife has sent me to tell you that if you don't come down at once, sir, she will have the carriage driven off and you can walk home in the mud, sir."

Samuel Johnson threw back his great head and roared. "The man who acts, huh? Did ye hear that, Davy? The man who acts! Ha, ha! Go along. *Signora* Garrick is a forward kind of body. God bless me, but she does make our Davy jump!"

David Garrick smiled mockingly at Johnson. "My wife is a sensible girl. She would not have me stain my shoes. Well, then, Samuel, will you not come to see my *Henry VIII* when I put it on?"

"You know I will not," said Johnson, "and I cannot conceive why you bearded me here in my den today to beg me to attend one of your odious performances at Drury Lane. I know of your butchery of Shakespeare. There will be far more of Davy Garrick's work than there'll ever be of Shakespeare's once you've worked on that unfortunate play. I may rest easy on that. And you know, although I wish you heartily well, I do detest actors. You are the sole exception. No sir, Davy, you'll not see Samuel Johnson at your Drury Lane."

The actor shrugged his shoulders and winked at Richard, as if to ask whatever did one do about such a surly bear as Samuel Johnson. "I shall take my leave then, Samuel," he said without anger. "I'll not argue with a man who roars so against me, but will hope to see you, even if you give me cruel usage, at Old Slaughter's coffee house next week again."

"That you shall, for I shall have the relish for it then," promised Johnson. "And, now, Davy, take up your fine hat, you peacock of a man, and take up your fine cloak and get yourself down to your lady before you have to walk. Who can imagine the elegant Garrick walking! I do believe that *Signora* Garrick would let you go by shank's mare, too. These Italian creatures have their distracting ways."

With unusual grace Garrick walked over to a chair where he'd hung his gold-laced hat and his black velvet cloak. He put them on with a flourish that dazzled Richard. Samuel Johnson watched and chuckled. "Ah, Davy, you have a spellbound audience. Put a bit more artful conduct in the throwing of the cloak. A bit more of a dash over the left shoulder, I do believe, sirrah. It was a fine gesture and suitable to a Falstaff as played by Garrick, I would say. Or perhaps it would do for Richard III."

"Do you really think it was?" asked Garrick, frowning seriously. "Should I flick my wrist a little more?"

"Oh, go along, Davy. Let me get back to my labors!"

Bowing slightly, David Garrick moved elegantly past Richard, then clattered down the steps as if he'd been as young as the boy himself.

Samuel Johnson stared at Richard, waiting for him to speak.

"I really came to ask your advice, sir, on an important matter," Richard began. "I only ran into Mrs. Garrick and carried her message by accident. I met you, sir, on the steps of St. Sepulchre's Church some weeks ago. My name is Richard Larkin."

"I don't remember you," came the rumbling reply.

"But you gave the little girl with me a penny."

Johnson waved his hand as if Richard were a bothersome fly. "I do that constantly. It is my besetting sin to give pennies to waifs."

"I'm from Pennsylvania Colony," said Richard, desperately trying to identify himself.

Johnson's heavy face brightened. "Ah, yes, the boy who spoke of the savage Delawares! And why do you come to me, sirrah?"

"You said if I ever needed it you would help me and to come to you at your house in Gough Square."

"And so here you are." Johnson heaved a massive sigh. "Well, what is it? Out with it! Is it a cruel master? Ah, you've been caught theiving—a matter of the heart—a brother in Newgate or Fleet prison—a sister in Bridewell prison beating hemp—your uncle in Bedlam Hospital, or what have you?"

"I believe, sir, that it's a matter of treason," Richard answered.

"Aha, treason! Well, that is an unusual thing, lad. And what are you, pray, an agent of the Pretender?" Johnson grumbled and then chuckled, waving at the two men in the corner, who went promptly back to their work.

Richard felt his face getting red. Johnson did not believe him. He left the doorway without Johnson's permission, pulled up a chair and sat down. Johnson eyed him tolerantly and said nothing. "Send those men away, please," Richard said softly. "I don't belong in Bedlam with the lunatics, and I do know what I'm talking about. I don't want anyone else to hear me but you. I'm not an agent of the Pretender. If anything, I think the Jacobites want to kill me, too, sir."

Samuel Johnson smiled. "Well, well," he said, "I do believe you ought to aid Tobias Smollett with his novels or write one yourself. Such a fine imagination and taste for drama! *Roderick Random* is not a bad book, lad. Have you read it yet?"

"Oh, sir," Richard begged again, "you must believe me. Alexander Murray plots with other men to kill King George. I overheard him and six others conspiring for the Stuart Pretender night before last right here in the city. I saw them kill a man that night and now they're hunting for me, and I know they've killed another man this morning."

Johnson shot a hard glance at Richard. "And what man did they murder the other night, lad?"

"I hear he was a London merchant, sir, who gave money to help the Jacobites and who fought at Culloden. He was a nervous little man, dressed all in black."

"Carlton!" exclaimed Samuel Johnson in a strange choked voice. "Your description is quite apt. I mark the man well. Tell me of the second man."

"He was an agent of the King's," explained Richard, "at least that's what he told me yesterday, and he was found this morning with a dagger in him, too. Just the way Mr. Carlton died, I know. I saw Carlton stabbed."

Johnson was suddenly in a state of agitation, his face jerking, his large hands twitching. "Gilman, Hay!" he called out. "Go take a pot of ale, lads. The dictionary can wait for a few moments."

The two men grabbed up their hats, looking curiously at

Richard as they hastened out of the door. When their footsteps died away, Johnson leaned forward, his hand clasped like a vise on Richard's arm.

"Who else knows of this perilous business, Larkin? Tell me at once. Tell me the whole story."

Though Richard was frightened by Johnson's manner, he kept his wits about him and did not implicate Jeremy Belcher or Timothy Quayle. Nor did he mention Chiswick or Hogarth. He reported only the conversation among the members of the Society of the Stars, the murder of Carlton and his meeting with Saturn. He decided too not to mention Saturn's wish that he take service with the Earl of Burlington. As Richard ended his story he sighed with relief. "No one but you, sir, knows anything of this now that Saturn is dead," he finished.

"You've not gone to a justice of the peace or to the watch?" Johnson released his grip on Richard and drummed his fingers on the chair arm.

"No, sir, I don't know where to go or what to do, and I don't really understand anything that is going on, either. This is why I came to you. I don't dare go to anyone who is an officer of the King. They'd put me in Newgate even if I didn't steal the alderman's snuffbox. What's my word against an alderman's?"

Johnson nodded in agreement, pushed his vast jerking body out of the chair and began pacing the attic. His head shook as he did a little involuntary dance. He looked both pathetic and funny and made Richard feel, in spite of his own troubles, like laughing. At the same time he remembered the man's terrible temper and kept his face straight.

"I will tell you the story of that sad and accursed House of Stuart," Johnson began, "but only if you come and walk with me, for it is a tale of so much wretchedness, treachery and misery that I cannot bear to sit at my ease and speak of it. Perhaps when you have listened to it you will understand more of what you have heard and seen." Samuel Johnson paused in his stride and stood for a moment, pulling at his lower lip. "The melancholy history of the Stuarts is a long and complicated one involving many factors, boy, so I'll try to give you as short an account of it as I can. But first, do you know who the Stuarts are? Tell me how much you know of all this."

Richard shook his head. "I know very little of it, sir. I was taught little history although I do know the Latin poets. My schoolmaster didn't like England very well, I'm afraid. All I know is that the House of Stuart once ruled England and that they don't rule any longer, for King George II is a Hanoverian."

Johnson made a grotesque face. "Hanover!" he snorted in contempt. "Aye, we get to that detestable odious breed soon enough in my tale. Too soon! Now come walk with me, sirrah."

Richard paced alongside the huge swaying man, back and forth across the attic; under Johnson's great weight the floor creaked with every step.

"The trouble really began, young Larkin, in 1685 with the death of King Charles II, which gave the thrones of England, Scotland and Ireland to his brother, James II, a Roman Catholic convert. Now, a convert to a faith is always much more violent and strong-willed than the man who is born into the religion. You must remember that England is a Protestant country with a long history of suspicion and hatred of the Catholics. The full strength of that hatred can be measured by how long it has taken England to change to the new style calendar used by the rest of Europe for years—all because the English thought the New Calendar was some sort of Catholic plot. It was adopted here only a few weeks ago, as you surely know. Now, as I have said, James II was a Catholic. He used his position as king to put Roman Catholics in high places, ousting Protestants, and also seeming to give additional strength to the Roman church. Bless me, lad, I forget you come from those barbarous American wildernesses and very likely would not even know what a Protestant or a Catholic might be! Do you know?"

Richard nodded, faintly angry at Johnson's question. He himself was a Protestant and had been taught at an early age that Roman Catholics were agents of the devil. Though after meeting Timothy Quayle, he found this hard to believe.

A great sigh came from Samuel Johnson. "To go on, even this was not the final reason for the flight of James to Catholic France. It was, curiously enough, the birth of a son to him that did this. James had two full-grown daughters and both were Protestants married to Protestant princes in Europe. The English would have put up with James and his Catholicism if it had not been for this innocent newborn babe, but they rejected the prospect of a line of Catholic kings and chose to have the daughters of James II rule in place of James or his baby son." Here Samuel Johnson waggled a finger at Richard. "But remember, too, that by the strict laws of succession, James was the rightful ruler of England and his son, also named James, although you may have heard of him as the 'Old Pretender' or 'Jamie the Rover' or the 'King Over the Water,' is still the rightful king in the minds of many. His son, Prince Charles Edward, is the heir apparent. Those who feel James to be the rightful king, be they Protestants or Catholics, are called Jacobites after the Latin name for James, which, as you may know, is Jacobus. These Jacobites have made many attempts to restore what they sincerely believe is the man chosen by God to be the ruler of England."

Richard interrupted. "But how does Scotland figure in all this?"

"Do not break into my story, boy!" Johnson bellowed at him and went on. "The greatest source of strength for this movement and of the various armed uprisings which have taken place in the last sixty years or so has been in Scotland. Originally the Stuart kings came from there, and clan loyalty is very intense. Scotland, for your information and the furtherance of your lamentably deficient education, is one of the most dreadful places in the world—bitterly cold, windswept, craggy, barren and constantly drenched in rain. It produces nothing but oats, cattle, and a particularly tenacious fortitudinous sort of man who, for some inexplicable reason, loves his impossible land with an insane passion. A Scot is exactly the type of person I find intolerable, sir. I find Scots even worse than you colonists, and I find you quite despicable. Not one of you understands the true noble order of things. I would exercise my prejudices and send you away at once, wretch that you are, if you had attained years of reason and had not that chapfallen look about you that cozens me so. I abominate the American colonists."

Richard opened his mouth to protest, but Johnson silenced him with a mighty roar. "Quiet, sirrah! Do not inflame my temper. Now, the Scots almost succeeded in gaining the throne for the House of Stuart in 1745, as many of us can attest. But, finally, in 1746, at Culloden in Scotland, this last gallant uprising was crushed in a most cruel and monstrous manner by the present King's brother, the Duke of Cumberland, more often than not referred to, even here in London, as 'Billy the Butcher' because of his brutal treatment of the defeated Scottish Jacobites. It was as a result of this uprising, called the '45, that Lord Lovat, Lord Balmerino, Lord Derwentwater and Lord Kilmarnock were beheaded for treason."

Richard could not contain himself. "But the House of Hanover, sir? How did they get to the throne?"

"By invitation of Parliament," said Johnson sourly. "When the two Protestant daughters of James II died without leaving children, the Hanoverians were called from Germany. The only reason they were summoned is because they had a claim to the throne by way of a Stuart ancestor and because of the fact that, if they have any religion at all, it is convincingly Protestant. This is the only reason why anyone would put up with those gross German swine. Still and all, they remain usurpers. It is a great crime that the 'Old Pretender' is not our king, for he is a goodly sober man, even if afflicted with fits of melancholy, but I cannot cavil at this as I suffer from that malady myself. Prince Charles Edward, his son, the lad who lost at Culloden Moor, is everything that England could ask in a monarch." Johnson's face grew purple. "But there is still the old rub. Aye, the 'Old Pretender' is a strong Roman Catholic and will not renounce his faith. In spite of the martyrdom of the Scottish lords and the defeat at Culloden, the Jacobites' hope is still high. Ultimately the rightful, legitimate king of England will be restored to his rightful, legitimate God-given throne!"

Samuel Johnson ended on a triumphant note, almost braying the last few words. He stopped his pacing and turned to stare at Richard with bulging eyes.

"It's a dreadfully confused business, sir," confessed Richard, his head awhirl. "I'm not accustomed to thinking about so many kings all at once, and I'd never thought about a king's throne being given to him by God."

"You have in that statement, Larkin, given me the proof of my comments about the barbarity of you American colonists. Only God can give a king to a throne or a throne to a king. It is part of the order of things! But I refuse to entangle myself in a religious argument this day, for you would surely not understand. Let it suffice to say that this is the reason many of the wisest, clearest-headed men in England favor the return of the House of Stuart."

"Men like Alexander Murray?" Richard asked in all innocence.

"No, not that man!" Johnson thundered. "The thought of his meddling in Jacobite affairs appalls me. He is a Scot, and as I have told you, they feel strongly if they feel anything at all. There are cool heads among them even so, but Alexander Murray is a violent wild man, and I fear the fortunes of the Stuarts are once more in bad hands."

"But what am I to do?" asked Richard. "Can you help me?"

A strange twisted little smile visited Johnson's thick lips. "I am a Jacobite, and some believe that I was out in the '45, Richard Larkin. Not that I will admit the latter, for I could still be taken up for my participation."

"You'd be beheaded?" Richard was horror-stricken. "If they knew you were a Jacobite, they'd chop off your head?"

"I'd not lose my head," Johnson rumbled confidently, "but I would be hanged, very likely. The ax and Tower Hill are reserved for the noblemen and great lords, not for the likes of me. But that is how it should be in the order of things."

Richard shook his head, thinking that "the order of things" took in some very strange ideas. If this was a privilege of rank, he could not comprehend it. He asked again. "What am I going to do?"

Samuel Johnson shook his head and sighed. "I cannot advise you on this. Ask me whatever else you will, and I can try to tell you what is my studied opinion. But I cannot tell you what to do, for I am a Jacobite, sirrah. Would you ask me to suggest you betray a conspiracy formed to return the House of Stuart? Even if I believe that given the complicity of Alexander Murray, it is a hare-brained scheme?"

"But if I went to a magistrate, I wouldn't mention your name. Honestly, sir, I wouldn't!"

"I believe that you would not implicate me, boy, but what chiefly concerns me is the plot. Now let me ask you what you think you are going to do? Before you make your decision, lad, remember the sufferings of the men who have devoted their lives and their fortunes to the rightful cause. Think of the agonies the supporters of Prince Charles Edward Stuart endured in Scotland, and consider the loathesomeness of the Hanoverians, who are not Englishmen at all, who barely trouble to learn the English language, who look upon us as people to be exploited." Johnson raised a great fist and shook it at the ceiling. "By God, sir, the Hanoverians eat up England with their greedy, grasping favorites from Germany, and to think a man like King James lies just over the water patiently waiting while a monstrous bag of tripes, called George II, squats toadlike on the thrones of England and Scotland."

Richard stood aghast as Johnson grew even more purple with rage. His face was engorged with blood, the veins in his thick neck throbbed. He swung like an angry bull and thrust his face into Richard's as he hissed, "Do what you will! If I throttled you, I would throttle the chance of your betraying a conspiracy I wish to succeed, but that would be a crime to sit on my conscience. If you speak, you'll be the death of many men, and if you keep silent, you'll rid England of a festering wound, those damnable Hanoverians. You can do

England a service by your silence and, if you were an Englishman at all, you would do so. Now leave my house, Larkin, and don't come back here again; I shall never know you after this day. I feel that an attack of melancholy will afflict me the moment this anger has passed—an attack which matches my anger! Get you gone before I become so full of spleen that I can never climb out of the pit of melancholy."

Richard turned and fled.

It was all he could do to deal with William Hogarth's frame-makers, the Brothers Gosset in St. Martin's Lane. He remembered to ask for the letter to the painter, saying that the frame would be ready at the proper time. In his misery he could think of nothing else to do but return to Chiswick and Hogarth's house. At least he knew the Hogarth family and Betsy Lewes and felt that they would not desert him as Samuel Johnson had done. Richard did not realize until now how much he had counted on Johnson's advice. And now that the man who had once befriended him turned him away, he was crushed. He rode dejectedly through the heavy rain, his head down, water running off the brim of his three-cornered hat. They moved out of the cobbled streets of London and headed into the mired, rutted turnpike that led to Turnham Green and Chiswick. The horse finished the trip at a dull jogging trot, splashing mud on both of them.

As they turned into the Hogarth yard Betsy Lewes came hurrying out, a shawl flung over her head. The moment Richard dismounted she led the wet, shivering horse inside and threw Richard a large coarse cloth. Then she filled a wooden pail to the brim with oats and put it down before the horse while Richard removed the saddle and bridle.

"No, no," Betsy warned him, as he began to rub down the horse. "That is a clean cloth from the kitchen; wipe your face and hands. They're black with London grime. I'd barely know you. I'll rub the horse down later. Master Hogarth's most particular about this beast. Go give that wet cloak and hat to Hannah to dry and take the frame-maker's message to the master. He's been asking me where you've been so long."

Richard nodded, wiping his face, astonished at the filth that came away on the cloth. He handed it to Betsy and started out the stable door when she called out softly, "How did your affairs go in the city, Dick?"

Richard shook his head sadly.

"Oh, Dick," Betsy said in a tender voice, "then you are in trouble, aren't you?" Her voice rose in concern. "Are those men following you here? Do you want me to tell the master to call the magistrate right away? You know, Dick, there's a pair of pistols in the kitchen, hidden up in the corner cupboard. Would you be needing them? No one would ever know they'd been taken, I'm sure."

"No, Betsy. I don't know that pistols would do much good now."

"Well, then, why not tell me what the trouble is? After Master Hogarth has his message and tells you to go, you can come back here and help me with the horses. They all need currying."

Richard had to smile. It was not Betsy's job to look after the horses. No servant girl or cookmaid did such work. The horses already shone like satin, and the harness, the saddles and even the carriage were polished and bright, the leather gleaming and the brass glittering like the sun. If there was anything at all old Matt liked and did well, it was to look after the stable and its tack. But Betsy's suggestion was not a bad one, even though Richard knew she could not help him. How could a girl of his own age do that, when he couldn't even help himself? But she cared and would be understanding and at that moment this counted for a good deal.

He decided then to tell her. After depositing his borrowed cloak with Hannah Charke and seeing that Abby was napping peacefully in front of the hearth, he delivered the framemaker's note to the painter and returned to the stables. He turned over two empty wooden pails, beckoned to Betsy to sit down, and there in the warm lantern-lit stable he told her his story.

Betsy frowned as she listened and, even when she murmured at the mention of the murder of Saturn in Chiswick, her eyes did not leave Richard's face. When he came to the explanation of Jacobite, Betsy held up her hand. "No, Dick," she said. "I know all about that, I think. Anybody knows that. I've known lots of Jacobites who aren't fine folk at all. But what are you going to do? It seems to me that you have to choose which side you're on."

"I'm in the middle, I guess," Richard observed, sighing. "I don't know what to do. I don't know anything about the Jacobites really, and I know even less about the House of Hanover. It just seems to me that neither of them considers anyone except themselves. They fight each other, chop off people's heads, and murder one another without feeling guilty about it at all. They're far worse than the Delawares or the Mohawks back in the Colonies."

"Maybe they are," Betsy said bitterly. "The noble people don't care if they wound people who are poor. They don't see things the way we do. I suppose it's because they never look at the ground. I think that they really believe that anything they do is all right as long as it gets them what they want."

"Well, I've had a stomachful of fine people. If Alexander Murray, Antares, Spica, and the rest of the Society of the Stars are the sort who fit into Samuel Johnson's 'noble order of things'—well, I don't see anything fine or noble about it!"

Betsy hunched forward, leaning on her fists. Her black eyebrows drew together. "I think you've forgotten one thing, Dick. Everyone else seems to be trying to get what he wants except you. The Society of the Stars wants to put 'Jamie the Rover' on the throne. The Hanoverians want to stay where they are, and no one cares for anyone else. What is it *you* want most of all?"

"To get back to the Colonies," Richard answered quickly. "But Betsy, I need a good deal of money for that."

"And how could you get that money?" she asked. "Not by working for pennies here. You'll never get home to Pennsylvania that way!"

"That's right," Richard agreed. "I never would, and I could never take you and Abby then, could I, unless we all went as bound servants?"

Betsy bit her lip and spat out, "Not me, Dick Larkin! I don't choose to be anyone's bound girl. For that matter, I don't intend to be someone's servant forever."

"Well, I don't want to be bound out either, and there'd be nothing we could do about Abigail. She's too little to work yet. You know, people say in the Colonies that being a bound servant is worse than being a blackamoor slave. Do you suppose that Mistress Hogarth would keep Abby?"

"She might. She dotes on her, heaven knows, for Abby has pretty ways; but the mistress is fickle-tempered and she might tire of her and get the master to send her to the Foundling Hospital or leave her behind in the Leicester Fields house some summer. I wouldn't want to say how she'd fare at the Hospital or in the city. It's dreadful unhealthy there in the summer months."

Richard was shocked. "But would William Hogarth allow that?"

"He gets so tied up in his painting that he might not notice. Oh, he's such a kind man, but Mistress Hogarth is the one who really says who lives in the house. If I had Abby as my little sister, I'd get her out of London." Betsy looked at Richard and her brown eyes grew dark with sadness. "You know, Dick, if you live to be apprenticed here, you're very lucky."

Richard shivered, recalling the chimney sweeps outside the Bishop of Ely's palace. Some apprenticeships did not strike him as being lucky, and Betsy's attitude sometimes surprised him; but perhaps being a Londoner made people hard.

"If I were you, I'd go to see about working at Lord Burlington's estate the minute Master Hogarth goes to the city, and he's leaving for Leicester Fields soon now, Dick. Hannah, Moll and Mistress Hogarth have already started packing. I'd keep my eyes and ears open like that old man Saturn told you.

That's how to get our passage money together."

"But, Betsy, Saturn's dead. I haven't any way to pass on anything I find out, and it will be dangerous."

Betsy laughed almost contemptuously. "You silly goose. You've forgotten something. Not that you'd like to have a girl point it out to you, I suppose. But Saturn told you he watched the steward on Lord Burlington's place, didn't he? And didn't he say that there was a Hanoverian agent who came up the river to take information from him?"

"Yes, he did say both of those things," Richard said, puzzled at her meaning.

"Well, when they find out Saturn has been murdered, they'll send somebody else, won't they? I'll look out for new people in the village for you, and you keep a sharp eye out at Chiswick House. That's where they'll likely put a new agent. They surely wouldn't have anyone new as the church gravedigger, would they? That would give the whole thing away, and he'd surely be murdered, too."

Richard looked at Betsy with new respect. She'd thought faster and deeper than he, and her words were sensible—far more so than he'd expected—and strangely enough her comments about not taking advice from a girl didn't bother him.

"How do I get out of going to Leicester Fields with Master Hogarth?" Richard asked, gratefully. "For that's what I'm going to do, Betsy. It seems to me that ever since I've been in England people have had their way with me. Everything has happened all around me, and I haven't done anything at all except run away. Now, I think it's time I did something, too."

"Good!" Betsy smiled in agreement. "Don't you worry, Dick, about going to Leicester Fields. I'll think of something."

As it turned out, it wasn't necessary for either of them to do much thinking, for that evening Abby refused to eat. She whimpered constantly, and was feverish to the touch. Hannah Charke looked at her chest and arms and nodded wisely. "'Tis no teethin' fit, lad. Th' wee poppet has taken somethin' 'less I miss me guess. Look'ee, lovey, see these big red spots."

Richard held a candle close. Hannah was right. There were red spots on Abby's arms. She wailed when Richard gently touched one; then she dug at it with her sharp little fingernails.

"'Tis a pox," Hannah went on. "'Ave yer 'ad th' pox, Dick?"

For a moment Richard was terrified, but then he realized as Hannah smiled at him that she did not mean the dreaded smallpox, but very likely measles, chicken-pox, or cow-pox. If it had been smallpox, Abby's chances of living would have been very slight, he knew. He decided then and there to have her inoculated, even though this would mean taking a pock from a person suffering from the disease and embedding it in a little cut on Abby's arm. His mother had seen to it that he had been inoculated in Pennsylvania, and he was relieved now that it had been done.

Richard watched thoughtfully, as Betsy bent over to comfort Abby for a moment. He caught himself staring, struck by something warm and lovely, for at that moment with the red lights of the hearth fire shining on her face and dark hair, Betsy was beautiful.

CHAPTER 6

In the Path of Spica

THE yellow buttons of the tansy plant dotted the October meadows as Richard walked along on his way to the Earl of Burlington's Chiswick House. The high dew-damp grass soaked his stockings and shoes. His head was bowed, his mind troubled. He did not want to go to the Earl of Burlington's estate on this gray morning, even if he did know that this was the only way. The thought of deceiving Hogarth again was painful for him. No matter how he excused himself, he knew that he had not been a good servant to the painter. He had not really earned his wages and he had lied again and again to the man, and now he was about to attempt to join one of Hogarth's worst enemies, the antiquity-worshipping, Italian-loving Earl of Burlington. Richard was certain this would be the last straw, as far as Hogarth was concerned. The painter would surely consider this desertion and treason, and Richard would not be welcome again at Hogarth's pleasant little brick house. But Hogarth, afraid of Abby's pox, had hurried ahead with the rest of his family to his town house and perhaps he would never find out. If Richard was lucky, he could earn his passage money and leave England without the painter ever learning that he had entered the Earl of Burlington's service. Betsy had said that she had any number of ideas that might keep them from joining the other servants at the Leicester Fields house. Richard straightened his shoulders. Perhaps it would work out all right after all.

By now Richard had left the meadows behind him. He stopped to brush the drops of water from his stockings and to make sure that his hat sat straight on his head. Then he carefully touched the black bow that Betsy had tied for him. She had lectured him all the while in her most serious and sarcastic fashion about how he must make as good an impression as possible, if he hoped to work for such fine noble folk as those at the Earl of Burlington's villa.

Richard stepped forward as boldly as he could around the reach of the high brick wall and stood for a long moment. Before him loomed great iron gates, open now for a stylish carriage to pass through. Beyond them a few hundred yards was the white stone villa.

It was a small building, much smaller than the huge red brick house that stood to the right behind a row of tall trees. This white house was the Italian villa that Lord Burlington had erected and that William Hogarth found so detestably ugly. Richard walked closer and stopped just outside the gate; he had never seen anything like this villa in all of his life, and he didn't know yet if he agreed with the painter or not. The building, small as it was, had a dome on top, two staircases and a front rather like a picture Richard had once seen of a Greek temple, for it had six columns on the second story. Four chimneys poked their way into the gray sky on each side of the roof. Marble statues sprouted up from everywhere —on the sides of the staircase and on the pointed roof over the columns. A long line of statues lined each side of the courtyard in front of the villa.

"Wat yer think uv th' plice?" asked a wizened little man, leaning against the gateposts. From his maroon livery uniform, Richard guessed he was one of the Earl's servants.

"I don't know," Richard said. "I never saw any house like it before."

The servant nodded. "'Tis the supremest piece uv art in Lunnon, they says," he confided.

"Does the Earl of Burlington live inside it?"

"In that there alablaster plice? Naw, 'e lives in th' big 'ouse to th' right uv them trees, 'e does. Nobody lives in th' villa."

"But what's it for then? If nobody lives in it?"

The gatekeeper looked at Richard in great contempt. "If yer wasn' but a lad, I'd say yer was a tom-doodle ter ask sech a stoopid thing. This is wer th' Earl keeps 'is pitchers und give 'is routs und parties. That's all th' villa is fer."

"You mean to say," Richard exclaimed, not quite believing this even though he'd heard it from Betsy before, "that he built this house just to give parties and hang paintings in?"

"'Tis th' way uv th' great folk, 'tis indeed." The man's attitude suddenly changed and became businesslike. "Well, that's th' time uv th' day, lad. What am yer arter? What am yer up ter?"

"I thought there might be a place for me to work here in the garden?" Richard said hopefully.

"There might be," stated the gatekeeper, holding out his hand in a way that could mean only one thing. Richard handed over three of his pennies unhappily and watched the little man pocket them, snarling at the smallness of the vail. "Go along, bob, be'ind th' villa, und ye'll likely find Tom Bell, 'is lordship's 'ead gard'ner. Yer kin tell 'im I sent yer, und that I found 'im a boy ter work fer 'im, und that 'e kin pay ma fees to me for th' sarvice."

"Your fees?" Richard asked.

The gatekeeper shrugged. "Tom Bell, 'e asked me ter find some lads ter rake up th' leaves fer 'im, und I got 'im one, didn' I though? Tell 'im 'e owes me a shillin'. That'll be vail enough. Now get along, less'n I take a shillin' from yer, too."

Richard looked at the gatekeeper in disgust, but the man only laughed and strolled over to pull in one side of the gate as a girl came riding in. Richard watched her approach.

She was as unusual as the villa itself. In some ways she seemed to fit the strange building. She rode on a handsome dapple-gray horse, her long skirts of deep green cloth draped gracefully over its back. Her costume was almost as dazzling as David Garrick's clothing had been, for she wore a waistcoat of bright green trimmed with silver. At her neck was a lace cravat and on her head a little black hat edged with silver and topped by a white plume. Her dark red hair was tied with a silvery ribbon. She reined in, nodded haughtily to the gatekeeper and swept Richard a cool look from slanting hazel-gold eyes. She was the prettiest girl Richard had ever seen and beside her all others seemed common, if not low-featured. She cantered away up the cobblestoned courtyard that led to the villa, leaving Richard to stare in admiration. As the girl turned the horse's head in the direction of the great house, she swung around in the saddle and gave Richard a long look. A moment later she had disappeared behind the trees.

Richard walked slowly up the courtyard, craning his neck to see the red-haired girl, but she had vanished. He looked up into the branches of the tall trees that bordered the courtyard and then downward to the long line of odd white marble statues standing under them. They really weren't statues at all, he thought, only heads and shoulders stuck on plain pillars. He had no idea what they were called, and in any event they were most peculiar looking.

In a few more steps he had reached the white villa itself and stood gaping at it, unmolested by the liveried servants that hurried past him. Richard walked to the left on the inside of the iron fence and marveled at the tall windows of the second story and at all the fine detailed decorations. When he reached the rear of the house, which seemed to him to be very like the front except that it had no templelike columns, he was stopped by a servant who demanded the nature of his business.

"I came to see Tom Bell," Richard said, determined not to pay another vail. But he didn't need to worry. This man was breathless from hurry and carried a trowel in his hand. He had no time to ask for money.

"'E's down with 'is lordship by the wall. So's ever'one else in Chizzick," said the servant nervously, darting away. Richard followed him, feeling that this was what he was expected to do.

A group of men clustered about a section of wall that was being torn down. Most of them wore the maroon livery of the Earl of Burlington, and they stood quietly by as three other men soberly examined a section of the wall. One man, a tall long-faced person, richly dressed in a brown velvet coat and breeches, with a yellow brocade waistcoat and ornate wig, caught up the trowel from the servant and glared at the wall. His heavy-lidded eyes and thin mouth showed nothing but rage; even the tip of his long pointed nose seemed to shake with anger.

"That miserable pettifogger. That abandoned miscreant.

He had no more brains than an ass," he shouted. "Just see this wall and see how he plumed himself on being a mason. A giddy-headed girl could lay bricks better than he. And Elliott, do not tell me any tales of where you found him. This mason's work smells strongly of Thames Street."

A tall heavily built man, dressed in sober gray cloth and a plain cravat, shook his reddish head. "No, my lord. He was vouched for in London as being one of the finest masons in all England."

"Well, you've been properly bubbled, my fine steward Elliott," the Earl of Burlington said dryly. "See that it doesn't happen again. You can't make a good wall if you try to save on the mortar, and that's what your fine mason did."

"I shall order it repaired at once, your lordship," assured the red-headed steward.

"Nay, Elliott. I shall do it myself and see that it is done properly this time. Let this be a lesson to you never to indulge in cheapness in the men you hire. 'A laborer is worthy of his hire,' remember." The Earl bent to a wheelbarrow filled with gray mortar. "Now we shall see a wall as fine as any ancient Roman would have built—far better than your mason could do."

Richard watched as the Earl went to work, a brick in one hand, a trowel in the other. The servants winked at each other and began to drift away from the wall. The crisis was over, and the Earl of Burlington seemed happy. Richard looked curiously at Elliott. The red-headed steward of Chiswick House stood, his arms folded, staring down at his master with a strange expression on his face.

Then he caught sight of Richard and glared back at him in irritation, his hazel eyes alight with anger. "What do you want here, lumpkin?" he demanded.

Richard removed his hat. "I'm looking for Tom Bell," he said.

"Thomas Bell, you mean to say, don't you, idiot boy? Thomas Bell, the gardener?"

"Yes, but I'd heard his name was Tom Bell." Richard looked hard at the fierce steward, recalling Saturn's warnings about the man who was to raise the Irish chairmen in London.

"To you he is Thomas Bell, and remember that. Here, Bell, you'll see to this brat. See what he wants and get rid of him before I set the dogs on him or have him whipped for his insolence." Elliott jerked his head toward a smock-clad brown-skinned man, who had stood listening curiously to Elliott's conversation with Richard. The man smiled a toothless smile and hobbled over.

"Come along, boy," said Thomas Bell in a harsh cracking voice. "You'd be a'comin' to do a piece of work, wouldn' you, I s'pose. Come away wi' me, and we'll see if ye'll do at a'rakin' the leaves."

Tom Bell was bent like an old tree root and was very talkative. His yellowish cloudy eyes darted a glance at Richard. Then he chuckled, looking quickly over his shoulder at the brick-laying Lord Burlington. "There's not another fine gentleman in England who could build hisself a house or lay a brick, I'd be willin' to bet. For all that, some of the great folk smile at him for it. He knows more about such than most of the masons who ever lived. You know the old saying:

'When Adam delved and Eve span,
Who then was the gentleman?'

Well, he can work with his hands and if the worst come to the worst for him, he'd be worth somethin' more'n most fancy gentlemen, who strike me as bein' like clingin' mistletoe on an oak that's dyin'."

Richard followed along by the side of a tall green hedge listening to the old man's babbling talk.

"Take no mind back there of Valentine Elliott's tongue. He's the Earl's steward, and he thinks he's a god or somethin' —hisself, I mean, not the Earl. You call me Tom Bell, boy. Ever'one else does. Even William Kent, the greatest gardener England ever had, called me that, and he set out these gardens. I worked under him afore he died a couple of years back, not that I held with his plantin' of dead trees to make the place look more natcheral. Do ye come from Chizzick village, boy? Yer speech don't show it, if ye do."

Richard said that he did but did not mention Hogarth or try to explain his accent. The gardener nodded acceptingly and seemed pleased that Richard was a Chiswick boy. "There's no more room for servants in the big house," he said. "Ye'd just be comin' here by the day then, and you won't have to wear the Earl's livery. That's good. I won't wear it neither. This place is swarmin with gawks of servants, all lookin' like purple parrots and bowin' and scrapin'. If the gatekeeper wasn' a friend of mine, he'd have sent ye to the great house to make a footman out of ye, and then ye'd wear the livery and work in the house or mebbe in the stables. That's no life for a strong healthy boy. 'Tis better for a lad bein' out-of-doors, I says."

"You owe the gatekeeper a shilling for me," Richard blurted angrily, remembering the three pennies that had been taken from him at the gate.

The gardener sniffed. "I'll pay him soon enough. 'Tis his custom, and he makes the best of it too—too good, sometimes, if ye ask me."

Tom Bell seemed friendly and willing to talk, so Richard decided to question him as they walked slowly along the tall hedge.

"The steward's name is Valentine Elliott?" he inquired casually. "Has he been with the Earl a long time?"

"Not more'n seven years," was the reply. "Take some advice, lad, and don't get in the steward's way. He has a bad temper and hard ways even if the Earl don't seem to notice it. Aye, he's a sad harsh dog, the steward is."

"Is he Irish?" asked Richard, thinking of the Irish sedan-chair carriers.

"I wouldn' know that. He doesn't talk like any Irishman I've ever met. The family of the Earl is named Boyle, and they come over from Ireland a long time back. That much I do know, but I don' know of no other Irishers hereabouts."

"Are there any other new servants or staff here. Besides me, I mean?"

Tom Bell shook his head. "I don' think that there be, but I don' know ever'one who works in the big house."

Richard's face fell. How would he ever contact the Hanoverian agent now? And how would he recognize the agent if he had been sent? There was no special phrase and no mark that Richard knew that would identify him. About the only thing he could do would be to mention Saturn's name to people and see how they reacted. It was most unlikely that Tom Bell would be an agent of King George II, but Richard decided to test him, feeling ashamed of himself for using the kindly old gardener.

"Have you heard about the murder three days ago down at Chiswick Mall?" Richard asked. "People say that there was a touch of the evil planet, Saturn, in that business."

The gardener didn't pause in his hobbling steps. He shot Richard a disgusted glance and croaked, "I didn' know you'd talk so silly, boy. There's murders so many, even in Chizzick, that I takes no notice of 'em. Whatever Saturn, or whatever you said, has to do with 'em, I wouldn' be knowin'. Tom Bell cares for nothin' but his trees and his plantin' and for hard work. I'll tell ye a truth, boy," he suddenly turned and pointed a gnarled knotted finger at Richard. "Men like Tom Bell, who spend their years workin' with things that are green-growin' don' be havin' much time for what men does. Most men like me don' even have much use for people. I just puts up wi' their doin's. I was goin' ter stake up a young plant when the Earl took his notion to see ter that wall. My time was a'wasted, and I don' like it a bit. Come along, boy, and we'll get back to work."

Bell was certainly no agent; Richard was convinced.

"Them's William Kent's gardens," announced Tom Bell. "There's nothin' like 'em anywhere's else in England."

Richard looked at the beautiful wide sweep of green lawns, the masses of feathery trees, and the curving little river that lay in front of him. A small herd of fallow deer, tame as house pets, grazed several hundred feet away, and a peacock walked with slow pride up to the gardener and spread its magnificent tail to its fullest. Tom Bell laughed. "See the pretty popinjay," he said.

"Is this all natural?" Richard asked.

"Naw, it's all made. 'Twas set out by William Kent, I been tellin' you. 'Tis a 'artificial wilderness,' they calls it. Wander around and look at it for a spell. You see the Greek Temple over there by the serpentine, which is what they calls the canal? You see the round pond and the big rock p'inting up out of the water? In the summer the Earl has me put orange trees in wooden tubs around the pond, and that is a raree show with the peacocks walkin' in and out, I tell you. Go along, look around for yourself. There's plenty of leaves to rake ever'where hereabouts. Though the Earl likes things to be natcheral, jest as they'd be in the autumn, he hasn' a fondness for brown leaves." Tom Bell scratched his head. "That don' seem so natcheral to me."

Richard didn't hesitate, but set out down the slope from Tom Bell and his attending peacock toward the Greek Temple. To his surprise this little building was in the first stages of falling apart. Then he remembered what Bell had said—that William Kent planted dead trees and he realized that it must have been built that way. What foolishness, Richard decided—to build a ruin and plant something dead. But he had to admit the little temple was beautiful. Richard turned away to walk down an avenue of tall dark trees that led to a group of statues all clad in Roman togas. Richard shook his head, wondering why Roman statues should stand in an English garden, even so strange a garden as the Earl of Burlington's.

Three very long treelined or hedged avenues led out from the statues, and Richard peered down them to the white stone buildings at each end. All were quite different from each other, but like the central villa, they seemed to be too small to live in. As Tom Bell had said, there was much work to do, for the paths were all ankle-deep in yellowish autumn leaves. Richard sighed in homesickness. Autumn in England was yellow and brown, not red and gold as in Pennsylvania. He found it a much sadder time of the year than he'd ever known it to be before.

Richard walked on to the left again where over the treetops he saw a tall white column topped by a statue of what he guessed was a Greek or Roman goddess. He went on to look at a small brick house that, like everything else, seemed to have no purpose. Beyond this he spied the glass roofs of a greenhouse where Tom Bell must have raised the Earl of

Burlington's oranges, and in front of that was a brown withered garden set out with such precision that it seemed quite unlike the rest of the estate's careful naturalness.

Retracing his steps, he passed by the rear of the villa and the great house and, after explaining to several haughty servants what he was doing, he went down to the serpentine. Ducks and swans greeted him with hissing and quacking as they begged for bread. There, at a place where the height of the ground rose sharply, a pretty little two-level waterfall tumbled in three streams of water into the canal. Richard smiled as he crossed over it on a little wooden bridge; no natural waterfall ever looked like this miniature one, but again he had to admit it was pretty.

A very tall white shaft loomed up ahead of him, and Richard went toward it, following a path that slanted diagonally along the high brick wall that surrounded the entire estate. The shaft towered high over Richard's head. Although he'd given up expecting to find any purpose for the things he found on the Earl's estate, he spent some time looking at the shaft. There was a carving of a man, a woman, and a small child at its foot. The shaft mystified him.

"It's a gravestone, silly," came a piercingly sweet voice from behind. Richard turned and looked into the gold-hazel eyes of the girl who had ridden past him at the gate. "It's an ancient Roman gravestone," she went on. "Can't you see the man and his wife and their baby at the bottom of it?"

"It's the strangest marker I ever saw. Why would anyone put a Roman gravestone in his garden?" Richard said, embarrassed by the girl's boldness.

"Well, you don't know much about art, then, and you've never been to Rome," the girl's tone was superior.

"No, I've never been to Rome. Have you?" Richard asked.

The girl looked at him coldly. "I ask the questions around here, my boy. My father is the Earl of Burlington's steward and if you're to dally on his property you'd best be civil to me, for I am Venetia Elliott, and I've come to feed his ducks." She shook a cloth bag under Richard's nose.

"Whose property?" Richard asked quickly. "Your father's or the Earl's?" Richard found Venetia Elliott not only the prettiest girl he had ever seen but also the haughtiest and the rudest.

Venetia gasped at the question. She was about to answer, but something checked her words and Richard smiled, remembering once more what Saturn had told him. It was not hard to guess what the Earl's Jacobite steward would demand for his part in the plot to unseat King George II. It was well known that the Earl of Burlington was a loyal supporter of King George. Chiswick House would be the red-headed steward's prize.

"It's the estate of the Earl of Burlington, just as Burlington House in London is," she replied with so sweet a smile that Richard could hardly believe how waspish she had just been. "Here," she added, "perhaps you'd like to learn some Latin, that is if you can read. I have some easy grammars I could lend you. You seem so interested in this Roman grave marker."

"I read Latin well enough; that seems to be all that I do know," Richard grinned, remembering Samuel Johnson's comments on his education. There was no reason to take offense, for so few boys his age could read that her remarks were only natural.

"What are you doing here?" Venetia asked, kicking at some leaves. "Are you going to be a footman in the great house?"

Richard shook his head. "No, I'm going to work with the gardeners."

Once more the girl laughed prettily, showing off dimples and little white teeth. Richard noticed that she laughed often and knew its effect very well. "Oh, Tom Bell," she said, "He's a bit daft, you know. He talks to the trees—really he does. I've eavesdropped and heard him."

Privately, Richard thought that Tom Bell's trees were much better company than most of the people he'd met in London. But he only smiled and kept his silence while Venetia pointed out the view from the Roman marker, which she told him was an obelisk. The view was lovely through the trees across the serpentine to the Greek Temple. "Have you seen the Rustic House, the Ionic Temple, the Doric column and the Deer House, or the two pavilions, the River House and the Casino?" she rattled away.

"I think I must have seen them all, but I don't know which is which. What do they use them for?"

"Oh, you are silly!" Venetia giggled. "They're just to be seen, you know. Nobody lives in them. Don't they look elegant among the trees? No one lives in the villa either, although guests sometimes stay there. You should see how beautiful the villa is inside. On the outside it's like a villa in Italy, and on the inside it is wonderfully like fairyland. When I'm married to a rich man, I'll go to Italy and look at hundreds upon hundreds of beautiful statues, paintings and buildings. All I have to do is find a rich husband and then I can do anything I like. I don't suppose you're rich, are you; but that was silly of me to ask, wasn't it? If you were rich, you would have come here on a fine horse, and worn a velvet suit, and you certainly wouldn't be working for Tom Bell, would you?" Venetia looked frankly at Richard. "You are handsome, though. It's a great pity that you aren't rich. I don't suppose you'll ever be rich, will you? Papa wants me to marry a nobleman, or a knight at least. But I think I'd even marry a merchant, if he was rich enough and handsome, too."

Richard was astonished by the girl and by himself. He found it hard to take his eyes off Venetia Elliott. She leaned against the Roman gravestone, smiling and showing off her dimples to full advantage. "Oh, come now," she said softly, "you're old enough to know what the world is about, aren't you? I want a coronet on the door of my carriage, and I want lackeys in my husband's livery to stand behind it. My father says that I'm pretty enough to catch an Earl at least, but if I can't get what I want by marrying, it can be done other ways," and her pretty little laugh pealed out again.

Richard's face became stern as he thought of the sinister road Valentine Elliott traveled as a Jacobite plotter, and he quietly changed the subject. "Do many great folk come here?" he asked, and then added. "Would people from the King's court come here?"

The girl nodded. "Oh, yes, nearly everyone who is important in England comes to the routs and gambling parties that the Earl and his lady give. I've seen most everyone at the court here at one time or another."

"Does Lady Primrose or Lord Elibank, or his brother, come here often?" Richard asked in casual tones, looking up at the cloudy sky.

Venetia paused for a long moment and then said, "No, I don't think I know who they are. Or, at least, I don't know them by sight. When Lord Burlington opens his villa, there are so many people coming and going and there's such a crowd that I don't try to remember anyone under the rank of Earl. Are they Viscounts or Barons, do you know? Where did you meet them?"

"I don't know what they are." Richard was truthful, and then, thinking swiftly, he added. "I was thinking of going to the city to work for Lord Elibank or Lady Primrose as a stableboy until I thought about working here first. This is closer for me."

"You live here in Chiswick?" The girl walked away from the obelisk, pulled a yellow leaf from a bush nearby and shredded it in her fingers. "You didn't say how you got to know the Murrays and Lady Primrose?" she asked pointedly.

Richard caught her use of Murray, the family name of Lord Elibank, or Sirius. He thought frantically for an answer. Venetia Elliott was obviously not a fool, for she pursued an idea with skill. "I rowed the three of them on the river," he lied quickly, "when they were coming up to Chiswick from London. I thought I wanted to be a waterman once, but the work's too hard. I talked to them then. They were very kind."

Venetia's face grew hard as she said, "If you thought rowing on the Thames and a waterman's work too difficult, you might not like it here at Chiswick House either. Tom Bell is a taskmaster. You'd better find him instead of standing about talking, for I don't think he approves of me, not that I really care. My father is the steward and old Tom is only the gardener. But you'd better go if you want to stay around here, boy." She smiled prettily and her tone softened. "I wish you would stay. There aren't many handsome lackeys here right now. Tom Bell should be over by the bridge at the cascade talking to his trees. Better go find him." With these words Venetia Elliott smiled sweetly and sauntered down the avenue that led to the serpentine.

Richard swung around, heading back the way he came. Sure enough, there was Tom Bell standing on the wooden bridge, frowning and talking to himself as he watched the green-clad girl throw food to the ducks.

"You've been wastin' time with that jill-flirt, that bubble, haven' ye?" he growled. "Well, take a rake here and come along with me and don' let me catch ye talking to her agin.

She don' bring nothin' but trouble ever'time I spy her out. She jest talked with ye because she finds ye well-favored in the face. She'll seek out and talk to any lad who's well made. Did she tell ye she was out to catch herself a duke or a marquis to husband?"

Shame-faced, Richard nodded his head. Tom Bell grunted. "Not her fault, I guess. Her da' put that idear in her addle-pated head when she was a poppet. To be fair, I can't be blamin' the lass. Oh well, 'tis none of my business if she don' get in the way of my plantin' and prunin'."

Still grumbling and shaking his head, he put his rake over his shoulder and led Richard up the path past the obelisk, where great drifts of sodden fallen leaves covered the ground.

That evening after they had eaten and put Abby to bed, Richard recounted everything that he had learned to Betsy Lewes. She sat quietly on a stool in front of the hearth as Richard spoke of the Earl of Burlington and the faulty wall and of Tom Bell. When he came to his conversation with Venetia Elliott, Betsy snorted in disgust.

"I know that jade!" she spat out. "Riding about like a fine lady on that gray horse of hers, showing off her gowns to the likes of me and the other servant girls in Chiswick, with only one gown to our backs. Studying music, Greek, Latin, and what have you, to raise her up to feel she's something better than she is. Her father's a steward, but that's still a servant, isn't it? I suppose you think she's well made, Dick? Most boys in Chiswick do."

Richard was about to reply that Venetia was the prettiest creature he had ever seen, but he caught a glint in Betsy's eyes and replied with a yawn, "Tolerably, Betsy. I guess she's tolerably well made. I didn't take much note of her except when she slipped about not knowing Lord Elibank and then called him Murray."

"And she's plotting against King George, too," Betsy said darkly. "That could almost make me a Hanover, knowing that Elliott shrew was for 'Jamie the Rover.' "

The fire blazed up on the kitchen hearth as the autumn wind came down the chimney. Richard was silent. Girls had odd notions about politics, he decided. To be for King George just because Venetia Elliott was a Jacobite was ridiculous, but he knew Betsy meant it. Richard sighed. The work for Tom Bell had been hard, and he was tired. The woods and gardens at Chiswick House, strange and different as they were, had made him ache for America and his home.

"Homesick, Dick?" Betsy Lewes suddenly asked, guessing his thoughts. Richard nodded yes, and she went on, "Well, we just have to go along with what we've started anyway. We're in too deep now to stop."

In the days that followed Richard did not learn anything new at Chiswick, and he did not see Venetia Elliott again. For one thing it rained constantly and for another Tom Bell kept him so occupied with raking the masses of dead leaves far from the occupied houses on Lord Burlington's estate that he saw very few people at all. He despaired of ever questioning anyone as he watched the days march swiftly on toward the tenth of November.

One wet afternoon he was sent by Tom Bell to the kitchens of the great house to ask for a large wicker basket, and as he came away from the kitchen and stable wing of the house he walked along behind the summer parlor and the building that linked the villa to the great house. Richard looked out and to his surprise saw David Garrick and Madame Garrick strolling along in the downpour with the Earl of Burlington. The Earl was busy pointing out some new piece of statuary. David Garrick was looking distinctly and magnificently bored. He also seemed angry, tapping his small elegant foot on the ground and glowering first at the Earl and then at his wife as if to say that they ought to come in out of the rain, if they had any sense at all. He frowned and flicked drops of rain off his cloak and looked right through Richard, who stood dumbfounded. It was hard for him to believe his eyes. He had not been surprised to find the famous actor in the eccentric Samuel Johnson's garret. But in the few months he'd been in London, he'd learned that actors weren't the sort of people who usually associated with great lords and ladies. However, it very definitely was the great Garrick, and it was clear, too, that he did not remember Richard.

Madame Garrick turned around, holding the hood of her scarlet cloak close around her dark hair. She put her hand on her husband's arm. "It is getting cold, Davy," she said in her strangely accented speech. "Why don't you go inside, if you want. I would really like to see his lordship's newest statue from my beloved Italy."

Garrick was suddenly gallant. "No, my love, my Dulcinea," he said frowning furiously. "No man will say that Roscius entered the house because of the elements and the fury of the tempest—particularly while his flower of a wife, the mistress of his soul, braved the terrors of the storms."

"I wonder if he always talks that way?" Richard asked himself.

The Earl of Burlington sighed loudly and then laughed. "All the world's a stage, all the time, isn't it, my dear Garrick?"

"And why not?" commented the actor. "I do firmly hold that we act out parts throughout our lives. Fate has cast the play, and fate gives us our lines and prompts us, too. Struggling against what the mighty playwright, Fate, ordains is useless. Only the dullest fellow in the world would attempt it."

Richard listened closely, wondering if the man really meant what he was saying, for it was impossible to tell with all the gestures, postures and face-making that accompanied his philosophy. If it was really true, thought Richard, then there was little hope for him. Considering the way events had taken shape, Richard Larkin's fate could lead only to a dagger in some black corner.

"La, the lad is marvelously taken with the fine free show you put on," teased the Earl of Burlington, nodding toward the passageway where Richard stood.

"A country blockhead, no doubt, my Lord, who will not broach the farthings to come to Drury Lane to see me," said the actor, steering his wife away toward the entrance of the link building. "Insolent sauciness of the country lout to gawk at his betters! What is the world coming to?"

"I'm not a country lout," Richard shouted. Garrick's words stung and bothered him. He was tired of insults and tired of being ignored.

Lord Burlington and both Garricks stood in utter surprise, for no servant ever spoke back.

"Good heavens, who is this creature?" the Earl demanded, raising his eyebrows. "And do you belong around here?"

"I'm Richard Larkin from Pennsylvania Colony, and I rake leaves for Tom Bell," Richard's reply was almost defiant.

"Ah, that explains it all," David Garrick laughed. "He's from the savage wilds where there are no people of wit and fashion."

"He's a saucy wretch if he's from the Colonies or not," remarked the Earl sternly. "And he'd better not speak up again if he knows what is good for him unless he wants a taste of my steward's lash."

"Oh, love, do not have them whip the boy," Madame Garrick pleaded with the Earl. "I don't think he knew what he did, and Davy did provoke him. I like a proud lad, and I like the look of him."

"For you, my dear, I would grant anything," said the Earl. "You know that Lady Burlington and I are slaves to your every pretty whim."

"Come then, dear man," she said. The Earl put his arm around her and led the way back into the house. David Garrick followed, prancing like a horse, shaking his cloak free of raindrops.

Richard watched them enter the link building and shivered a bit in spite of himself. He didn't know that they whipped servants in England the way they did bound servants and black slaves in the Colonies. In his heart he thanked Madame Garrick for coming to his rescue even if she hadn't recognized him. Then, suddenly he remembered the basket and his errand. He hurried back to the grounds where Tom Bell waited patiently for him. He found the old gardener murmuring tenderly to a sickly looking plant.

"Do David Garrick and his wife come to Chiswick House often?" he asked the gardener as he put down the basket.

"Oh, that they do," Tom Bell answered. "In a way Mrs. Garrick is related to the Earl, or so people say. He knew her family in Italy. She was a dancer in the Italian opera there. Violette was adopted by Lady Burlington and lived here at Chizzick House for a spell before she married that actor fellow." The gardener grunted. "Lord and Lady Burlington had no relish for the match, but Violette and Garrick were set on each other. After some years the Earl give in, but if I know the Earl, and no man knows him better, he don' really relish the idea yet, he don't."

"Mrs. Garrick is the best lady I ever knew," declared Richard, picking up his rake. "She saved me from a beating just now."

"Aye, that's her way," Tom Bell shouldered the basket and asked no questions. "Nobody can see what she sees in that Garrick. Lord ha' mercy upon us, he's a silly fellow and plays the fool more'n any man I ever heard tell of."

"I suppose he is the greatest actor who ever lived, though," Richard murmured.

"Actors!" Tom Bell snorted. "They're the greatest bubbles that ever lived. Ye can be makin' yerself easy on that, boy."

The next day Venetia sought Richard out as he worked. She stood near him, her eyes narrowed. "I hear that his lordship fell into a violent passion because of your sauciness yesterday, Richard Larkin." She seemed happy as if the thought of beatings pleased her.

Richard did not comment and Venetia came closer, so close that he could smell the scent of lavender on her clothing. "Would you like to see the inside of the villa, boy?" she asked. "The Earl of Burlington and his lady are going into the city this evening to the theater and then to a rout at the Duke of Newcastle's house, and I know how to get inside the villa." She paused, looked down, and drew a design in the dirt path with the tip of her pretty red shoe. "Of course, if you're afraid to come after you've been threatened with a beating, you don't have to." Venetia glanced swiftly at him from under her long brown lashes. "It will be your only chance to see the villa. The Earl doesn't like to leave Chiswick House for his town house very often, you know."

Richard looked at her thoughtfully; it was true that he did want to go inside the villa. Every time he went by, he tried to peep past the velvet curtains. Sometimes he was rewarded by a flash of gold ornament or a glimpse of crimson wallpaper. Going there wouldn't serve his purpose in finding the Hanoverian agent, but there couldn't be a great deal of harm in it. Besides, Betsy Lewes would like to hear about the wonderful things inside.

"It is very fine, I suppose?" Richard said tentatively.

"Oh, yes, it is monstrous fine," she breathed. "I've seen it lots of times, and I could spend hours just looking at the paintings. Can you meet me at the rear of the link building just at dark, Richard? I wouldn't want anyone to know that we were inside the villa."

"Not even your father?"

"Oh, no, Richard," she said, giggling and turning away from his eyes. "He'd be in a rage if he knew that I went inside and even more full of spleen if he knew I took a gardener's boy with me. Even if I told him that we didn't touch a single thing and that we only wanted to look at the paintings, he'd have both of us punished. He'd have you whipped until you dropped, and he'd lock me up in our house for months. So, you mustn't tell anyone at all and certainly not Tom Bell or anyone in Chiswick. You have no idea how people talk about me around here." Venetia gave Richard another one of her pretty smiles.

"I won't tell anyone," Richard said thoughtfully.

"All right," he whispered, feeling like a conspirator. "I'll meet you at dark."

Venetia giggled and held a finger to her lips. She turned on her heel and ran swiftly up the avenue that led to the small brick house she shared with her father. Her dark gray cloak billowed out behind her.

Richard bent to his raking, wondering if he should tell Betsy Lewes of Venetia's invitation. He decided that it would be wiser not to. He did want to see the inside of the famous villa, and he had a very good idea what Betsy would have to say about an escapade with Venetia. He'd have to make up some sort of excuse to leave the house.

That evening when supper was cleared away, Richard told Betsy that he had to meet Tom Bell about ordering flower seeds for the spring. Betsy commented acidly on how odd it was that he should concern himself with such things when he would not even be there next spring to see the plants come up. Richard explained that he had promised, and after looking at the nearly healed pox on Abby's face he set out for Chiswick House and his appointment.

I won't worry about Hanoverian or Jacobite agents tonight, he told himself as he entered one of the little gates that led into the grounds. Tonight I'll just enjoy looking at the wonderful things that the Earl of Burlington has collected and put in his villa. The sun had been down for about fifteen minutes and as Richard reached the rear of the link building, the white villa was barely visible in the pale light of the early November moon.

Someone whistled from the side of one of the doors of the summer parlor, and Richard walked quietly toward the sound. Venetia's white little face looked up at him from inside the hood of her cloak.

"Richard? Dick?" she called softly.

"Yes."

"Take my hand. I don't dare light a candle until we get inside, and then, with all the curtains drawn, it will be safe enough, I guess."

Richard put his hand into her small cold one, and she drew him inside the link building, softly closing the door behind them. She led the way with assurance down a dark corridor and then in through another door.

"This is the villa," Venetia whispered. "Wait until I light a wax taper." She let go of Richard's hand and he heard her fumbling with tinder and flint. A second later he was blinded by the flash of the spark in the darkness. "There, that's done," she said with satisfaction. In front of her smiling face she held a candle in a silver candlestick holder. With the other hand she loosened the neckstrings of her dark gray cloak.

Richard stared at the magnificence of her dress, gold brocade with silver and green flowers scattered over the square-cut bodice and full skirt. Green stones shone in Venetia's ears. Richard felt sure that they were emeralds.

She laughed at his confusion and grasped his hand once more. "I always dress in my finest gowns in the evenings, even when there's no one around to admire me. But I have you here now," she said. "Do come on, Dick. This is only the lower floor, or the Earl's library. What we want to see is upstairs. That's where the paintings and all the other important things are."

Venetia and Richard passed swiftly through the series of fine apartments upstairs. Each was ablaze with color—red, blue and gold. Every time Venetia held the candle aloft, Richard craned his neck to see the elaborately painted ceilings that showed scenes from Greek mythology. Sometimes she held her candle at arm's length to show a beautiful chimney piece or a particularly fine cabinet, table, or chair. Richard was dazzled. She led him into the domed salon where tall classical and historical paintings hung high over pedestaled busts of ancient Roman figures. She held the candle up as high as she could to show off the elaborately designed and decorated dome. He was astounded at all the gold and wealth he saw.

"This isn't all, Richard," Venetia said loudly. "There's one more thing I want you to see. You'll find it the most interesting of all."

Once more she caught his hand, and Richard noticed that it was damp and clammy. Venetia was nervous. But, after all, she was running a risk, too. Why shouldn't she be?

She hurried him across the domed salon and into another room. The walls here were covered with green velvet and the gilded and decorated beams gleamed in the light of her candle. The girl hurried over and set the candle down on an ornate mantelpiece. The light shone up on a huge painting of Cupid among many flowers.

"Here he is, father!" she said breathlessly.

Richard turned. A spark was struck at the far end of the green chamber. A second candle was lit and put on a second mantelpiece, this time illuminating a painting of Cupid and a goddess. But it was not the painting that held Richard's terrified attention. It was the smiling figure of Valentine Elliott, who stood with his back to the fireplace, beckoning to the side. A tall thin man in a plain scarlet coat, a black military stock, buckskin breeches and top boots of black leather walked out of the deep shadows.

The skin of his brown face was drawn taut over his cheekbones, and his cold dark eyes gleamed as he looked at Richard. Spica smiled, just as he had smiled when he stabbed the unfortunate merchant, Carlton, at Jeremy Belcher's Seven Stars.

CHAPTER 7

Vega Rises

"Is this the boy?" Valentine Elliott asked in his harsh drawling voice. "Are you sure?"

"I do believe it could be. The very devil's spawn!" was Spica's reply. "The light is not fine, but he looks the same lad."

Venetia said nothing. Hurriedly she crossed the room and stood beside her father, her eyes intent on Richard, her pale cheeks flushed with excitement. "Take him!" exclaimed the girl biting at her knuckles in agitation. "Let Sirius see him, father. If he's the boy, and I think he is, Sirius will reward me, won't he?"

Swiftly the two men came over to Richard, who waited frozen with surprise and terror. He could not escape through the blackness of the villa. After the first few yards he would have been hopelessly lost in the maze of dark rooms. Like a frightened animal he waited while Lord Burlington's steward and Sirius' hired assassin caught him by the arms and dragged him the length of the Green Room and out the door. Venetia paused to pick up the candles, then stepped ahead of them, lighting their way. Once outside Venetia left them, melting into the darkness without a word.

A carriage was waiting in the courtyard and Spica and Elliott heaved Richard inside. Spica jumped lithely in behind him. Elliott's voice called to the driver, and seconds later with a screech of iron wheels the carriage moved forward.

"Where are you taking me?" Richard asked, picking himself up from the floor of the carriage where Spica had shoved him.

"Oh, do not be troubled on that head, dear lad," was the lilting and frightening reply. "'Tis not far ye have to go on any road that lies before ye, is what I'm thinkin'. Now, not another word out of ye, or I'll cut your throat right here."

Richard sank down in his seat, while the carriage jolted its way over the rutted muddy November roads. More than once they were almost mired in the deep ruts left by the heavy passenger coaches, but always, with the driver cursing and cracking the whip, the horses were able to pull the carriage free, and they were on their way again. They were traveling east along a route Richard did not recognize. Once they passed a gallows where a long-dead criminal hung in chains, his form swaying blacker than the black night.

Spica saw the gallows, too, and chuckled, but did not speak. Instead he kicked the boy with his boot and laughed again.

He can't frighten me, Richard told himself to bolster up his courage. He can't scare me with the threat of the gallows. I haven't murdered anyone. The gallows is for him and his kind and the block and the ax for his betters. Richard thought bitterly of Samuel Johnson, who had let him down, and of Johnson's "noble order of things."

He sensed that Spica was not a particularly important member of the Society of the Stars. More than anything, he was Alexander Murray's hired servant. Murray, the Society's Sirius, was the key man and decision-maker.

Richard kept his silence. He did not want to speak with the murderous Spica. He felt certain that he was being taken to see the other plotters for final identification and decisions. Spica would not act without the approval of the others and he seemed to be in some doubt about whether Richard was the boy who had witnessed the crime. Richard's hopes rose a little. This was all the more reason not to give anything away. He made himself as comfortable as he could, and his thoughts wandered to Betsy, Abby and William Hogarth. If he could only get word to them. William Hogarth would help, if he knew. He should have told him all about this back in Chiswick. Betsy would be worried sick when he didn't come back; perhaps she'd go to Leicester Fields and tell Master Hogarth. And then, a dreadful thought chilled his heart. Suppose they kidnapped Betsy and Abby? Even more likely Antares might come after his letter if he was told by the Elliotts that Richard was living at Hogarth house. Richard had not told Venetia where he lived, but Chiswick was a little country village, and everyone knew everyone else's affairs. Betsy and Abby were in a danger as fearful as his own.

I've got to keep calm, Richard told himself. The carriage clattered over the cobblestone streets now and into the city of London. Keeping quiet and denying everything was the only hope for him and Betsy, too.

They turned into the crowded web of city streets and wove in and out among the throng of coaches, sedan-chairs, carriages, and torch-carrying linkboys who shouted for the crowds to make way for the gentlemen they preceded.

Once more they turned and then the carriage slowed while Spica leaned out the window to call to the driver, "This would be the Strand now?"

"Aye," came the answer. Spica grabbed Richard by the collar, and the carriage came to a halt in the Strand, that street where only the wealthy and noble lived.

"Now, harken to me, boy," hissed Spica. "Ye walk beside me to the house and to the proper door that suits the likes of ye as a servant brat. If ye do a thing amiss or say a word to anyone, I'll have to be puttin' a knife in ye and be thinkin' no more upon it than if I wrung the neck of a fat young goose. Do ye hear me, now?"

Spica jumped down. Slowly Richard climbed out of the carriage and stood in front of the house.

It was as fine as any of the others in the Strand—tall and narrow of red-brick with a white door and iron railings on each side. Tall link extinguishers stood before the house. Four linkboys stood gossiping while they waited and three sedan-chair carriers sat on the curb, throwing dice to while the time away. As Richard walked away from the coach he noticed a black carriage further up the street, under a street lamp. To his horror he recognized the painted coat of arms on the door. It was the black carriage he'd seen in Chiswick. Either Vega or Sirius must be nearby.

"Come along, brat," murmured Spica, linking his arm firmly with Richard's. "Me boy, you and I'll enter as brothers, if not friends." He dragged Richard along to the side of the house and up a short flight of steps and pushed open a small plain door. "Ah, 'tis quite a night for a brat like yourself," whispered Spica, "to be seein' the sights in Chiswick House, as well as the house of one of the greatest ladies in England.

And all in the same night. You should be thankin' us. And," he added, "can't a common lad like yourself be takin' great comfort knowin' that it was such a fine pretty lass that was the means of your enterin' both places?"

Richard hadn't thought much of Venetia's treachery. "Jill-flirt!" he said angrily.

"Take care, boy," Spica warned. "Take care when you look into a pretty face. Fine men have been caught with fine words and the flutter of a fan. Ye mean the Elliott hussy when you say that, and no man'd go against ye in sayin' what ye do. But now you're to meet a great lady, and ye'd best be civil to her and tell her whatever she asks you, tellin' her the truth. And tell it swift if ye know what's good for ye, and what's wise and proper."

They passed through a large dim kitchen with whitened plaster walls glimmering in the light of a few tallow candles and a glowing hearthfire. They went into a hallway off which Richard could see a large room ornately tiled in black and white. Then Spica pushed him along up the plain wooden staircase reserved for the servants and onto the next floor of the house. Voices came from one of two rooms on the second floor. Spica rapped on the first door. Richard looked about him with one quick agonized glance. There was no way to escape. A clock as tall as a man stood ticking loudly away at the end of the hall between the two rooms. It seemed strange to Richard that except for the low hum of voices in one parlor and the tick of the clock, the house was utterly quiet. There had been no one about on the ground floor, not even a servant to open the door. There did not seem to be a servant in the house. Then he realized that they had probably all been sent away for good reasons, reasons that Richard did not find comforting. His heart began to pound.

Spica rapped again and Richard heard quick light footsteps. Then the door opened slowly. "The white rose will bloom even in the winter," Spica whispered.

"Even in the snows of England," came the reply in a slightly nasal woman's voice. The door opened wider and Lady Primrose stood on the threshold. She looked much as she had when Richard saw her in her carriage outside William Hogarth's garden gate. Her hair was powdered and elaborately curled, with black plumes in a diamond holder towering above her curls. She was dressed all in heavy black brocade while a diamond necklace glittered on her yellowish throat and diamond buckles shone on her satin slippers. A black fan hung from her wrist on a cord. She caught it in her hand and opened it slowly, then folded it with a snap, and tapped it against her chin.

Lady Primrose was not pretty, Richard decided, and she could be any age at all. There was an air of power and command about her that he'd never seen in a woman before. Her face was more square than oval, with a thin mouth and straight dark eyebrows. Her nose was more aquiline than straight and her eyes, of some indistinguishable color, had neither softness nor gentleness. Richard sensed that Lady Primrose or Vega was a woman as dangerous as any of the men who plotted against King George.

Spica bowed low to the lady. She looked down on him sardonically and asked, "This is the boy that Elliott minx found?"

"I do believe 'tis the lad," Spica answered.

"Bring him in here then," she ordered and swung around, and clutching her rustling skirts with each hand, she swept ahead of them into the parlor like a huge black swan.

Richard and Spica entered. Spica immediately went over

and leaned against a wall that was brilliantly decorated by a red damask hanging. Richard stood alone in the center of the room. Vega pointed wordlessly with her fan for him to remain where he was, while she backed across the room and seated herself on a little gilt chair, never taking her eyes from him.

There were six chairs in the large high-ceilinged room. Four of them were occupied. Richard looked about with numb curiosity and recognized three members of the Society of the Stars. There was the fat, hog-faced man called Arcturus and the swaying, slovenly old man known as Capella. Across from Vega sat the glowering, Indian-headed Sirius or Alexander Murray. They wore black cloaks and looked dramatically sinister in the many-mirrored parlor with its gilded furniture, crystal chandeliers and heavy blood-red hangings.

Vega's voice was sharp. "Are you satisfied now? Is this the boy, my dear Sirius and my dear Arcturus? If you must use my house on this business, tell me quickly, is this the boy? And if it is, get him out of here, and if it isn't, release him at once. He knows nothing of our affairs if Spica and the Elliotts have not spoken."

Alexander Murray gave her a hard look. "I do not enjoy looking at tavern boys and potboys," he said in a voice that Richard remembered only too well, "but I say that he is the same lad."

"The room is ablaze with wax candles. You could have no better light to recognize him by," Vega put in crossly. "I should think you could save me the trouble of sending away my staff while you go about this sorry business in my parlor. Why didn't you take him somewhere else? Why not to your house or to your brother's, pray?"

"You run few enough risks for our cause," was the sharp

reply. "My brother has gone to the Duke of Newcastle's, as you very well know."

"Where *I* should have been tonight myself if it weren't for your commandeering my house!" Vega retorted.

"I doubt if old 'Hubble-Bubble' misses your ladyship," Murray remarked coldly, "unless it is that he doesn't have to pay his agents to keep an eye on you when you are in his parlor. I doubt even more if you received an invitation."

"To see that little man 'Hubble-Bubble' scuttling about, picking at his ears and covering his face with a handkerchief because he fears someone will breathe on him and give him the ague." Fat Arcturus rumbled and laughed. "I do not believe our glorious Vega could stoop to such a thing. Only a Hanover could support the Duke of Newcastle's manners, and our gracious Vega is not one of that loathsome breed."

Vega inclined her head and smiled at Arcturus. "You are not of noble birth, Arcturus, but your manners put to shame those of another I could name."

Suddenly, Capella came to attention. "I know that brat," he croaked, leaning forward and leering drunkenly. "That's the very potboy—the boy who stared so at me."

"You were gallows lushy," Arcturus shot at him, "as you are now. You wouldn't remember a Barbary ape from that night, I'll warrant."

Capella shivered a little. "I remember some things I've never seen before that happened that night," he said thickly, his little eyes rolled toward Spica, who still lounged against the wall.

"Hold your drunken tongue!" Murray thundered. "Is this the boy?"

"I say aye," came Spica's lilting voice.

"It is," croaked Capella.

"I do believe he is," Arcturus agreed.

"And I, too, say aye," stated Murray, his eyes on Richard's face. Richard did not move as Murray continued. "Were you some time ago at the tavern, called the Seven Stars just off Fleet Street?"

Richard shook his head, unable to trust his voice.

"Are you sure it is he?" Vega inquired, her voice rising. "I don't like questioning the boy in my house. If you're sure, take him away."

"I do believe that the female is more deadly than the male, after all, my dear fellow stars," Murray said maliciously, and bowed his heavy head to Lady Primrose. "Or has our dear Vega grown cool to our cause? If this is the boy there is much to be learned from him. Before killing him we must know if he talked to anyone—and if so, to whom."

"If this is not the boy, you speak too much," retorted Vega, her face, even under its heavy coat of white paint, grew pink with anger.

"Spica," ordered Alexander Murray, "we must give Vega the proof she desires, tiresome and time-consuming as it is. Bring Jeremy Belcher here at once. We will play our game accurately and patiently."

Gracefully Spica moved from his spot against the wall and sauntered out the door. Richard watched expressionless. Surely, it was all over for him now, for Jeremy Belcher was a Jacobite and would have no doubts about his identity.

"Do something about that boy," Vega demanded. "He vexes me standing there in the middle of my best carpet."

Murray drawled, "If he so vexes you, I should suggest that you bring him a chair."

"I've done enough servant's work this night, acting as my own footman." She snapped open her fan, fluttering it in rage before her face, and her eyes shone above it like bits of stone. Murray smiled back mockingly. "And I do not like this affair," she put in hotly. "There have been things in it that Regulus and the Sun would not fancy. I do not like bloody work, Sirius, and you know it."

"Ah, you are willing to share in the spoils, aren't you, dear lady? But you do not want to dirty your white hands unless it's to dip them in gold."

Vega bit her lip and was silent. Alexander Murray had won a point. In the silence Richard looked curiously at the four people. Arcturus and Capella had carefully kept out of the quarrel between Vega and Murray. Arcturus was not a nobleman, and was wise enough not to offend one of them. As for Capella, it was very possible that he was too drunk to even hear what had been said. One thing was certain, though; the plotters were falling out. Richard remembered the bitter quarrel he'd witnessed between Antares and Sirius that night in the Charles Wain.

Vega finally spoke to Richard. "Sit down on the floor, boy, if you'd like. There's no need to stand so long."

"Such *tendresse*," Murray sneered. Richard sat down on the floor and Vega picked up a book from the little table beside her and began to read.

Richard found the sudden quietness much harder to take than the bitter words and questioning. It gave him time to think about the real danger of his situation. He was his own worst enemy, for he had stupidly alerted the clever Venetia Elliott by his clumsy questions about Lady Primrose and the Elibank brothers. She had reported this to her father, who must have known that the Society of the Stars hunted for the potboy who had seen Carlton murdered. By his own foolishness he had brought the killer, Spica, directly to him. He couldn't have done it better if he'd stepped out and shouted to them that day Lady Primrose's carriage had passed by. Alexander Murray must not have seen him after all. If he had, he'd have sent Spica to kidnap him long before this. Very likely Murray had no idea that Richard had been contacted by Saturn. At least, Richard hoped not. Well, thought Richard grimly, that's one thing they won't learn from me—not that it matters much anyway now that Jeremy Belcher is coming to tell them who I am.

They waited while the hall clock ticked on, Capella snored softly, and Lady Primrose turned the pages of her book. A door closed below stairs and footsteps came up the stairway. Lady Primrose sighed and shut her book.

"Get up, boy," she commanded.

Richard scrambled to his feet and stood waiting. Spica opened the door quietly and came in, followed by Jeremy Belcher. Belcher was much the same, perhaps a bit tired and somewhat thinner. He'd come in great haste, throwing a rug coat on over his tavern-keeper's apron, and from the way his eyes popped when he saw Richard, it was plain that Spica had told him nothing. Jeremy Belcher was a most surprised man.

"Do you know this filthy brat?" Murray barked. "Did he ever work as a potboy at your inn?"

Belcher scratched at his chin with one hand and narrowed his eyes. "Aye, there is a certain resemblance," he muttered, "but I am not certain that it is the lad. The city is full of thieving brats, and my potboys come and go so quickly, either from fevers or smallpox or running away, that I pay small mind to them anymore."

Murray was annoyed at this and struck hard with his fist

on the arm of his chair. "Well, make sure, little man," he shouted. "How can you tell? Did the boy who stole the gold snuffbox have any physical marks that you remember? This is vastly important to me, sirrah. There's a bag of gold in it for you if you can set our heads easy on this matter."

The host of the Seven Stars shook his head. "There was nothing that I recall, my lord. Perhaps my wife would . . ."

"Hang your wife!" thundered Murray. "Is that the boy?"

"Ah, there was something now," said Belcher brightly. "The lad I hired was from Bristol and spoke like a Bristol man, and, too, he walked with a slight limp. I had the devil's own time with him falling over men's feet in the common room with full jacks of ale in his hands."

"Walk, boy," ordered Alexander Murray. "Walk the length of this room."

Richard's hopes rose as he walked swiftly from one end of Vega's parlor to the other. Had Jeremy Belcher confused him with another tavern boy, or was Belcher trying to protect him out of kindness?"

"Nay, there is no limp," said the tavern-keeper finally. "Does the boy have a Bristol way of speaking, I wonder."

Without a word Lady Primrose passed her book over to Richard. "Do you read, boy?" and when Richard nodded, she said "Good. This is *Amelia* by Henry Fielding. Read aloud the passage that I've marked."

Richard read wonderingly. "Fortune may make thee often unhappy, she can never make thee completely and irreparably miserable without thy own consent."

"Well chosen, madam," said Murray. "You will give the boy courage and comfort, it seems. I wonder even more if you've not cooled to our great cause."

"That's no Bristol speech," said Jeremy Belcher, shaking his head. "I pride myself on knowing every kind of speech in this isle, and that's one I never heard."

"Where do you come from, my boy, and what is your name?" Arcturus asked.

"I come from the American Colonies," said Richard, "and my name is Richard Larkin." There was no reason to lie at this point. Many people in Chiswick already knew this much about him, and Jeremy Belcher had obviously never told them his name.

"That settles the matter," said Jeremy Belcher. "My boy was called Alan something or other, and this boy is too dark to be Alan. It's Alan that you want, I warrant. He stole the snuffbox and offended you gentlemen. This is not the lad."

"'Tis more than the snuffbox, host," Murray stated harshly. "You know our political complexion well enough. If you don't know it, sirrah, we know yours. We want to find the boy for a matter that hinges upon our cause, not because of some silly trinket he may have filched from one of us. Come, for the last time! Is this the boy we seek? I say he is. There is gold in it for you if you can satisfy us."

"Do you want me to say this is the lad when it isn't and have this upon my conscience all my days, just to earn your gold, your lordship? I have said what I could say and I have told you what I know." Belcher looked him straight in the eye.

Alexander Murray shifted in his chair. "The gold will be sent you at your place of business, Jeremy Belcher, but not as much as you might have gained by more cooperation."

"I have done my best," stated Belcher bowing.

"Are there others in your inn who would know this lad?" asked Lady Primrose.

"No, I don't think so, my lady. My other potboy at the time, an Irish lad, has gone back to Dublin to be with his widowed sister, and the cookmaids are brainless jilts and would have no memory of him."

"You mentioned your wife?" she persisted.

"Ah, but she would agree with me," said Belcher. "She mentioned the affair of the stolen snuffbox to me just the other day and called Alan to mind, describing him to me. I couldn't remember him at all. It's my wife's description of Alan that I judged upon today."

Alexander Murray was disgusted. "See that this little man gets back to his place of work," he commanded Spica. "Our Prince is not well served by his London friends, high or humble."

Belcher's eyes glittered with anger at this insult to his Jacobite sympathies. "There was a murder in my inn the same night the snuffbox was prigged, my lord," he said smoothly in his best host's voice. "I will remind you of that unhappy event, if I may. The King's watch favors my inn with much attention these days, and my hands are tied to do anything for the cause. I do not know but what I was followed here tonight."

Vega gasped and Arcturus adjusted his gross body uncomfortably on his tiny gilt chair. Murray silenced them with a look.

"Go back to your den, hyena," he ordered wearily.

Belcher drew himself up and once more bowed but this time only to Vega. "If I have your ladyship's permission?" he asked.

"Good man," she said, "you will not speak of this or of anything happening in my house, I believe? This is for the cause we all embrace."

"Nothing occurred at all this evening," said the tavern-keeper, and without a single glance at Richard or at any of the others, Jeremy Belcher stalked out of Lady Primrose's red and gold parlor. The quick-moving Spica followed close behind.

For a long moment there was silence and Richard looked happily from face to face. Jeremy Belcher had lied to save him. They'd have to let him go now. Alexander Murray caught his happy look and glared at him.

"Fortune is not your friend," he growled. "You know too much of our business now, even if some say you aren't the boy we search for. We have all the more reason not to let you go now."

Suddenly Capella woke up again, sneezed, and looked at Richard with bleary eyes. "The very spit of the boy," he croaked.

"And I do still believe he is," added Arcturus.

"Our host of the Seven Stars is a liar," Murray declared. "For fear of the Hanover rats and the watch or for reasons of sentiment, Belcher lied to us."

"But the tavern-keeper positively identified him as not being the boy," Lady Primrose protested.

Murray put up his hand to quiet her and turned to Richard. "For the last time, Larkin, were you a potboy at the Seven Stars?"

"No," Richard answered.

"There are ways to find out," Murray threatened. "Now, why did you ask about Lord Elibank, Lady Primrose and myself when you were at Chiswick House?" he asked sharply. "We know that you mentioned those names to the Elliott jade."

Richard stuck to the story he'd told Venetia. "I rowed

these people up to Chiswick, and I spoke to them about working in London."

"I happen to know that the people you asked about have never been to Chiswick by way of the river," Murray exclaimed triumphantly. "There, Vega, he's been caught out in his own lies."

Vega arose and walked nervously about the room. She circled around Richard enveloping him in a cloud of heavy musky perfume. "I'm not satisfied yet," she stated icily, stopping before Alexander Murray. "I'll grant you the innkeeper may not have told the truth just now, but I am not convinced, Sirius, and I must be sure."

"And if you hear it from his own lips? Would that suit you?"

Lady Primrose nodded her head slightly. "If you can give me proof?"

"When Spica returns, the boy shall confess to you that he was at the Seven Stars and he shall tell our dear Arcturus that he took his snuffbox, too. I promise you these things within ten minutes after Spica re-enters your house, dear lady." Murray said this with a joyous grin.

Vega shuddered. "Don't hurt him badly, I pray you, and certainly not here in this room, sirrah." She picked up *Amelia* again and began to read. Suddenly she laughed and lowering the book, looked directly at Murray as she recited from the text, "The devil himself contrived this wickedness."

Once more Richard waited, trying hard not to show how frightened he was. Vega did not seem to be as cruel as the others, but there was nothing to be gained from her, either. She could not help him far.

Spica was a long time coming back from the Seven Stars. They waited for what seemed an eternity to Richard. The clock ticked on until once more they heard a door open below. But this time the door slammed shut and heavier footsteps came up the stairs. There was a loud sharp rap that startled the silence.

Vega put down her book and swept to the door, opening it to a man in a long black cloak. He made a low and elegant leg to her.

"My provoking, bewitching Lady Vega," said this late arrival. Richard recognized him with new despair. It was the blond Antares. "You are ever a more distractin' beauty," and he kissed her hand with great gallantry and practice.

"Come in," Vega said crossly, almost snatching her hand away.

"Ah, I see that I am not to remove my raven's cloak even though I have just now come from my tailor's," Antares smirked and looked at the three cloaked men. He shot one rapid glance at Richard and went on with his chatter. "'Tis a pity, for he made up some new pink silk from China for a silver fringed waistcoat that I would willingly show off."

"Peacock, popinjay," Murray rose and pushed aside a hanging to look down into the street.

"Are you expecting someone, dear Sirius?" Antares calmly drew off his gloves and blinked after Alexander Murray.

"Spica is returning from some business," Arcturus volunteered, eager to please the elegant newcomer.

"Aha, so our dear Spica is out doing a bit of work. Now, I wonder what kind of work that can be? So, then we have six stars in the firmament tonight, have we?" Antares' voice was soft and accented. He chuckled. "We have myself, our lady, Vega, Capella, Arcturus, Spica and, of course, Sirius, last but surely, my dears, not least!"

Murray did not rise to the bait. With his back still turned

he protested mildly. "God help me! How I detest your ape's airs and manners. Come awa' now, be an honest Scot if you can."

Antares laughed. "I confess I do not know an honest Scot in England. I've looked everywhere. Very definitely I have, but I find not one hereabouts in London society."

Murray was weary. "Look at that boy there," he ordered, turning around. "Do you know him? Have you seen him before?"

Antares circled Richard slowly, pulling at Richard's hair to see if he wore a wig or not, peering into Richard's face, staring at his hands and feet, and feeling the cloth of Richard's coat between his fingers.

"Never saw him before in my life," he said, taking an enamel snuffbox from the pocket of his coat. "The cloth of his coat is good, but the cut is of last year even if the coat seems new enough. Here, have a pinch of snuff. It's the very nicest I could buy in this quite barbarous city. Paris is much better for such purchases."

"Stop this ridiculousness at once," roared Murray. "Am I to understand that you do not know this boy? You never saw him the evening we met at the Seven Stars?"

"My old friend, my friend! You wound me. My midriff quivers with woe that you should bring up such a painful thought. My condition was such that I have no recollection whatsoever of our first meeting as a society." Antares waggled a white finger at Murray. "I was, to put it in a low manner, gallows-lushy, as you may remember. That particular evening is a positive blank to me."

Richard breathed freely once again. It was true. The foppish Antares had seemed very drunk that night.

"Insignificant puppy. Lout!" said Alexander Murray in

bitter tones. "What can be gained from you in our cause, I wonder."

"I support our princely star, Regulus, as strongly as you do, dear Sirius," Antares smiled. "I happened to be inebriated that evening. My clan has supported the fortunes of Regulus and his family for generations, but what of yours? Were you out, sir, in the '45? What have you done that compares with what I have done? Who is closer to Regulus? You or I, sirrah?"

"You. Closer than a leech," Murray said coldly. "Today you are a rake in clothes that would shame a peacock's vanity, but a few years ago you sold the very buckles off your shoes for food and an attic room. How do you come by such prosperity? By pouring lies into the ears of Regulus against the rest of us and being rewarded for them with the little gold he has left?"

Antares was angry now. He and Murray faced each other. Richard and the others were quite forgotten. "I sold some property if it is any of your affair," he answered.

"What have you to sell? Your property in Scotland is in the hands of the Hanoverians. What did you sell, sirrah? Jewels the Prince gave you? Perhaps some of the rubies of the Prince's dead mother found their way into your hands or, better yet, it could be that a good number of the gold pieces of the Prince's Loch Arkaig treasure became yours. I have heard rumors and tales about that treasure. They mention your name more than once."

"When the Prince left Scotland after the failure of the '45, he entrusted much to me as a loyal and devoted follower," Antares' voice was deadly serious. "Among others, I was given the secret of the Loch Arkaig treasure, and concerning it, I did the Prince's bidding, not that this will be believed by you. Some will say that I have dipped my hands into Stuart gold, but this is a lie, and these men who say it will have reason to regret their words, I promise you." Antares reached to his side and halfway drew his sword from its scabbard.

"Put your sword away," cried Vega. "The hospitality of my house has been abused enough this night. Do you want the watch up here the minute they hear the sound of your duelling?"

"Vega is correct, as always," added Arcturus. "Pray sirs, do not quarrel now. The time is short until we strike our blow. We must not fall out with one another."

"This is the second time you've almost drawn your sword against me, Antares," Murray commented coldly. "The third time I shall surely kill you, even if I do it under the eyes of the Prince himself."

"If you suggest once more that I use the Prince's friendship for my own profit or that I have used Stuart gold or the Sobieski rubies to line my own pockets, I'll call you out," warned Antares. His face grew white with strain. "My resources are my own affair. I do not question yours."

"There is no need to question mine," retorted Alexander Murray. "Even when I joined the Prince and his men in France last year, my motives have always been open and clear. I do not skulk about in secret on dark business. I do not disappear for days at a time."

Antares' mouth dropped in a furious gasp. "My skulking, as you call it, is done upon the Prince's affairs. You don't know everything that goes on. You're pricked with envy because Regulus prefers and trusts me to you. He knows you have little head for secret and weighty matters, so he entrusts more to me. It only pleases him to let you consider yourself chief of the Society of the Stars."

Dark blood came to Murray's cheeks. He put his hand to

his sword, but Lady Primrose clapped her hands and cried out, "Stop this perilous business at once, I beg you. There's much work ahead of us and no time for fighting among ourselves like beasts. What of this lad? Four of you claim to know him. Antares says he doesn't recognize him, and the host of the Seven Stars agrees with Antares. The hour grows late and we have settled nothing yet."

"The boy will tell us what we want to know soon enough," Murray promised, glaring at Richard.

Antares waggled his finger at Murray. "You will get nothing from tormenting this poor boy, Sirius. If Spica hurts him badly enough, naturally he'll say what you want him to say, but you won't know whether he is really the boy or whether he's claiming he is, just to escape Spica's tender attentions."

"Do not preach to me through your nose," Murray remarked with a little smile. "Preaching does not go well with your face and fine laces and satins, not to mention your character."

"May I speak to the lad alone?" asked Antares of Vega.

"There'd be no harm in it until Spica returns," Vega agreed, and Murray shrugged and turned away to peer out the window once more. "Put yourself to rest on one matter," he said. "No one is watching this house. Spica and the landlord were not followed."

Antares walked over to Richard and in a friendly manner led him toward the opposite end of the room. "I do not believe that this fine braw boy can have any mischief in him; such sweetness and candor of expression is not often found in boys like yourself. Ah, you are a bold lad and a lucky lad, and you'll let Antares help you certainly." Antares kept up his soothing conversation until they reached the end of the parlor where no one could hear them, then suddenly he tightened his grip on Richard's arm, his face came close to Richard's, his pale fishlike eyes bulged. "Now, lad, be quick about it. Where is that letter?"

Richard was not unprepared. From the moment Antares entered the parlor, he had been thinking about that letter, hidden away in the wall at Hogarth house.

"I don't know what letter you mean, sir," replied Richard.

"Don't mince words with me, boy," Antares said quickly. "I wasn't so deep in wine that I don't mark you well." He gestured toward Capella and Arcturus, who were sitting silently across from Lady Primrose, "These fools marked you, too, and Sirius is positive that you were there."

"I haven't understood anything that's gone on here all evening," Richard looked at Antares blankly. "I didn't even know where the Seven Stars tavern was until that tall man over by the window told me that it was just off Fleet Street. They brought a man that I'd never seen before to look at me, and he said he didn't know me either. They talk about me as if I stole somebody's snuffbox, but I never stole anything in my life. For some reason you call yourselves by the names of stars, and that's all I do know except that you ask me odd questions I can't answer. I don't even know who you and your friends are, sir."

"Come away from this nonsense," Antares hissed in Richard's ear. "I know you, boy, but I want my letter more than I want you identified as that Seven Stars potboy. I'll stick to my story that you aren't the right lad if you'll tell me where you put my letter. I know you have it. I saw you pick it up, though other matters kept me from claiming it at the time." A strange look of fear came across the man's face and his voice quickened. "I've hunted for you, myself, unbeknown to the others. I can save you. Spica will be here any minute now.

He'll get the truth out of you. Nothing pleases him more than this kind of employment, believe me, boy."

Richard was stubborn. "I don't know anything about any letter. How can I tell you what you want to know when I don't know what it is myself you want? What am I supposed to have done at the Seven Stars, sir? First they talk about a snuffbox and then about a murder!"

"Fool, idiot! There isn't any time to lose. They're going to kill you anyhow, I know that much. Don't you? They don't give a devil's farthing for the stolen snuffbox or even for what you are supposed to have seen or heard at the Seven Stars. What they really want to know is if you've told anyone else about it. They have you now, but they want anyone else who knows, too. Spica will find out if you've talked. Some of us are touchy where murder is concerned, particularly Regulus and the Sun, but others would slit your throat and dump you in the Thames without a second thought. As for me, I want to save you. I don't like murder either."

Richard looked at the wheedling Antares and remembered the dagger that had killed Carlton and possibly Saturn. Antares had been warm for at least one murder. "You'd save me because of the letter?" Richard asked. "It must be a very important letter."

Antares' eyes gleamed. He clutched at Richard's shoulders. "Ah, that's better boy. That letter has a sentimental value to me—a deep sentimental value."

"But I didn't say I had any letter!"

"Never mind. I'm satisfied that you do have it. Now, keep your tongue and your head and let me save your life," Antares advised.

"For a letter you'd save me?" Richard repeated, seeing the game he had to play.

"Not entirely," came the blithe mocking reply. "Say rather that I'm taken with your bonny face and would not like to think of you lying dead in the mud of the Thames." Antares patted Richard's shoulder and steered him back to the group at the other end of the parlor.

Murray turned from the window and glared gloomily at Richard and Antares. "Spica is coming up the Strand now," he said. "What have you learned from the boy, if anything at all?"

Antares removed his hand from Richard's arm and clapped the boy on the shoulder. "I have questioned him sagaciously, dear Sirius. He has never been a potboy. His education is sadly deficient in the knowledge of wines and ales. I believe that he has never even been in a tavern. I detect nothing but a boundless innocence in him."

"Bah! Gammon, all gammon!" snorted Murray. "There is no innocence in him. He's taken you in, but some of us are not so gullible or heedless in the Prince's service."

Arcturus got up ponderously from his chair and came over to Murray. "This takes too long, sir. We must have an end to this affair, I regret to tell your lordship. I beg you that we make a speedy dispatch of it and depart separately and in safety. I have weighty business yet tonight for the Prince in a meeting with others, who favor our cause."

"And I agree," added Vega. "I do not like my house to be used for such purposes, but if I must, I must. I ask you, Sirius, to end this quickly. Capella," she shook the dozing old man. "What do you say?"

"It is the boy. Kill him," Capella mumbled and closed his eyes again.

Despite his own fear Richard heard the sudden intake of Antares' breath, but the elegant young man said nothing.

"I have been thinking. It is more than possible that this boy is a Hanoverian agent," Murray said slowly. "He has not behaved like any Fleet Street potboy I have ever known. I am convinced that he saw the assassination we were forced to commit at the Seven Stars. I believe that he was aided in his escape by someone in that tavern, if not by Jeremy Belcher. I shall make it my business to find out who has played against us there and punish them as soon as our current business is at an end. This spawn of Satan was at the Seven Stars and then he reappeared at Chiswick House to ask questions about Lord Elibank, Lady Primrose and myself. Now why does he show up at Chiswick House, unless he was planted there to spy? The more I consider it the more certain I am that he has been approached by some Hanoverian agent and enlisted in the King's service. We know that 'Hubble-Bubble,' that very noble Duke of Newcastle, is always alert for plots against the Hanoverians and that he maintains a vast army of spies and that he would even stoop to enlisting children. Sometimes I suspect our own ranks—perhaps even here in this room. Someone, besides the boy, is in the pay of the Duke of Newcastle."

Arcturus, Vega and Antares stiffened involuntarily.

"My lord," protested Arcturus, his fat face turning even pinker, "if you suspect me or my loyalty . . ."

Murray held up his hand and moved it wearily for quiet. In that silence they heard the rush of Spica's feet on the steps.

"I say that we should kill the boy at once," Murray declared. "Spica has come."

Spica hurled himself into the room, brushing at his scarlet coat. "Your pardon, noble sirs, for being so late. I left the host at the door of the Seven Stars, making sure that no one followed us, and started back to the Strand, but I was caught first in an apprentices' game of ball and could not cross the road and then I was trapped in a doorway while two chairmen fought with clubs over who should carry the passenger who weighed the least and could pay the most. Then they dragged me into it."

"We have business for you here," Murray silenced him impatiently.

"What sort of work would it be, your lordship?"

"You must do away with this boy. Though we want to know what he's told to others of our affairs, there is no time for that now. We'll watch the Seven Stars and hunt up his companions in Chiswick and learn from them what we need to know. He may be a spy, so he must be done away with now."

Spica moved forward, smiling evilly, but Antares stepped quickly in front of Richard. He struck a dramatic pose, worthy of David Garrick. "No, sirrah," Antares exclaimed. "No one will harm this boy. You all know where Sirius and I journey before dawn tomorrow, and you know with what favor this deed will be looked upon. And I have every intention of telling the Prince what went on here tonight."

"You insolent dog!" Alexander Murray bellowed. "You'll put all of our heads on the block with your foolishness."

"I *will* tell Regulus," Antares warned.

"Well, then, just what do you propose we do?" asked Lady Primrose, looking at Antares with distaste.

"There is room in the fishing boat for three, as well as two."

"You'd take the lad to Regulus?" she asked in disbelief, and then added slowly as an afterthought, "Regulus does not like murder. You are right there. It is well known that he has a tender conscience. Perhaps you are right to do this."

"Idiocy!" shouted Murray. "Regulus won't thank us for this piece of nonsense. He has greater matters on his brain than the fate of a wretched spying boy."

Arcturus was thoughtful but silent. Slovenly Capella

snored while Antares and Murray faced each other once more. Spica had not moved since Antares had put forth his amazing idea, and now he looked at Murray waiting to see what he should do.

"The course is a clever one," Lady Primrose argued. "You and Antares leave London tonight. Take the boy with you and let Regulus make the decision. Regulus has ways to inspire devotion. Perhaps he can find out what the boy knows and what he's told without hurting him."

"Nonsense," Murray frowned and sighed wearily. "However, I allow it against my saner judgment and, then, only to save time. We'll take the boy."

"I wish you three a most pleasant journey," Lady Primrose said mockingly. "I hear the crossing is lively this time of the year, and you'll have each other for company. Indeed, what could be pleasanter?"

Alexander Murray growled wordlessly at her and stalked over to the open door, motioning to Spica to follow him. He rearranged his black cloak and started down the hall without a word of farewell.

"Come away with me, boy," Antares soothed Richard. "Didn't I tell you that I would save your life?"

"Where are you taking me?" Richard asked, dazed by all that had occurred.

"Why to Regulus, of course," Antares confided, crooking a white eyebrow at Richard and winking at Lady Primrose. "To Regulus across the English Channel. Or rather, should I say, dear laddie, to 'Bonnie Prince Charlie' in France?"

Antares inclined his head to Arcturus, bowed elegantly to Lady Primrose and kissed her hand, took Richard companionably by the arm, and they followed in the steps of Spica and Alexander Murray.

CHAPTER 8

To Regulus

A STRANGE tall coach waited in the Strand below Vega's house. Antares made his way toward it, mincing along, the perfect elegant fop, heedless of the grins and nods of the waiting sedan-chair carriers and linkboys. Alexander Murray sat inside the coach alone. Spica was nowhere to be seen, and Richard immediately felt lighter of heart, as Antares ordered him into the coach.

Antares got in fussing about his cloak and seated himself by Richard, across from Alexander Murray. The blond man bounced on the hard leather seat and sighed. "I fear it will be a vastly uncomfortable journey, lad. Our traveling companion is of but a melancholy disposition, it seems, but you are in good hands, have no fear." He reached over to pat Richard almost affectionately on the hand. "No one will harm you."

"You have suddenly become over-tender," snarled Murray. "You are very squeamish now, but you were not always so chickenhearted, not when it was your own dirk that killed

Carlton and your own hand that killed that old fool of a Hanoverian spy turned Chiswick gravedigger."

"Dear me," Antares answered languidly. He pulled a scented lace-trimmed handkerchief from his sleeve and waved it delicately under his nose. "So open in your speech now that we've left the others! Think of the things this poor innocent boy will learn from you. You'll terrify him. What makes you think that I murdered any man in such an out-of-the-way place as Chiswick, sirrah? The ideas you do entertain. La, your brain does work strangely, Sirius."

The coach rumbled forward, as the horses stepped slowly through the crowds of the Strand.

Alexander Murray answered confidently. "Spica has assured me that he did not kill this gravedigger. The man had drawn suspicion on himself by too many questions, just as the boy here did. Valentine Elliott pointed him out and Spica was sent to dispatch him, but when he arrived, he found that someone else had found the old man first."

"Really?" Antares yawned.

"Oh, but there is much more. Spica saw the man's body as he lay on the bank of the Thames and he recognized him as a Hanoverian agent of some reputation. He also recognized the dirk in his back."

"Do go on, pray," Antares sniffed at his handkerchief. "Truly, these fevers and nauseous odors of London do distract me."

"We are almost certain too that he was the man who spoke to you and Spica in the hall of the Seven Stars the evening that you chased this potboy."

"And?" inquired Antares.

"I had mentioned to you that there was an old man who dug graves in a churchyard in Chiswick and that Elliott suspected him to be a Hanoverian agent. And, Antares, I told no one else of this."

"So?"

"I put it to you, dear Antares, that you went to Chiswick without informing anyone, somehow recognized the man and for reasons of your own, killed him and kept this secret from me."

"Now that is most interesting, Sirius. I've not been so diverted for some days now. Do you think that I would deprive Spica of his pleasures?"

Alexander Murray did not answer. They moved out of the Strand and into the complex of narrow London streets. Finally he said, smiling at Antares, who still held his handkerchief to his nose. "You may bubble the others among us who consider you an idiot as well as a graceless rake. You act at every opportunity, but your talents are wasted, Antares. You should walk the boards at Drury Lane. But I am not taken in by you. I know you and I know your family. You come from an ancient Scots line, loyal to the Stuarts. You are not the fop you pretend to be, and you must be the assassin of the Chiswick gravedigger."

"And why me, pray? Why not Arcturus or Capella, or even Vega?"

"I told you just now, Antares, that you are the only one who knew of that agent's existence, outside of Spica and myself. Capella is a drunken animal; Arcturus is a pompous fat frightened fool. You are the only one who has the stomach for murder. The others are cowards and whining idiots."

"La, I had not realized you thought so well of me, Sirius," mocked Antares.

"I do not think well of you at all, and I heartily wish you were not involved in our cause. If Regulus did not favor you,

I'd have Spica follow you some night as you slip in and out of your London haunts doing what you term the Prince's business. Where is your dirk, Alastair?" Murray suddenly demanded.

"Stolen, alas, stolen weeks ago but I have another. It was not an unusual pattern. No great loss." confessed Antares. "I had it prigged when I came home gallows-lushy one evening. London is alive with pickpockets. 'Tis a positive sink of crime and criminals."

"'Tis a great pity the stolen dirk wasn't left in your back as it was in that gravedigger's," said Murray bitterly.

Antares turned to Richard. "Have you ever heard the like, boy?" he asked. "He'd like to see me dead, I do believe!"

Richard gazed in astonishment at Antares and Murray. Was it true that Antares had killed Saturn? Alexander Murray seemed honest, even if a hard and vicious man. It was quite possible that Antares had put two and two together and realized that Saturn had helped conceal Richard when he ran from the Charles Wain apartment at the Seven Stars. Antares could possibly have seen him in the hallway, recognized him again at Chiswick, and then killed him to get the letter. Antares' motives always came back to that letter. He would have to be even more careful with Antares than Alexander Murray, Richard decided. He'd learned a good deal tonight that he hadn't known before. Antares had responded to the name Alastair, so that his real name might not be Alec Guthry. And if so who wrote the letter?

Murray leaned forward, his hands on his knees. "Watch what you do with your dirks, Alastair, from now on."

Antares leaned toward him and said in a voice so soft that Richard had to strain to hear. "I shall, dear Sirius. I promise you, that I shall."

The coach left London, the coachman cursing and cracking his whip over the horses' heads all the way. Once they had reached the open countryside of Kent, the horses broke into a steady gallop.

Antares touched Richard. "I would suggest, boy, that you sleep. We'll not be reaching the area around Folkestone until an hour before dawn."

Richard studied Antares by the light of the waning moon. How could the man actually think that he would be able to sleep?

"Aye, lad," came a rumbling comment from Murray, invisible in the darkest corner of the coach. "By all means sleep. You're but a wee broth of a lad, you know, to be a Hanoverian spy. It will be a great comfort to you to know that I dispatched Spica to look after your friends in Chiswick. They will soon be safe in his tender care."

Richard sat horrified, glad for the blackness as a cloud covered the moon. Tears came to his eyes. So that was where Spica had gone—to Chiswick to spy out Betsy and little Abby.

"I have no friends in Chiswick or anywhere else in England," Richard said as steadily as he could.

Murray laughed sharply. "Aye, sleep, boy. If you can. There'll be precious little rest for you when you're brought to the Prince."

Antares giggled in the darkness. "And will you be thinking of sleeping, too, Sirius?" he asked sweetly.

"Not with you in the same coach with me!" came the snapped-off reply.

"Ah, boy, he is my countryman, and yet he does not trust me. Isn't that a sad story?" Antares spoke to Richard in mock sorrow.

"Deil scowp wi' ye, Alastair. Shut your loon's mouth," Murray roared.

And after that outburst there was silence. Richard sat in

the dark thinking about his own stupidity, the danger he was in, and, most of all, about Betsy, who didn't even know of her own peril. Finally he fell asleep curled up in the far corner of the seat. He slept fitfully for some hours, despite the rocking carriage and the changes of horses at relay posts.

Some hours later Antares shook Richard to wakefulness. "Come away, laddie. We're nearly there and we'll be leaving this rattlebones of a coach for a boat. We're not far from Folkestone."

A few moments later the coach stopped. Richard, Murray and Antares got down into the dark windy night. The sound of surf was not too far off. Antares spoke to the coachman, who grunted a reply, cracked his whip and was off again northward.

"Down here, lad," Antares caught Richard by the hand. "'Tis an hour before dawn and we must be in the channel at sunrise. Hurry, there'll be no lanterns to light our way."

Richard realized that he must be near the edge of a cliff, for Antares held him firmly and pulled him away once or twice as they hurried along. "The path is not hard," Antares told Richard. "There is a bank on one side so keep your hand on it. Feel your way. You follow Sirius. He and I know this path well."

Richard did as ordered, thinking sadly of the great care Antares took of him because of the letter. He wondered if he could bargain with Antares for his life and Betsy's? Did Antares have the power to call off Spica or did Spica obey only Sirius? As they reached the foot of the cliff, Richard remembered something that Betsy had mentioned, William Hogarth's pair of pistols in the corner cupboard of the kitchen. As far as Richard knew, Hogarth had not remembered to take them to Leicester Fields with him. Richard's brow furrowed. He was not at all certain that Betsy would know how to prime and fire a pistol if Spica did find her.

Alexander Murray stopped short at the bottom of the path. "Bring the brat. Where is he?"

"Here," Antares replied softly, pushing Richard ahead of him onto the sandy beach. "See that bobbing red light out there, boy? That's the boat we're to take. We'll have to wade out to her and make quick work of it, too. She's not far out and she draws little water. We'll not get very wet, I hope. Sink me and curse me for wearing my new pink silk waistcoat, but I fear there's no help for it. Now hurry! The wind bids fair this dawn for France."

The sky was brightened by the light of the false dawn, as Richard and the two men waded out into the icy November water. The sands gleamed white behind them. Richard could see the little fishing boat tossing gently up and down in the quiet water of the isolated cove. They were knee deep in the surf when they heard someone from the boat singing softly. "Here's him that's for awa', Willie, Here's him that's for awa'."

Murray replied, whistling the tune that had just been sung, then adding the next line in his deep voice. "And here's the flower that I love best, the rose that's like the snaw."

"What is the color of the rose that blooms in November?" came the soft call over the water.

"White as fallen snow," Murray sang out.

"Come away, then," said the voice from the boat. " 'Tis a wasp's byke here, so close to Folkestone, and I like it not."

Murray and Antares floundered quickly through the water, and Richard followed them. In moments they had been hauled aboard the boat by strong hard hands. They stood shivering on the deck while a man raised the anchor and another set the sails. A third man, evidently the master, conferred with Murray. "Ye have three. That's one ower what I was ta carry," he protested.

" 'Tis a boy who has business with the Prince," Murray explained.

"It'll cost more siller," said the master. " 'Tis one ower."

"The Prince will pay you, my man," put in Antares.

"Oh, aye," was the sardonic comment from the master. "The Prince'll pay me—someday."

"Hold your tongue," ordered Alexander Murray sharply. "Take us to the coast near St. Omer. You know the place. You've done the Prince's business more than once, and you know he expects us."

"It'll cost more siller. By the look of last evenin's sky and this mornin's wind, this crossin'll be wild wark and cauld wark," said the master stubbornly. "Ye'll soon be even more drookit from the waves than ye be now. Go below. Ye'll find blankets in the cabin to keep ye from the ague. Yer to keep to the cabin too, for safe-keepin'."

Richard followed Murray and Antares to the hatchway that led to the tiny cabin, just barely visible now in the grayish light of the true dawn.

" 'Tis misty in the cove; that is favorable and will keep our sailing hidden," Antares looked about before he went below.

Alexander Murray was gloomy. "It will not last," he said. "No weather has ever aided the cause we serve. No wind has ever blown in the right direction at the right time for the Stuart cause." He clumped below, pushing Richard before him.

But this time Murray was wrong. The little fishing smack moved swiftly under the cover of the mist and sailed boldly out into channel waters. The moment they reached the open sea the wind hit with such force that they nearly capsized, and Richard fell, sprawling over Murray in the tiny cabin.

"Get off me, you devil's brat!" he kicked Richard aside, then leaped up the steps bawling out to the master and the crew. "Idiots! Fools! Are you trying to drown us all?"

The master, a weather-beaten man with gold earrings and a red stocking cap, bellowed back, "I'm master of this smack. If ye want a swift passage, ye'll take my orders, noble lords, or no. No man tells a Kerr what to do."

Murray returned to the cabin scowling. The look and color of his face matched the gray clouds and high gray seas. A fine hard wind lashed the channel with a needle-spray of ice-cold rain.

"*Sassenach*!" spat Murray, wrapping one of the blankets about himself and sitting down on a keg.

Antares, who had been examining his pink waistcoat with tender concern, laughed and explained to Richard. "He called our inestimable master a *Sassenach*. That means he's an Englishman or a Lowland Scot, laddie. The Kerr clan is Lowland."

"They are the same nasty breed," snarled Murray.

"Ah, not so fast, Alexander Murray," said Antares. "There are as many Englishmen and Lowlanders as there are Highland Scots in this venture of ours. It is London we raise while Polaris and Deneb are to go into the Highlands. We could not succeed without the English who back the cause. The failure of the '45 should have taught you something."

"Sometimes I would that it was all honest Highlanders in this," vowed Murray, moving from his keg. He sat down on one of the small bunks to brace himself better against the rolling and pitching of the little fishing boat. "And by honest Scots, I don't mean *caterans* like you either, Alastair."

"He calls me a Highland robber, laddie. I am honored." Antares preened proudly. Richard, who was heartily sick of their quarreling, cared little about the meanings of *Sassenach* or *cateran*. Besides, he was tired, hungry, and frightened of the channel storm and even more frightened of what was in store for him.

"How long will it take to cross the channel?" Richard asked. Antares took the second bunk and motioned for Richard to sit on the keg Murray had just vacated.

"Four to five hours," Antares shivered as a great wave broke over the boat and sloshed down into the cabin. "By this evening, if all goes well, and the horses await us in France, you shall have been presented to 'Bonnie Prince Charlie."

"I'm hungry, sir," Richard said, and Murray and Antares roared with laughter.

"So are we!" remarked Antares, still laughing. "You haven't crossed the English Channel, I can see that, or you wouldn't talk about eating. Once in France we shall stuff you like a goose ready for the oven, but there'll be no food on this passage. The wise traveler doesn't eat on a rough day in these foul waters."

For the first time Alexander Murray was jovial. "You may have crossed the sea from the American Colonies, brat, but you don't know the Channel. You'd not have food in your midriff long enough to taste it. Let your gizzard growl away."

Richard sat back and tried to relax in the bare little cabin. The fishing smack bore them onward to France and Regulus. Before long Murray and Antares buried their heads in their blankets. Richard leaned queasily against a bulkhead thinking to himself. What chance had a plot in which the major conspirators hated and distrusted each other with such fierceness? Samuel Johnson had been right about Alexander Murray, and what would he think had he met Antares and Vega?

A pale cold sun broke through late in the morning and stood directly overhead. The drenched master stuck his head into the cabin. "France is in sight. I've seen yer Frenchies through the spyglass. They've a coach on the cliff for ye. Ye'd best hurry. I want ta take aboard a load of brandy and salt afore dark ta have somethin' ta show for ma day 'a braw honest work as tha best smuggler in tha business."

They scrambled out of their blankets. Antares straightened his queue, pulled out a tiny looking-glass from the pocket of his sea-ruined pink coat and carefully affixed a black beauty patch to his chin. Richard watched in astonishment.

"Popinjay, 'tis a pretty sonsy cratur, aye," said Murray as he left the cabin. "'Tis no man. 'Tis but a cunning laddie, who puts his dirk in men's backs in the dark, Alastair Ruadh."

Murray's harsh comments did not bother Antares. He smiled into his mirror, put it back into his pocket and beckoned to Richard to follow along. "Laddie, we're in France," he declared, "the land where food is fit to eat—the most civilized country in the world." He swung around, his pale blue eyes intent on Richard's face. His voice was soft and conspiratorial. "And, boy, do not forget that letter. If you value your life, do as I tell you and keep your tongue in your head before the Prince."

Some moments later the little boat lay at anchor under the yellowish cliffs of the French coast. Murray, Antares and Richard waded ashore, their backs to a cold wind, the water icy on their legs. Richard shivered as they crossed the narrow beach and climbed to the top of the cliff where three men and a coach waited for them.

The moment Alexander Murray set foot on the wind-swept

brown grass of the clifftop one of the men came forward. Richard recognized him. It was the one-armed man who had also been at the Seven Stars the night of the murder.

"Betelgeuse!" exclaimed Antares, pushing Murray aside he moved toward the man and held out his hand.

Betelgeuse ignored Antares' gesture but bowed stiffly to him and then more deeply to Murray. "The Prince is waiting." He had an accented voice much like Spica's. Richard remembered that Timothy Quayle had marked the one-armed man as Irish. "Who is the boy?" he asked looking at Richard with curiosity. "I feel I've seen his face before."

"You remember the potboy from the Seven Stars—the boy we've hunted and scoured London for?" Murray shot a triumphant glance at Antares.

"Ah, it could well be the very boy." Betelgeuse stared hard at Richard now. "Has he joined our cause, then?"

"In a manner of speaking," Murray said dryly. "We've brought him to see the Prince."

Betelgeuse nodded and turned on his heel, leading the way to the coach where two men stood waiting. They were magnificently dressed. The first wore a gold-laced hat, blazing blue cloak over a dazzling white uniform and the most elaborately powdered wig Richard had ever seen. The second man was dressed in a scarlet jacket with a multicolored scarf thrown over his shoulder and caught with a brooch, a blue bonnet with a feather on it, and most astonishing of all, a short skirt that stopped above his knees. The man saw Richard's eyes on him, laughed, and swung up onto his horse in a whirl of skirts.

"I see that the French king has sent us an escort," commented Murray as he got into the coach. "To find an officer of his own troops and one from Ogilvy's Regiment of loyal Scots is honor indeed."

Betelgeuse jerked his head toward Richard and then asked Murray, "Do you talk freely in front of him?"

"There is no reason now for silence. The boy is a prisoner and knows a good deal already. He can't get away so I see no reason not to speak now that we are here in France."

Antares had been silent all this time, but Richard noticed that his eyes had missed nothing. He had glanced briefly at the soldier in the kilt, and both had looked quickly away in mutual disgust.

The French officer had said nothing and seconds after the Scot had mounted his horse, the Frenchman did the same. Now they cantered easily alongside the lumbering coach as it turned away from the cliffs and the channel. Richard sat next to Antares and as Betelgeuse and Murray spoke quietly together, he looked out the coach windows at France. It seemed older even than England. The little-traveled muddy road was lined by withered brownish hedges, and beyond the hedges were old gray stone farmhouses with slate roofs and stone pigsties. Now and then he saw hogs walking sadly about in the yellow mud looking up at the gnarled gray fruit trees, hoping, he supposed, that it wasn't too late in the year for an apple to fall.

They rode on for about an hour and Richard stared listlessly at the countryside. Now and again he saw a great gray stone chateau on a hilltop and wondered idly whose house it was and if this might be where he would meet the Prince? But always the coach pushed on.

Richard was exhausted and depressed, and he sensed that Antares was experiencing the same difficulties. The presence of Betelgeuse and the two officers had not lifted Antares' spirits and once more Richard felt that the conspirators hated one another. Betelgeuse was not, like Spica, a tool of Murray's commands, and he did not even bother to show his dislike of

Antares. Antares and Murray treated Betelgeuse with more concern than they had shown Capella, Arcturus and Vega back in London. It was clear that Betelgeuse was closer to the Prince than the other plotters. Now Betelgeuse said something that caught Richard's attention. "The Prince has perfected his plans now. Do you have the Westminster mob ready to rise? And has Valentine Elliott made a signal for the sedan-chair carriers?"

"Aye," was Murray's reply. "All is in readiness, I believe, to bring off our business in London."

"Is there any threat to the plan?" inquired Betelgeuse.

"Not unless this potboy has blabbed of what he heard and saw at the Seven Stars. We have him safe enough here but what of the people he's contacted since he left the tavern? How much has he said to them of our business? He could very well be a Hanoverian spy."

"What do you know, boy? You'd better tell us," commanded the one-armed man. "It will go better for you if you talk now, I promise you. We have great plans, and no one must stand in their way."

Antares began to cough delicately into his handkerchief while Richard said, "I'm no spy. I don't know anything but what I've heard these gentlemen say in the hours I've been with them."

"Little lying devil," growled Murray. "I would have let Spica have him and save the Prince all this trouble."

Betelgeuse gave Murray a look that Richard could not fathom and turned his face away to look out the window. "We are in St. Omer," he announced. "The Prince will be waiting for your report. I'll keep the boy close prisoner until the Prince is ready to see him."

They were jogging down the only street of a small town.

The street was lined with more of the tall stone and stucco houses. People in sober dark clothing walked about. They looked with open interest at the coach and its oddly assorted outriders.

"The people of St. Omer are not accustomed yet to the presence of the Prince and his staff," explained Betelgeuse. "I don't believe they approve of his wild Irish and Scots, although, as you know, the French King procured a large old farmhouse for the Prince's headquarters."

The coach rumbled to the left and into a small deeply rutted road that led to a sprawling gray stone building, much like those that Richard had seen all along the way.

"'Tis not St. James's Palace in London, and we are cramped, but it will do until the tenth of the month," Betelgeuse said with a knowing smile, "and then we have St. James's and London, too, don't we?"

Murray grunted in agreement as the coach jerked to a stop. The door was flung open by another kilted Scot, in the same multicolored cloth that the escort had worn. Murray leapt to the ground and greeted him coldly. Betelgeuse, Antares and Richard climbed down after him and stood in the sticky mud. Kilted soldiers stood guard outside the massive wooden doors of the house while others lounged against its walls, each wrapped in the bright red, yellow and blue plaid of the Ogilvy Regiment. One or two of them nodded to Murray and Antares, but no one came forward.

"I trust the Prince gives us a warmer greeting," said Murray bitterly to Betelgeuse, but the one-armed man did not comment.

Instead he motioned for Antares and Murray to precede him inside and then touched Richard on the shoulder, telling the boy to come along with him. They entered the large lower room of the house. Betelgeuse led Richard off to the massive hearth at the far end. The others turned to pass through a knot of men clustered around a great wooden table set before a second fireplace at the other side of the room. Their footsteps rang loud on the stone floors and reverberated against the vast beamed ceiling. The group of men moved away from the table to allow the London plotters to approach a tall slim young man, who came forward to greet them.

"Bring wine for my friends from England. Bring wine for everyone," the young man called out in a high pleasant voice, and a boy in a kilt hurried out of the room.

Murray and Antares bowed very low to the tall young man and swept off their hats.

"Is that the Prince?" Richard asked Betelgeuse. Betelgeuse frowned as he watched the meeting.

"Yes," was the short reply, and then he added, rather kindly, seeing Richard's white face. "When did ye sup last, lad?"

"It was a long time ago, sir," said Richard. "I don't really remember. So much has happened to me since then."

Betelgeuse snapped his fingers and a servant appeared. "Fetch this boy wine, bread and meat," Betelgeuse ordered, and then more softly to Richard. "Sit before the fire. You're shivering with the cold. It will be some time before the Prince will see you. Eat and get warm. Many of us do not make war on children."

Richard did as he was told, seating himself on a corner of the large fireplace. The servant brought him dark bread, slabs of cooked pork and watered sour red wine. The wine warmed him and even made his head swim a little as he looked across the room at 'Bonnie Prince Charlie' and his staff.

Most of the men who clustered about the Prince wore uniforms of one sort or another—the white of the French King, the kilts and blue bonnets of the Scots, the black, green or red coats of the military. Some of the men were in ordinary dress. In the middle of these Richard spotted Rigel, the sad-faced elderly man, the last arrival at the Charles Wain. And now while Alexander Murray talked to the Prince and pointed to a map spread out on the table, Rigel walked slowly over to Betelgeuse and stood for a long moment gazing at Richard.

"Yes, I've seen this boy before, I believe," he said. "What is his business here?"

"He was the potboy at the London tavern—the lad who escaped, sir, you remember?"

"Oh," was the comment. "Then he has business with the Prince. Tell me of these matters, boy," and Rigel sat down alongside Richard, eyeing him mournfully. Suddenly he looked up at Betelgeuse. "So young to be in this business," he sighed.

"There's nothing to tell you, sir," said Richard firmly. "I've been kidnapped, that's all."

"Nothing to tell? The Prince will be the judge of that," reprimanded Rigel. "Wait until the Prince calls for you." He got up quickly, dismissing the boy. "Does the lad tell the truth?" he asked Betelgeuse.

"Sirius says that he lies."

"Bah! Alexander Murray!"

"He is a friend to the Stuart cause."

Rigel smiled sadly. "The Prince has one friend he values more than all the others, one that has been faithful to him for some years—a friend he values far more than Alexander Murray," Rigel nodded significantly to Betelgeuse and inclined his head toward the Prince, who was lifting a glass of wine to his lips.

"Aye," agreed Betelgeuse, "wine is no friend to kings even though it can be kind to a poor man in distress."

"The Prince was a poor man, hunted and ill in Scotland after the '45," said Rigel coldly. "He had little to eat and much to drink. He developed a taste for strong spirits. But this is 1752, not '45, and we, who are with him day and night, see him drink more and more with each disappointment."

"And there have been plenty of disappointments," Betelgeuse nodded.

"Seagraves, only a weak man salves himself in spirits. I say to you that the Prince has little heart for this London venture."

Betelgeuse was silent for a moment. Then in a grave, sad voice he said, "Like the others: without a miracle it will fail. Even with the aid of the great Frederick of Prussia, it will fail."

Rigel shook his head and drifted slowly back to the Prince. He stood there quietly, looking dolefully at the men, who drank with his master to the hope of the Stuart cause.

Suddenly a silence fell on the group, and it was obvious that something was expected. The Prince's voice broke the hush, shouting, "Murray, I told you that there shall be no murders done in my name."

Richard started at these terrible words. The Prince shouted again. "Usurper though he is, German George, my cousin, shall not be killed. Kidnap him and hurry him and his family out of England, but murder, no! I do not like murder, as you well know."

Richard leaned back against the chimney, weak with relief, and the Prince went on. "We shall take the Tower of London, secure the family of my cousins from Hanover, and raise Scotland. Archibald Cameron and MacDonald of Lochgarry have gone to Scotland already. All of England and Scotland will be ours in two weeks." The Prince's voice faltered for a moment and he took a large sip of wine. "We shall not fail, I trust. And it shall not be said of King James, my father, that he condones murder—even of usurpers."

Alexander Murray bowed his head. His face was scarlet. Richard caught Antares' quick grin at Murray's embarrassment. The Prince called out. "Alastair Ruadh Macdonnell, here, has the head for this kind of business," and he strode forward, to clap Antares on the shoulder. "Now give me a quick victory in London. London is the key to the scheme this time, not Scotland." The Prince lifted his glass to the men around him, "and now with the favor of Sweden, Prussia and our gracious friend, the King of France, who shelters us, why should we fail?" Bonnie Prince Charlie drank deeply. He bent once more to the map, wine glass and wine bottle never far from his hand. He talked to Antares, while the men in uniform gathered close about him, pointing and disputing. Alexander Murray hovered glumly on the fringes trying vainly to get the Prince's attention.

It was late afternoon before the Prince had Richard brought to him. In that long interval of time Richard had watched Prince Charles Edward Stuart closely, knowing that his life depended on what this man would decide. He determined that he would say nothing that could further endanger him or Betsy.

Betelgeuse and Rigel stood with Richard before the Prince, who sat at the end of the long table. The men in the bright-colored uniforms had drifted away across the room, talking in little groups. Antares and Murray stood close by, one on each side of the paper-strewn table. The Prince held a glass to his lips while he and Richard exchanged long, careful looks. Bonnie Prince Charlie was still a young man. His reddish-blond hair showed no signs of gray and his handsome oval face was tanned and unlined. His brilliant hazel eyes bored into Richard's eyes, brighter and more feverish than any Richard had ever seen before. Richard remembered Samuel Johnson's words that except for the Catholicism of his family, this was a man who was everything that England could ever ask in a king. The only fault that Richard could see in this handsome face was the mouth. It was too delicate and prettily shaped for a man.

"I believe the lad marks me out well," the Prince said, turning to Rigel, and laughing a little.

"This is the potboy, who overheard our plans in London, your Highness," explained Alexander Murray. He spoke swiftly before the Prince could silence him. "We have not learned yet if he has told anyone else of these matters."

"Fool, to meet at a tavern! Even more fool to have a potboy hear you!" the Prince's tones were icy. He turned abruptly to Richard. "Well, have you talked?" he asked.

Richard recited. "I am Richard Larkin of Pennsylvania Colony," and then he bowed as deeply as he had seen Antares and Murray do. "I am not a potboy but a gardener. And I don't know anything that would interest anyone here. I've been kidnapped."

The Prince smiled at Richard's reply and low bow. He held up a long brown hand for quiet, and deep lace ruffles fell away from his green sleeves. "He makes a decent enough courtier, it seems, and he is well spoken. A potboy, do you say?"

Murray stepped forward. "If I have your leave, your Highness. He has been identified by myself, Capella, Arcturus, Betelgeuse, Rigel and Spica."

The Prince spoke sharply to Antares. "What have you to say about this, Macdonnell?"

Antares spread out his hands apologetically. "I do not know the boy."

The Prince swung back to Murray. "Where is Spica?" he asked coldly. "I do not see your shadow with you this visit, Sirius."

"He has been sent to find this devil brat's friends where-ever they are," Murray explained. "The boy will not tell what he knows, and I've not had the time to persuade him yet. But there are other ways to find out how much he has told, in spite of Alastair's idiotic ideas."

"From the boy's friends, I suppose?" said the Prince, putting his empty wine glass back on the table. "Have we come to that, my friends, that we torment a child and a child's playmates?"

Murray pressed the point. "He is old enough to do a day's work, your Highness—a day's bad work for us. He jeopardizes the entire plot. If he has spoken of what he's heard, and it comes to the ears of the Duke of Newcastle or of his brother, Henry Pelham, we have lost everything we've planned and worked for these last two years."

"We could lose Polaris and Deneb in Scotland, your Highness," advised Rigel in concerned tones. "The Hanoverians could catch them."

The Prince waved away his advisors and spoke directly to Richard. "You are marked, boy. Why not tell us what you know? I shall not have you hurt, but it is vital to me that I know. Trust me."

Richard looked into the Prince's compelling eyes. More

than anything else, he wanted to believe and trust Charles Edward Stuart. If he had been alone in this danger, he would have told him everything, but how could he protect Betsy, with Spica hunting for her in Chiswick? The Prince looked at him with sympathy, and Richard wanted to tell him but could not.

"The boy is a Hanoverian spy, I am convinced," Murray insisted. "He is a devil. The Stuart charm, as your Highness well knows, has made many friends out of former enemies, but it can't avail against this monstrous boy."

"They say I saw a murder," Richard said and glanced appealingly at Antares, who was gazing moodily at the beamed ceiling. Antares, for all of his promises, had been of no help since they landed in France, and now that Murray spoke of him as "Hanoverian spy" Richard felt the net closing in about him.

The Prince shot out of his chair, nearly overturning it. The whole room turned at the commotion. "I have told you over and over again that I do not like murder. A thing that begins in blood ends in blood, and you well know it, Sirius. Must I do all of your thinking for you? Who was killed?"

"It was found necessary, your Highness, to do away with a London merchant, who was invited into our society, and who opposed our plans. We were also forced to kill a notorious Hanoverian spy in Chiswick," Murray spoke with dignity, not looking at Antares.

"The death of this spy does not greatly concern me," said the Prince, "but who was this merchant?"

"Carlton, your Highness," volunteered Antares, grinning before Murray had a chance to speak.

The Prince put his hands over his face, visibly shaken, and for a long moment was silent. "An old friend and a true friend. A wise head that I needed so badly. We have so few left who serve us honestly." Then he removed his hands to look at Murray. "So this is how I am served in London by my supporters! And I am not told of these things. So Carlton would not join my cause." The Prince sank back into his chair.

"He would not join you and he could have betrayed us all," Murray pressed on, beating his fist on the table. "It was necessary that we silence him, your Highness. We stopped him before he had a chance to speak to others. That is not the case with this boy. He has had weeks to talk—weeks in which we sought everywhere for him. We know it is the boy," and he stopped to glower at Antares, "even though for reasons that no one but a lunatic could fathom, Alastair Ruadh swears he has never seen him before. This boy may have all of our necks on the block right now."

"What do you suggest we do with him?" asked the Prince calmly.

"Wring the truth from him!"

"I do not torment children," thundered the Prince, rising again, "and I do not murder old men who have repeatedly shed their blood for the Stuart cause."

"Then, your Highness, the Stuarts will fail this time, too," said Murray boldly.

"And that we may," was the angry answer from Charles Edward Stuart, "but murder doesn't come as easily to me as to you, Alec Murray, it seems."

Murray was daring. "It is a fault in a king," he said.

The others, even Antares, were shocked, but the Prince did not lash back in anger. Instead he seemed to grow sober and more sad. "They tell me, Murray, that you have no head for matters, but I believe in this you are correct. Sometimes I feel that I come to the end of things."

Slowly the Prince walked over to a leaded window and looked out at the mud-filled dreary courtyard. Then he called softly to Rigel. "Goring, my very old friend, what do you think I should do?"

"If Spica is hunting for the boy's friends, he will find them," the old man said gravely. "The boy is no danger to us here in St. Omer. I say we should hold him here until we have played and won our game in London. Then, he can be safely released and you need not stain the White Rose with his blood."

"Betelgeuse?" queried the Prince.

"I side with Rigel. It is now the sixth of November; we won't need to hold him long, your Highness. Once you have won, he's of no importance, and we can trust Spica to silence others, if there are any. He'll suffer no harm."

The Prince nodded. "Good, that is what we shall do. We all know Spica and I would urge gentleness on him if I could reach him. He will find the boy's friends, if anyone can, and they will talk to him. He can consult Arcturus about what to do then. You will all be back in London by the ninth, in any event. This potboy is safer here with us than he ever was in England, if he has wit enough to know it." Charles Edward Stuart looked at Antares. "Alastair Ruadh, you disappoint me. I accept the fact that this boy knows much of our plans and that he saw the murder of our old friend, Carlton, but I do not understand why you insist that you do not recognize him."

"I was drunk, your Highness," said Antares, smiling and glancing toward the Prince's empty wine glass. "Perhaps I was mistaken in saying that I didn't know him."

"And Alastair was also the one who spoke too much before the boy at the Seven Stars," Murray said bitterly. "The others will bear me out."

Betelgeuse and Rigel chimed agreement while Bonnie Prince Charlie shook his head in bewilderment at Antares.

"You are not the Alastair Ruadh Macdonnell, fresh out of Scotland, that I once knew," he looked puzzled. "Often I don't understand you these days."

Antares bent low, his hand over his breast. "Always my heart and my sword answer the call of the King of England and Scotland. You know who alone deserves the allegiance of myself?"

"Of your clan, yes," hooted Murray. "But of yourself, sirrah, who knows?"

"Oh, take the lad and keep him prisoner," ordered the Prince, walking over to the table and pouring himself another glass of wine.

He beckoned and the members of the society moved close around the table. "I will speak openly," he began. "What this boy has seen today should be enough to keep him forever from the councils of kings. We fight among ourselves. We squabble. We struggle over a gold piece here and there. Yes, here we stand—loyal Scots, English and Irish with the hounds of Europe yapping at our heels! In a few days I shall sail to take London and then all of England, for we believe England will follow as a ripe prize. We of course must consider France, Sweden and Prussia, whose help I hate but must have. You marked my advisors here from all my good friends in Europe. They cluster like birds of prey at the end of this room. Mark their black, green and red uniforms. The Stuarts will never be rid of these foreigners. They will bleed us white forever, reminding us constantly that we regained our rightful throne because they gave us the help of their armies. And, worst of all, we hate and fear each other. Each star in the Society of the Stars hates the other, and sometimes I think that all ask more of Regulus, Charles Edward Stuart, than I can ever give. Oh, take the boy away!"

CHAPTER 9

Antares, the Red

RICHARD sat on the dirt floor, hands clasped around his ankles, trying vainly to keep warm. The moment that Prince Charles had dismissed him, Betelgeuse had dispatched two Scots guards and Richard had been taken away and put in this prisonlike hut.

The boy sighed. It was all settled now. He was not to be murdered, but only to be held until after London was taken by the Prince's forces. Lady Primrose had been correct; the Stuarts did not permit murder if they could help it. Richard sighed again. He should be very happy, he told himself, but the truth was that he was as miserable as before. Betsy was still in danger.

He knew enough about this plot right now to earn his and her passage money. But it certainly wasn't doing him any good sitting captive in this store room in St. Omer. Richard sighed again; he'd learned a lot. Rigel's real name was Goring and Betelgeuse was called Seagraves. Antares' full name was Alastair Ruadh Macdonnell, but for all of his fine talk he hadn't done much to help. He was so busy fawning on the

Prince that he hadn't given Richard a thought. But just the same, he still had the letter Antares wanted so badly. A disturbing idea crossed Richard's mind. Perhaps now that Murray had fallen from the Prince's good graces, Antares would not be so eager to get his letter back. Richard looked at the heavy oak door and then up at the tiny window in the gray stone walls. He thought about the letter and what it said. There was nothing much in it. He could almost recite it by heart, he'd thought about it so much. A letter written to Grandpapa didn't seem very dangerous, but then, he told himself sourly, he was new to this ugly business of spying. Antares had certainly wanted the letter badly enough.

Richard shook his head and reached for a piece of baked chicken that lay in a wooden trencher next to a mug of watered wine, a few feet away from him. There was nothing else in the store room. It certainly couldn't be said that the Prince meant to starve his prisoners. The chicken was well cooked and welcome, even if he couldn't say that he enjoyed the wine.

There were no guards posted outside the door of the store room. Richard had called out once, asking for a blanket but no one had answered. The exiled Scots who'd brought him to this place had been rough but not unkind. One had even tried to cheer him up, saying that he wouldn't be there very long and that the Prince didn't maltreat his prisoners, as did the English King and his son, the Duke of Cumberland. But they still hadn't brought him any blankets. Richard got up and went to the door again. He banged against it, but it was securely bolted. He jumped up at the one small window in the store room, but it was high above his reach. The store room was very cold and damp. If he was to get through the night, he'd have to have a blanket.

This time Richard beat on the door with his fists and shouted, but still no one answered. He went unhappily back to his place on the floor and picked up the chicken again.

The wind whistled through the window sending drops of cold rain down on Richard's upturned face. Again and again the gusts of wind came. Richard turned up the collar of his coat and huddled, hunched up, his head down on his chest, his face hidden by his hat.

Suddenly, Richard thought he heard a new note in the wind. He lifted his head to listen. Someone nearby was whistling the same Jacobite song he'd heard Alexander Murray sing in answer to the master of the fishing boat at Folkestone cliffs. Then there was a soft rapping sound at the store room door and a little folded slip of white paper came sliding under. Richard scrambled and snatched at the paper. "Who's there?" he whispered, but there was no answer.

He put his ear to the floor and listened, but there were no retreating footsteps.

Richard went over to the window and unfolded the note. It was late afternoon and nearly dark, but by straining he was able to read the few lines.

Richard Larkin:

The ship that sets its sails for France can set its sails for England. You are not friendless here. Do not sleep tonight. Destroy this.

There was no signature, and it was in handwriting that Richard had not seen before. Certainly it was not the writing on the letter he'd hidden in the wall at Chiswick.

I'm going to escape tonight, Richard told himself unbelievingly. That must be what it means. Slowly, in the last few moments of daylight, Richard tore the note into tiny pieces, eating and washing them down with the last of the Prince's wine. He sat down, and leaned back against the wall to wait. He faced the door, his ears alert for any sound.

The wind howled down the chimney of Hogarth's house as Betsy hurried Abby and old Matt through their supper. "Matt," she said, speaking as loudly as she could. "Will you look after the poppet?"

Matt stared at Betsy woodenly and cut himself a large slice of yellow cheese which he stuffed into his mouth. Finally he nodded. To make sure he heard, Betsy shouted again, "Will you look after the poppet, Matt? I've got to go to Leicester Fields. It's about Dick Larkin. He's in trouble. I have to see Master Hogarth. I'll take the horse he left us."

This time Matt nodded more violently and made motions on the table as if his fingers were horse's hooves. Abby was delighted with Matt's new game and began to copy him at once, calling out, "Horsie, Horsie!"

Betsy was satisfied. Matt had understood. He would look after Abby, and the child in turn would look after him. Abby was a careful little body, who minded boiling kettles and the hearthfire. Betsy hurried over to the pegs, put on her cloak, and snatching up a lantern rushed out into the darkness.

They've got Dick, she told herself for the hundredth time. There's no use calling the watch or the magistrate. No one would believe that something could happen to a gardener's boy at Chiswick House, and, besides, no one would care. I'll have to see Master Hogarth and tell him everything. Oh, why didn't we have the good sense to tell him the minute that Samuel Johnson refused to help? We were fools to think we could get by in this terrible business all by ourselves. I could have made Master Hogarth believe me. He's known me for such a long time now. Betsy stopped at the door of the stable. What would Master Hogarth have to say? He'll be so angry that we've kept things from him that he might even dismiss me.

Betsy pushed the thoughts away while she switched the lantern to her left hand. Then she unlatched the stable door and shoved it open. The black horse nickered softly as she stepped inside and into the arms of Spica, who clapped one hand over her mouth, and pinioned her against the wall. "Do not make a sound," he warned. "I have a knife. Now give me that lantern you're holdin'. Ye'd not be wantin' a fire now from a dropped lantern, would ye, my girl?"

Terror stricken, Betsy held out her hand and Spica took the lantern, putting it on top of one of the empty stalls. "I'd be after havin' speech with ye, girl," he said softly, "so I'll take my hand from your pretty mouth. If ye scream once, ye'll never scream again. Do ye understand me?"

Betsy nodded and Spica let her go, shoving her hard against the stable wall. Betsy glared at him. She knew at once who he was. Richard's description of the evil-eyed killer had been very detailed. She was deathly afraid.

"Ye'd be knowin' me?" Spica asked.

Betsy shook her head and did not answer him. She'd let

him do the talking. Perhaps she'd learn about Dick that way. Anyhow, she was too frightened to say anything.

Spica stood gracefully, his knife motionless in his hand, half-concealed by the ruffles at his wrists. "Well, that may be as may be. I've never seen ye before and th' devil's own time I've had findin' ye and th' house that Larkin spawn lives at. Th' folk of this fine country village have little enough time for inquirin' strangers, my girl. If I'd not put out a half-crown here and a half-crown there, I'd still be lookin' for me poor nephew from the American Colonies, who has just come into a great fortune. Aye, 'tis what I told 'em," Spica laughed, "and to think all the time the spyin' brat was under the roof of Hogarth, the painter. 'Tis the last place I would have thought to be lookin'."

"This is William Hogarth's house," Betsy said, finding her voice and speaking as firmly as she could. "If you've come here to rob Master Hogarth, you're too late. He's gone back to Leicester Fields and he took everything valuable with him."

"I'm no thievin' sort, my girl, I told ye. 'Tis about the Larkin boy I come."

"He's not here," Betsy spoke as defiantly as she could. "You've been told he lived here for a while and that's true enough, but you wasted your half-crowns. Richard Larkin hasn't been here for days. He doesn't live in this house anymore."

Spica corrected her. "Ye mean, don't ye, that ye haven' seen the lad for twenty-four hours?" Then as Betsy remained silent, Spica went on cruelly, "Ye see, my girl, I took him up that long ago."

"Where is he?" Betsy asked.

Spica shugged his shoulders. "Who knows? But he doesn' concern me now. 'Tis the likes of ye I'm after."

"Me?"

"Ah, 'tis ye and no other I come to seek—not the old deaf fool or the wee brat. It would be ye young Larkin would be tellin' his business to." Spica came toward Betsy. "And where were ye bound this night that ye come to the stable, girl? To go for a nice quiet ride to London and perhaps be talkin' to someone there about great matters?" Spica caught the girl hard by the wrist. "Ye'd be goin' to the Duke of Newcastle or to Henry Pelham, wouldn' ye, girl, to make a report? Or maybe ye'd be hurryin' to your William Hogarth to get him to help ye? 'Tis a dangerous thing for a girl to ride alone to the city in the night."

Betsy thought frantically. There was nothing she could say to Spica that he would believe. It was true that she would not be going into London alone unless it was some emergency and what sort of emergencies come up in the lives of kitchen maids? "One of us is ill in the house," she finally stammered.

Spica chuckled coldly, tightening his grip on her wrist. "There's no one ailin' there," he said smiling. "Th' wee girl has had th' pox and is well now. The old man is deaf as a tomb but hearty enough. I've had a full report of ye. A half-crown does that much. As for ye, ye're thick with the spy I caught at Chiswick House." The man added slowly, his eyes never leaving Betsy's white face. "I took him up while the steward's daughter showed him the villa. Would ye be knowin' that piece of news that he's thick with the Elliott lass, too? And now what do ye think of yer Larkin lad?"

Betsy gasped. She might have known Venetia Elliott was mixed up in this affair. Spica was trying to make her jealous so she'd babble, but it wasn't going to work. "What do you want of me?" she asked. "You say you have Richard and that he's a spy. Well, I don't believe either of these things, and I think it's pretty stupid of you that you ask me about the

Duke of Newcastle and Henry Pelham. What would I have to say to great lords like them? I'm only a kitchen girl. Let me go!" Betsy waited breathlessly, hoping that she would convince him.

"Ye're as stubborn as the boy was," he said, almost happily. "'Tis a pleasure I look forward to—teaching both of ye who's master. We know he's talked to ye, and we know he's a spy," Spica went on smoothly. "He confessed it, and he said that he'd told ye everything he knows."

He's lying, Betsy told herself. He's lying about everything. Dick would never tell them anything. She would have to trick this man. Betsy frowned as a plan came into her head. She spoke slowly, forming it in her mind as she went along. "I didn't know that Dick Larkin was a spy," she said, "but I did know that he was in some sort of trouble. He didn't tell me anything really about what kind of trouble it was, sir, even though I asked him about it once."

Betsy eyed Spica. He had not moved a muscle since she began to speak; nor had his expression changed. It was impossible to tell if he believed her or not. Betsy took a deep breath and went on. "He could have been a spy though, I guess. He was certainly mysterious enough about his business and where he'd been before he came here to Chiswick. I used to hear him walking around at night in his attic room worrying, and sometimes I'd hear him scratching away with one of Master Hogarth's quills. He borrowed ink, sand and paper from Master Hogarth, and the master laughed because he thought Richard was writing poems. I think that's what Richard told him, too." Betsy shook her head. "I don't think he wrote poems though. Dick wasn't half as much a poet as Master Hogarth thought he was." She finished, and looked at Spica innocently. "Could he have been writing secret messages, do you think?"

Spica drew in his breath, his eyes gleamed. "So the lad did some writin', my girl? Where are these fancy poems of his, if that's what he was callin' em?"

Betsy was stern. "I've hidden them," she announced. "When Dick didn't come back last night, I gathered them up and hid them."

"And why would ye be doin' that?" Spica demanded with suspicion in his soft voice.

Betsy looked down and smoothed her cloak. "I do like Richard Larkin even if he does fancy that Elliott hussy more than he does me. I suppose you may as well know. I looked at them to see if they were poems, sir, to Venetia Elliott, and they weren't. They were all strange and had numbers in some places instead of words. I didn't want Dick to get in any more trouble than he was already in. I was going to burn the papers as soon as I could, but when I got them down to the fire a neighbor came in, and I didn't get the chance to do it."

"Ah, ye still have them, then?" Spica commented with a wolfish smile. "Let me see them."

"No," Betsy cried and seeing the hard look in Spica's eyes added quickly. "You can see them if you tell me one thing. Is Richard all right?"

Spica assented gracefully. "He's no harmed and he's in safe hands now," he said.

"I'll show you the papers then," Betsy promised and Spica let go of her wrist. "Put your knife away, please. You needn't be afraid of an old man and a baby, and I don't think you're afraid of a kitchen maid like me, are you?"

The man was annoyed by this. Betsy could see it in his sulky manner, but he did as she asked and the knife disappeared up his sleeve. Betsy stepped over and took up the lantern from the stall. Spica watched her warily. She motioned for him to come along with her and pushed at the stable door.

"Do you know," she commented as calmly as she could as they walked toward the main house along the path, "I knew that Dick Larkin didn't like England very well compared to the Colonies, but I never did think he'd spy against our good King George."

For the first time Spica laughed—long peals of baying laughter that snatched away in the wind.

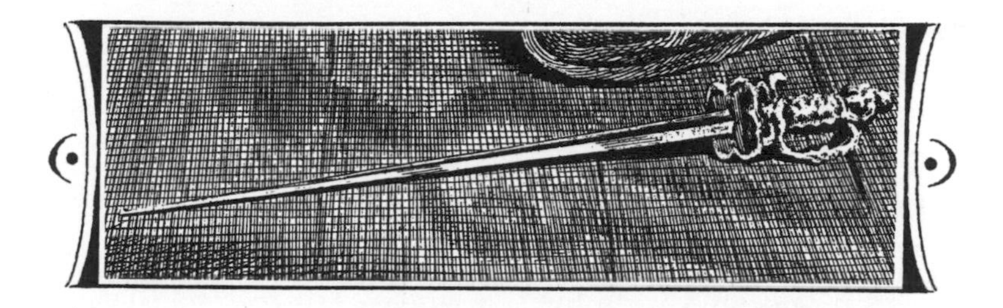

Richard had been in the blackness of the store room for what seemed like hours, when suddenly he heard the cautious rapping on the door again. He got up from his cramped position on the floor and replied with the same muffled rap.

Then he heard someone fumbling with the bolts and in a moment the door swung open noiselessly.

The moon was obscured by a dark cloud, and he could see no one. Then he heard a soft whisper. "Be swift about it, boy. 'Tis Antares the Red."

Richard didn't wait to hear more. He hurtled out of his prison and into the little enclosed courtyard that lay in front of the store house, under no illusions as to why he was being rescued.

"Come away, now. Hurry!" cautioned Antares. "They're all gallows-lushy by now. 'Tis midnight and the Prince has been at the wine bottle since noon."

"We're going back to England?" Richard asked in a whisper.

"Aye, where else, indeed? I have an appointment tomorrow night that I mean to be keeping—and before I keep it, I will have my letter," Antares added significantly. "Now come away quietly with me. I have horses waitin' for us, but first we've got to vault the wall here. Go first, Larkin."

It was inky dark in the courtyard. The only light came from the candle-lit windows of the farmhouse and that was barely enough to let Richard see the wall.

"Over it!" commanded Antares. "We can't be openin' a gate that makes a sound. I'm expected to be leavin' now, but they don't know I'm takin' ye with me."

Richard put his hands on the wall. Slowly he clambered up on it and sat astride for a moment. His legs ached from their long cramped wait in the store room.

Antares approached the wall and prepared to vault over it. At the same time a door of the farmhouse opened, and a tall black figure come out. Richard held his breath and sat motionless. The figure called out in a soft deep voice that was familiar. "Alastair Ruadh, ye have the boy now, have ye not?" In the light of the doorway, Richard saw the man lift a pistol.

Antares took his hands from the wall. "'Aye, Alexander Murray," he answered, "I have the lad with me. Are you plannin' to shoot him or me, Alec? Which is it to be?"

"I could kill you both here and gain nothing for it but the Prince's gratitude," said Murray levelly.

"'Tis been comin' up a long span of time between us, Alec, my friend," said Antares. "I've had my hand at my sword twice already to kill you and now you come at me with a pistol. Twice I've been deprived of my chance to duel with you. You owe me that as a gentleman."

"I'll kill you wherever you choose, Alastair. I'd ask a claymore if I could and if you were an honest Scot, but that you are not. I'll do it with swords, not pistols, then, and it will not be done under the Prince's roof. I have changed my opinion there. The Prince has had enough sadness already these days. Let him believe Macdonnell died still the Prince's man. There'll be no seconds or witnesses to this duel."

Antares chuckled. "So tender of the Prince's welfare and happiness, and you out of favor with him, too."

Alexander Murray ignored this statement. "You have horses ready?" he asked. "Where are they?"

"In the woods to the right of the house."

"Good, I'll meet you there in five minutes, but in the meantime, Alastair Ruadh, I want you to know that I know who and what you are. And when I kill you, the boy is mine, and he dies, too."

"Fairly spoken. And ye'll not bring the Prince or his guards with you?"

Murray's voice was scornful. "This is between us, Alastair. Ye'll be killed by a good Scot if that's comfort to ye and by an honorable man, if ye know what honor is."

"Oh, aye, I'd take great pleasure in that, indeed," Antares mocked, springing lightly to the top of the wall.

Richard watched Murray lower his pistol and move backwards into the doorway.

"What are you going to do now?" asked Richard, as he and Antares dropped to the ground.

"Get by the guards in front of the house," he flung one arm over Richard's shoulders and wrapped his black cloak around both of them. "Lean on me, boy, and pretend to be lushy. Keep your head down and don't speak."

Richard did as Antares commanded, and they lurched about in the darkness like drunken men past the side of the farmhouse.

"Who would that be now?" called a harsh voice from the shadows near the main door.

"'Tis a Macdonnell, laddie, doin' a good Scots deed. I have a young Frenchman here who can't take his wine. I'm gettin' 'im a breath of air."

"A Frenchman who can't hold his wine! Ha, ha!" came from the guard. "I know your voice, young Macdonnell of Glengarry, but what's the password? I've got to be askin' it, ye know."

"November the tenth and the White Rose forever."

"Pass on," called the guard out of the blackness.

Richard drew a deep breath of relief as they went away from the house, but the moment they entered the woods, fear caught at him once more. What if Antares lost the duel? Alexander Murray would surely kill him. "Is Sirius a good swordsman?" Richard asked.

"Are you worried, laddie? He's killed more than one man, but he's not measured steel with Macdonnell."

"Are you a good swordsman, sir?"

"The fools who have tried to find out do not speak overmuch of my skill now," Antares replied with a strange little laugh.

They entered the woods and followed along a short path. Two saddled horses waited tethered to a tree and quickly Antares untied them, and gave the reins to Richard. "Do not try to get away without me, lad. You'd never get to the sea, believe me. The countryside is alive with the Prince's men, and ye speak no word of French. Ye'd get no aid from the Frenchies."

Antares was right, Richard decided, and he obeyed. As he

stood quietly, holding the restless horses, he heard Alexander Murray's footsteps coming toward them. Richard glanced up at the sky. It would soon be light enough, for the black cloud was nearly past the face of the moon. And as Murray entered the clearing where Antares waited, the moon sailed out, bright and cold.

"Now, Alastair," Murray growled, and took out his sword, "is this light enough to kill ye by, do ye think? I'm thinkin' any light at all is good light for a good act."

"Aye, it will do," agreed Antares. His sword whispered its way out of its scabbard. Gracefully he sank to his knees, limbered up, arose, and flung off his cloak.

They stood a few yards from each other, Murray cloakless, tall and dark-featured in a red velvet suit; Macdonnell shorter and blond, still in his foppishly elegant pink, the silver fringe on his waistcoat gleaming in the moonlight. Alexander Murray has the longer reach, Richard noticed anxiously. Antares is younger and probably faster, but Murray still has the longer reach. Alexander Murray quickly changed his rapier from his right hand to his left. Richard's heart sank. The leader of the Society of the Stars was left-handed, too. There was no one more deadly than a left-handed fencer. Richard had gone several times to a fencing academy in Philadelphia and no one there had ever been eager to match swords with a left-handed opponent.

Antares saw that Murray had shifted his rapier. His eyes narrowed and his mouth grew hard. "Ye've been keepin' things from me, Alec," he said thickly.

"Much less than ye've been keepin' from the Prince. My left hand is my secret, but what is yours? Why are ye takin' the boy with ye?" Murray's voice shook with anger. "We know the Prince sends ye back to London to see Arcturus, but why does this spy go, too?"

"'Tis my affair, Alec Murray," said Antares coldly. "'Tis all I'll ever say."

"Aye, and there ye have the right of it," Murray almost shouted. "Ye'll not ever be sayin' another word when I'm done with ye." He rushed furiously upon Antares, giving him no warning, not even measuring swords.

But Antares was ready. Quickly he parried Murray's sudden lunge and stepped aside. Murray regained his balance at once and attacked again—this time coming in high, attempting with his superior reach to beat down the blond man's sword. Antares gasped and gave ground, but Murray followed him, pressing him, beating and slashing at him. The little grove rang with the clash of steel. The horses grew frantic, rearing and plunging against Richard's hold, their hooves striking the air above his head.

Antares was on the defensive and constantly giving ground, stepping backward from the ferocious attacks of Alexander Murray's long left arm. Richard watched in anxiety, dodging the maddened horses. Murray seemed to be tiring now. The fury of his offensive was less, and Antares had easier work parrying his opponent's feebler and more ineffectual thrusts. Antares stepped forward, pressing Murray to give way.

"*Cateran*, cur!" screamed Murray, his face distorted with anger. Antares shoved him back further into the trees.

Antares did not use his strength to reply to Murray's insults. Instead he struck savagely at the man. Then he made a feint Richard had never seen before. Stooping low, he struck down Murray's guard and plunged his rapier into Murray's chest and like lightning withdrew it. For a long moment Murray stared down at the spreading stain, a look of incredulity on his face. Then he folded slowly to the ground, his rapier falling from his hand.

"Did you kill him?" Richard asked, as Antares walked

swiftly back to the boy and bent to wipe his sword on his black cloak. He let the rapier slide back into his scabbard.

Antares shrugged his shoulders. "It is my fond hope that I did. I do not choose to leave people to testify against me, but 'tis of no matter. If I didn't kill him, he's hurt badly enough to have little to say for a long time. But we're not stayin' here to find out. Ye may be missed," he pointed to the motionless body, "and they'd be missin' him, too, and lookin' for him before long. Come away now, we ride for the sea and England."

"But your cloak?" Richard called out.

"Let it stay on the ground. That's over and done with," was Antares' enigmatic answer. And then casually, as if he'd just left some gaming table or coffee house in London, he swung up into his saddle. Richard followed him grimly, struggling to mount his frantic horse.

Antares calmed his plunging black long enough to call back to him, "Do you ride as well as you keep your tongue?"

Richard nodded; the rearing horse kept him too busy to speak.

"Come away," called Antares. "Follow me!" He loosened his reins, spurred the horse and like the wind galloped out and away.

Richard had no choice, for the instant Antares' black took the lead, Richard's bay gelding moved forward, its hooves pounding down the path. The Prince's horses were fine and young and more spirited than any Richard had ever known, wild with eagerness for a midnight run in the moonlight. No one could have stopped them as they raced out through St. Omer and into the countryside on the road that led to the sea.

Richard gasped as he watched Antares take a short cut, across a field toward a stone wall that looked eight feet high.

But the black horse cleared it as if flying and Richard's bay followed gaily, sailing over with Richard hanging on, teeth chattering, knees plastered to the saddle.

The sound of Spica's laughter chilled Betsy Lewes. She knew he would kill her the minute that he'd satisfied himself about Dick. Then, he'd kill Abby and Matt and Dick, too, if he hadn't murdered him already. It all depended on her now. Her plan had to work! Betsy said a silent prayer and put her hand on the knob of the kitchen door. "I hid the papers in the kitchen," she told Spica. "It was the best place and close to the fire in case I had a chance to burn them."

Spica's silence made Betsy even more nervous. Did he believe anything she'd told him? It was hard to tell. She'd have to be clever now and very careful, too. She couldn't afford to make a single mistake. Betsy turned the knob and went inside the kitchen. Old Matt and Abby were still at the table, finishing their supper. Betsy slipped off her cloak, acting as naturally as she could, and hung it on a peg, while Spica came silently inside behind her. She glanced at him, shaking her head, asking him wordlessly to let her do things her own way. He nodded shortly. "Abby, love," Betsy said, "it's time for you to go up to bed. Ask Matt to take your candle up for you."

Abby hopped down and tugged at Matt's sleeve. The old

man got slowly up from the table, groaned and went to a shelf to pick up a candlestick. Betsy hurried over, took the candle, and lit it for him. Matt was too slow, and Spica was not a patient man. "There, Matt," Betsy said. "It's lit. You take Abby up to bed now, and Abby, you say your prayers to Matt tonight, and don't forget to bless Dick and Master Hogarth."

"Bless Betsy, too?" Abby turned around, holding on to Matt's hand as he shuffled out of the kitchen.

"Oh, yes, bless Betsy, too," Betsy said, close to breaking with fear and terror.

The door closed behind Abby and Matt, and Spica stepped forward. "The papers," he said. "Give me those papers."

Betsy avoided his eyes and didn't answer. She caught up a stool and carried it to the corner cupboard.

"Are they in there?" Spica demanded.

He believes me, Betsy told herself triumphantly. She stepped up on the stool and carefully opened the cupboard door, her heart in her mouth. I can't do this thing, she cried silently. I can't, but I've got to, if we're to be saved. Her hand touched one of William Hogarth's pistols. How long had the guns been here? They might be crazy and foul. They might blow up in her face. What if they weren't primed and loaded? Even if she had time she didn't know how to load a pistol.

One of Spica's cruel hands reached up for her. She glanced down helplessly and saw the long-bladed knife. "Ye take too long. Give me th' papers," he said in his soft Irish accent. "If ye don't give me what's in that cupboard right now, my girl, ye know what'll be happenin' to a spyin' lass who's lied to me and what I'll be doin' to young Larkin, too."

Betsy's right hand closed hard around the butt of the pistol; she drew it out slowly, hiding it in the fold of her full gray skirt. "I have what you want now," she said. Betsy whirled about, cocked the hammer of the pistol with her left hand and snapped the trigger, firing into Spica's astonished face.

For more than an hour Richard and Antares sped on their way to the coast, finally slowing their lathered horses at the door of a crude stone building that nestled on a clifftop overlooking the sea. Here Antares swung down and clapped Richard companionably on the shoulder. The boy dismounted stiffly. "Aye, ye'll do, laddie," Antares smiled. "Ye ride like a plowman, but ye' stay on and ye'll do. Ye have talents, more's the pity."

Richard was too exhausted to worry about what Antares found so pitiful. "What's this place?" he asked.

"'Tis an inn. We'll not find our boat tonight. We'll take her in the mornin', the same smack that brought us to France. And the same coach will take us back from Folkestone cliffs to London. 'Tis all arranged."

"We'll go back to England in broad daylight?"

Antares laughed. "We'll not be bothered, laddie, put your trust in Macdonnell. I tell ye, I'm expected."

Antares strode on ahead and knocked confidently at the door of the inn. After a short wait an old man with a candle opened the door. Antares spoke swiftly in French. The old man shook his read repeatedly, muttering, *"Non, non monsieur, c'est fermé. Fermé."*

"Argent?" asked Antares, shaking a handful of silver coins under the landlord's nose. Finally the old man grumbled, motioned them inside and went to take care of the horses. Antares sat down heavily before the hearth fire and sighed with comfort. "'Twas all we required, Larkin—a seat by the fire and a place to wait for a time. 'Tis good the inn is empty save for us. Sit ye doon, laddie, and rest."

Richard sat himself across from Antares while the host of the inn re-entered and brought them each a cup of wine. Antares drank deep and then put his cup down with a ring of finality on the stone floor. "Now, laddie, we'll talk, won't we, you and I?"

Richard burst out, "Won't they look for us here?"

Antares shook his head, his thick blond hair fell over his forehead. "I have me grave doubts about that. The Prince knew I was going to England tonight; they'd expect me to be gone by now. They'll not connect my leavin' with your escapin' and they didn't know where I'd spend the time until the boat took me off to England. I did not favor you much when you spoke with the Prince. They have no reason to connect us."

"But they'll find Sirius, won't they?"

"If we are in luck, boy, not for a while yet. Not till mornin'. He's not that well beloved that anyone would seek him out in the middle of the night."

"They'll know you killed him when they do find him!"

Antares chuckled, flicking at the lace at his throat. "What? The fine fop of an Antares killing a great man like Alec Murray? It will be some time before they get around to thinkin' that. Aye, there were twenty more at the Prince's house in St. Omer who could have killed Murray, but not the silly London spark of a Macdonnell in an elegant pink suit."

"Other men hated Sirius, then?" Richard asked.

"Aye, that they did. He headed our little club, and they hated him for it. The Society of the Stars gives the lie to the notion that the heavens exist in harmony. We all hate each other, as you may have noticed. And there are many who would rather see the Society of the Stars fail than succeed, even in the ranks of the Prince's closest advisors. We Jacobites are a jealous lot." Richard nodded and Antares went on, "The cause of the Stuarts is nearly done, my lad. Ah, but it was glorious while it lasted. Ye should hear the tales they tell of the '15 and the '45, and ye should hear the pipers play the war songs of the clans. It would stir your blood, but those days have ended."

Richard thought sadly of Samuel Johnson and his story of the misfortunes of the Stuarts, but Antares did not let him ponder this long. "Now, about my letter, boy?" he interrupted in serious tones. "We'll get to London in the late afternoon and before I keep my appointment, I'll accompany ye to Chiswick and get my letter. Ye have it and ye have it there. I know. If ye had hidden it at the Seven Stars tavern, it would have been found long before this."

"I'll give you the letter, if you let me go, and I'll never tell anything I know to anyone. You can even keep me prisoner until after the Prince takes London. Will you make a bargain with me?" asked Richard coldly, yet afraid of his own words.

Antares looked amused. "Aye, ye'll not tell anyone. I believe I can rely on that," he said smoothly. "You're too clever a lad, and I don't think it will be needful to keep ye a prisoner. I'm not a man like the Prince, as ye may have guessed by now. Have no fear, Larkin. Once I have my letter, your troubles with the Society of the Stars are over and done with. Now, where is the letter kept in Chiswick?"

Richard shook his head. "I'll have to show you," he said. "I hid it."

Antares looked faintly annoyed, but assented with a quick nod. "There's time. It will be done as you wish."

"Does the letter concern the Prince?" asked Richard.

"That is none of your business." Antares frowned and gripped the arms of his chair. "I've not done anything since the '45 that did not somehow concern the Prince and the House of Stuart, if that tells ye anything." He passed one hand over his forehead, dropped it with a sigh, and stared into the fire. His face was masked in bitterness, his mouth twisted, and his eyes hard. "Aye," he spoke again "we have suffered for the Stuarts, but no one has suffered more than Alastair Ruadh Macdonnell of Glengarry, and by temperament there's no one less fitted to bear it. I was taken up as a loyal Scot and clansman after the '45 when I was not much more than a lad, like you. I lay in the Tower of London for long months until I was finally turned out, penniless. My family lands in Scotland were taken by the Hanoverians and heavy fines laid on them that I could not hope to pay. I had no fortune and no future, and having lost everything I had because of the Stuarts, I could do nothing more than throw in my lot with them once more." Antares beat his fist on the chair arm. "Ah, the ungrateful Stuarts! And now, boy, here is the rub. Ye've heard of the Loch Arkaig treasure, have ye not? Alec Murray would have dueled with me in Vega's salon in London because of it, do you recall?"

"I remember," said Richard quickly.

"The Prince trusted me," Antares went on. "With two

others he sent me to Scotland to retrieve the buried treasure and bring it back to him and to his father, King James III, 'the Old Pretender'."

"Why doesn't anyone ever speak of King James?" Richard asked.

"He's old and feeble. He will not live long, so we look to the Prince—that is, some of us do," Antares said laughing without humor. "Some of the treasure that was buried near the head of Loch Arkaig in Scotland was missing. Gold coins found their way into the hands of greedy men. The two other agents of the Prince who went with me to bring the treasure back to the Stuarts accused me, young Macdonnell of Glengarry, of stealing the gold, and I accused them of the same. One of them is Archibald Cameron, the fine Doctor Cameron, who goes to Scotland now to raise the clans to fight again. Aye, the clans might follow him. They love Archie Cameron as much as they hate Alastair Ruadh Macdonnell. Aye, they would follow Polaris, the North Star, but they despise Antares the Red."

Antares leaned forward and spat into the fire. Richard shuddered at the evil murderous expression on the man's face.

"But why do you stay with the Prince?"

"It suits my purpose well enough," Antares replied, settling back in his chair again. "The Prince trusts me, even if others don't, and I do well enough in his cause even if others go hungry. To do well by oneself, first and above all, is a lesson I've learned—for life is many-sided." He patted the velvet of his coat sleeve and smiled.

"I didn't see anyone who was hungry in St. Omer," Richard commented.

"Oh, they're not hungry for food now, laddie," explained Antares, "although most of them have wanted for that and for a warm place to sleep often enough, as they've followed the fortunes of the starveling Stuarts. The kings of France, Prussia and Sweden see to it now that there isn't that sort of want, but 'tis another kind I mean. They want their lands in Scotland back; they want the fines the Hanoverians have put on their estates remitted or canceled. They want to be able to wear their clan tartans and the kilt lawfully again. They want power. They want England to be Stuart once more. They want so much that the Prince could never satisfy them all. It has not been easy to wait for the Stuart star to rise—nay, it has been impossible."

"Will the plot to take London succeed, then?" Richard leaned forward.

Antares shot Richard a merry glance. "Aye, it could win," he said. "And are ye so interested? Have ye fallen under the spell of the Stuart charm, too? The Prince has more of it than any other Stuart has ever had, and he binds many men to him by it. Do ye want him to take England?"

"I don't care," Richard shrugged. "I don't want anything to do with this whole thing. All I want to do is go back to the Colonies where I belong."

"And you a Hanoverian spy and loyal to German George?" Antares mocked.

"I am no spy!" said Richard defiantly.

Antares chuckled again and picked up his wine from the floor. "Come on, brace up, boy. Haven't I just told ye that your troubles are nearly over. As soon as I have my letter and have paid ye off, they'll be ended, indeed."

"If I give you the letter, I'd also like enough money to pay for three passages back to the Colonies." Richard bargained.

Antares stared at him and raised his whitish eyebrows. "So there are three of you in on this?"

"They are both younger than I am," Richard explained.

"They can't interest you or the Prince. They don't know anything at all. I just want to take them out of England."

"Now, there's nothing quite like a lad of responsibility," Antares grinned. "I do believe now that I could manage to pay off three, as well as one—as soon as I have my letter in my hand, of course."

"Perhaps the Prince would pay you well for the letter," Richard ventured.

Antares' reply was icy. "The letter is mine! It is a personal note, as you probably know. I cannot conceive that you didn't read it. Was the Prince's name mentioned? Was there anything in it that had to do with Jacobite matters?"

Richard didn't answer and Antares lapsed into moody silence. I've committed myself, Richard thought. He knows for certain that I have his letter, and I'll have to produce it. Richard shivered. What sort of payment does Antares mean to make? Money for passage or murder for silence?

Richard closed his eyes, and leaned back in the chair. At least he could try to sleep for a while. Antares wouldn't be harming him until he had what he wanted. Richard's head nodded. Until that time came Antares would take care of him as if he were his best friend. Richard relaxed in his chair and fell asleep before the fire, a crooked smile on his lips.

CHAPTER 10

Dear Grandpapa

RICHARD and Antares left the inn on the clifftop just after dawn. They boarded the same little fishing smack, which waited openly for them in a large cove along with dozens of other small craft, all rolling up and down on the gray water.

Richard was puzzled about the horses. It was plain that Antares could not take them aboard the boat and when he asked about them, Antares replied curtly that it was no concern of his if the Prince got his horses back or not; they belonged to the King of France anyhow, not to Bonnie Prince Charlie. After this Richard stopped asking questions. Antares was a thief and a murderer, without scruples or sentiment.

The weather was a little better than on the first crossing, and the wind had veered around so that it was favorable. The skies were piled high with black thunderclouds, but as yet there was no rain, and the swells, although high, were not so rough that they held back the passage of the boat. They saw little of their ship's lowland Scot master until the late forenoon, when they spotted the white cliffs of England before them. "I spied a flash of red on the clifftops through the glass," he told them soberly. "It could be German George's redcoats waitin' fer ye."

"Aye, 'tis likely," Antares granted, showing no concern.

"We'd best be tryin' another place ta put ye ashore." The master looked worried. "I'd not be wantin' ta be caught by the king's soljers."

"Ye'd not be taken," vowed Antares. "Ye can put us in here in this cove. I'll take my chances with the redcoats. If ye like and are so lackin' in courage, we'll swim for it. That'll gie ye time to push off if they send a boat out after ye."

The master shook his head, ignoring this insult. "'Tis cold and the surf runs high, even this close ta the shore. I'll do as ye ask but ye'd best hurry about it. If the soljers take me and my lads, we'll all hang in chains on the cliffs."

Antares smiled. "Aye, we'd not be wantin' to lose th' best smuggler in these waters. Kerr, my lowland friend, if ye did'na bring in French brandy and laces, life wouldn' be worth th' candle in London. And think of the profits ye make, not to mention doin' the Prince's biddin'."

The master was angry. He all but threw Richard overboard. Antares climbed over the rail and dropped into the surf. The water was bitterly cold, almost paralyzing. Richard hung onto the side of the boat, gasping as a huge whitecap struck him in the face.

"Can ye swim, laddie?" called Antares, spitting out sea water. "If ye can't, I'll tow ye, heavy as my clothes be and cumbersome my sword."

Richard choked out, "I can swim," and struck out for the beach. Antares swam skillfully alongside him, watching him carefully. The moment the two swimmers had passed under her bow, the fishing smack turned about smartly and scudded, all sail spread, as swiftly as she could for the safety of the open channel.

Richard and Antares reached the shore exhausted and chilled. They lay on the sand for a time gathering their strength. Antares heaved himself up and hauled Richard to his feet. "The coach will be at the clifftop," he said. "Come away now. My appointment can't wait."

Half-pushing, half-pulling, Antares dragged the boy up the path to the clifftop.

"But the redcoats!" Richard gasped out in protest. "They'll be waiting for us. If they don't think we're Jacobites, they'll think we're smugglers. They'll hang us."

"Aye," was Antares' comforting answer. "That's the truth of it." And he grinned at Richard's worried face.

The coach was there, as Antares had said, not far from the cliff's edge. A band of redcoated dragoons sat quietly on their horses on a hilltop not far from the coach. They did not come forward as Antares and Richard got into the coach. As the coach moved away Richard noticed to his great surprise that the redcoats swerved in a body and moved down the hidden side of the hill.

"I told ye, laddie, they'd not bother us," Antares smiled.

"But why?" asked Richard.

Antares didn't answer, but began to pluck and straighten his ruffles and arrange his sodden pink suit as well as he could. "What a way to appear in London society!" he complained. "My coat and breeches are ruined, not to mention my new waistcoat. Ye can no launder velvet, boy. I must be changin' to my green brocade before I keep my appointment, but the pink will do for a country place like Chiswick, won't it? Now that it is no longer the season for gentlemen to live there."

Antares reached into his pocket, took out a very large silver watch, and shook it. "Aye, 'tis ruined, too," he said. "It could'na survive the swimmin', but it did'na cost me much," and he flung the useless watch out the coach window.

Richard looked in horror, for it was Saturn's large silver watch. Antares must have murdered the old Hanoverian agent even though he'd never admitted it to Murray. He'll kill me, too, when I give him the letter, Richard said to himself and shivered inside his wet clothing. He had to escape before they got to Chiswick. If he took Antares to Hogarth's house, he'd kill Betsy too, if Spica hadn't already found her. The silver watch settled it. Richard knew he couldn't bargain with Antares in this strange game, for the man couldn't afford to let him live.

Richard sat tense and wary, close to the door. Antares pulled a knife from his sleeve and began to pare his fingernails, whistling a jolly tune. Antares, amused at Richard's obvious interest in his knife, held it up for him to see. "Look, laddie. I could but wish it was a Highland dirk—the proper knife for a Scot, like me. I borrowed this flimsy thing from a kinsman of mine in France—a Macdonnell who hasn't disowned Alastair Ruadh of Glengarry yet. Not all Macdonnells are like me, ah, no!" Antares grinned evilly. "Ye see, boy, in Highland dress when you wear the kilt and the plaid, ye keep the dirk in yer stocking, under the garter, and if ye need it, ye just whisk it out. 'Tis a very useful thing, a dirk. Ye cut your meat with it, ye pick your teeth with it. Aye, ye can do many things with it—and 'tis silent as a ghost, too." His voice trailed off significantly.

Richard marveled at the many faces of this sinister young man. He looked and played the part of the elegant and fashionable young Londoner but was an expert swordsman, spoke three languages and possibly more, and was a man who killed with a knife and stole from his victim—a man of many moods and many voices. When Antares had been in Lady Primrose's salon, he had spoken pure English, when he was with the Prince and the Jacobites he went into Scots, and to Richard, he used a combination of the two. Antares was a person of unusual talents. It did not pay to underestimate him. Richard eyed the knife silently until Antares slowly went back to paring his fingernails, cursing softly now and then when the rocking coach caused him to prick himself.

As they traveled west, black clouds gathered in the deep gray sky and the rumbling of thunder sounded overhead. A flash of lightning made the coach horses whinny and skitter for a moment. Antares leaned out of the window to stare up at the heavens. "Aye, 'tis going to be a fit night to meet and deal with the devil, laddie," he commented, satisfied with the state of things. "But I fear it will be dark when we reach Chiswick. Do ye think ye can lay your hands on my letter in the dark and keep the takin' of it secret. I want no lanterns about me."

"I think so," Richard answered.

"I'd not be wantin' witnesses," warned Antares. "'Tis a verra private matter."

"There'll be none," said Richard.

Antares nodded, his eyelids drooping as he stared at the boy. Then he yawned and leaned once more out the window to shout at the driver, urging speed.

A few miles further on the rain began, and it continued in a heavy downpour that permitted Richard to see very little of the green countryside of Kent. It was raining even harder at Ashford and Chatham, where the horses were changed, and Antares and Richard did not leave the coach. The storm rode with them all the way into London. The flashes of lightning and loud bursts of thunder seemed to delight Antares. He sat whistling happily while the carriage entered the darkening London streets. Thunder rolled, and he laughed aloud with each new bolt of lightning. Richard shuddered to see how fever-bright his eyes were. I think he must be insane, Richard told himself. Antares howled with joy when a tall chimney, hit by lightning, split apart and exploded. The air was thick with the stifling smell of brimstone. Antares sniffed eagerly.

"Aye," he called out merrily. "'Tis the devil's own scent, laddie. 'Tis a fine night for the devil and for me."

Richard looked desperately out of the coach window. They were clattering along Holborn turnpike through the heart of the city, their iron-bound wheels screaming over the wet cobbles. London was almost deserted now, for few people cared to be out in the streets in such a downpour.

"There'll be empty seats at Drury Lane this night," Antares called out gaily to a pretty girl, who stood in a doorway, waiting for the rain to stop. "Will you meet me there, you provoking creature? Be there at 6 o'clock, sweetheart."

Drury Lane! The name caught at Richard even as the girl turned her head haughtily away from Antares, who leaned far out of the coach window laughing and shouting endearments to her. Why, of course, that was David Garrick's theater!

Richard glanced quickly at Antares, but the blond man had drawn his head back inside the coach.

He looked at Richard, gesturing with the knife. "All the same laddie, that jill-flirt will meet me. She marked me well, and I have a way with the lasses when I have a mind to——"

Suddenly the coach stopped with a sharp lurch that knocked Antares off balance, and he jabbed his finger with the knife. "Ye fool of a coachman," he shouted out the window. "Have ye gone daft? What is amiss with ye?"

"Look fer yerself," bellowed the coachman, pointing ahead.

A fine carriage lay overturned directly in their path. The horses lay kicking in their traces, and several women were shrieking inside. The driver lay outstretched on the cobbles.

"Back up and go around it," cried Antares. "If the fools drive a light rig in a storm, they deserve what they get. The looby of a coachman came onto the turnpike too fast."

"'Twas not his fault. 'Twas a runaway," the coachman called down, fighting to hold the skitterish coach horses.

"'Tis no matter of mine," growled Antares. "Let's be out of here. Back up, you tom-doodle."

Richard's eyes darted swiftly around. He knew where he was. The tall steeple of St. Giles-in-the-Fields Church lay just to his left. The turnpike was deserted except for the overturned carriage, and it was nearly dark. Richard cautiously put his hand on the coach door. Antares was busy ordering the coachman to back up. Slowly Richard's door gave way. Just as it opened, the leather creaked and Antares swung about, his eyes narrowed and suspicious. Richard didn't wait. Before Antares could get to him, Richard attacked, diving for the man's legs. Antares fell back onto the seat of the coach, falling under the fury of the boy's rush, the arm that held the knife flung wide, and the knife point buried itself harmlessly in the seat cushions. Richard jumped to his feet and leaped out the door just as the coach began to back up. He fell heavily to the cobblestones, rolling with the fall. Antares recovered and was after him. Jumping out of the coach, he stumbled to his feet seconds after Richard was up and running.

Richard sprinted, pounding into the maze of crooked narrow streets. The rain blinded him as he ran, and always behind, he heard the running footsteps of Antares the Red. Once he ducked into a dim alley and waited, his heart thudding; he listened, but there was no sound. After a time he came cautiously out into the street and leaned against a doorpost, inches away from a candle-lit window. Suddenly, and with no warning, a knife whistled through the air. Richard jumped aside as it thudded into the doorpost. Panicked, he ran deeper and deeper into the maze of courts, alleys and streets. He was lost, but he kept running until he sighted a party of the watch standing in the middle of one of the wider streets. Richard felt safer. Antares was a bold man, but not bold enough to kill him in the presence of the watch. Richard wasn't sure whether the storm had been a blessing or a curse; though there'd been no crowds for him to lose himself in, he'd had a free course in his run from Antares.

He limped up to the watch, gasping for breath. "Can you tell me the way to Leicester Fields or Drury Lane?" he asked. "Which is closer?"

A tall severe-looking man looked down at him. "What do ye be wantin' with Leicester Fields or Drury Lane?" he demanded. "That's where the quality are. Ye'd best be gettin' off the streets with all the stormin'. There'll be footpads out soon and 'tis a fine night for highwaymen."

"But I want to find William Hogarth or David Garrick, sir."

"To have your likeness painted, I suppose, or to act the part of Julius Caesar?" the man mocked. "Well, Drury Lane is but a few turnin's to the east from here, and ye'll find the great Garrick there now. We just saw his carriage go by. He'll not stir out in a rain. If ye'd walked south, ye'd 'ave found Leicester Fields, but Drury Lane is closer. Take your choice."

"Thank you." Richard turned quickly. There was no one in sight. He made up his mind. He'd go to David Garrick at Drury Lane and tell him everything. Garrick knew the Earl of Burlington, and the Earl must know King George. If anyone could help, they could. Richard looked back nervously and set off at a weary trot for Drury Lane.

It was completely dark by the time he reached the celebrated theater. David Garrick's carriage waited in the street under a flickering oil lamp, and Richard recognized it at once by its elegant gold trim and mulberry color. Quickly he climbed the steps of the theater and pushed open one of the large doors and stepped inside. The Drury Lane theater was very grand, and so were the liveried footmen holding seats for their masters. Richard came forward and stood for a moment, to get his bearings. He stared up at the three-tiered auditorium, the two tiers of boxes gleaming with gold and velvet, and the gallery at the top. Then he walked down the aisle into the pit, a place of backless benches covered with green cloth. It was too early yet for the play to start, but David Garrick must be there somewhere.

Richard marveled at the stage. Surrounded by candles in sconces, it was brighter than day. Suddenly an imperious voice hailed him from the wings, "What in the name of Bacchus do you want here, boy? You wear no livery and I doubt if you come to hold a seat. The performance is not to begin until 6 o'clock. Get out of here right now," and David Garrick, resplendent in a yellow satin suit, strode out onto the stage glowering and gesturing.

"Please, sir," Richard cried out. "I have to talk to you. May I speak to you privately?"

Garrick walked daintily over and peered down at him. "'Pon my word," he drawled, "'tis that wretch of a boy I saw at Chiswick House, the boy from the Colonies who has no manners at all. The brat haunts me, it seems. And what do you want here? I'm busy, too busy to talk to you now."

Richard shook his head. "May I speak to you privately? It's a matter of life or death, sir," he said, and coming closer, spoke softly. "It's my life, sir, and the King's life, too, maybe. The Jacobites are going to take London very soon."

"The King's life!" exclaimed Garrick laughing. "This is an excellent first speech for my next adaptation of Shakespeare. Your life and King George's life!"

"But it's true," Richard protested, "Prince Charles Edward and Alexander Murray are going to take London on the tenth of this month. Samuel Johnson believed me when I told him."

Garrick's jaw dropped and he bent on one knee to stare at Richard's face. "Of course," he said quietly and soberly, dropping his actor's manner. "I saw you there at Samuel's too, didn't I? And it was your visit to Samuel that put him in that foul melancholy. He's been more impossible than ever. So that's what you had to say to him. No wonder Samuel's so black these days, loyal as he is to the House of Stuart and aware as he is of Alexander Murray's wildness. Get up here, boy, and tell me. No one will hear us here. I half believe you already. Give me your hand."

Richard clambered up on the stage, half-pulled by the great actor, whose strong hands surprised him.

"Now tell me all," commanded Garrick, his eyes brilliant and piercing. He sat beside the boy in the circle of candles. The footmen stared at such an oddly assorted pair. Richard told him as quickly as he could what he knew of the plan of the Society of the Stars and of the participation of the Stuarts and the kings of France, Sweden and Prussia.

David Garrick's expressive eyebrows gathered into a deeper

David Garrick, resplendent in a yellow satin suit, strode out on the stage glowering and gesturing.

and deeper frown as Richard's story went on. When the boy had finished at last, Garrick whistled softly. "I do believe you, lad," he said, "and I'll take you to the Duke of Newcastle. He will be entertaining his brother, Henry Pelham, First Lord of the Treasury, tonight at chess. It is the Duke's custom to do this once a week."

"You know them? You could get in to see them?" Richard asked.

Garrick's smile was charming. "I am welcome anywhere in London," he stated. "There is no great house that bars its doors to me. They'll let me in, never fear, but I doubt if the footmen would admit you," and here Garrick pointed his finger at Richard's clothing.

Richard looked down at himself. He was a sorry mess. His breeches were torn and muddy, his knee buckles were missing and his stockings were dirty and pushed down about his ankles. His wool waistcoat and coat had shrunk in the water, and his sleeves stopped inches above his wrists.

Garrick arose gracefully. "Get to your feet, Richard Larkin. Crisis of state or no crisis, plot or no plot, you can't appear before the Pelhams looking like that. Can you dress in my carriage? My driver will be ready now. I'd planned to join my wife at the Earl of Burlington's town house, but she will have to wait, it seems."

"I guess I could," Richard wondered what Garrick was up to. The actor circled around him quickly and hastened off into the wings, his shiny yellow coattails flying.

He was back almost at once, carrying a splendid pale gray velvet coat with steel cut buttons and matching breeches. An azure waistcoat was over one arm and the other bore a white lawn shirt with ruffled wrists, a lace neckband and a pair of white silk stockings. "These are from my players' wardrobe.

They should fit a lad your size." He dumped them all into Richard's arms and sighed. "You'll have to wear your own shoes, though. I'm not sure I can fit you out there."

Richard protested as Garrick led the way down the steps. The suit was much too elegant, he thought. But Garrick would have none of it and insisted the moment that they were in the carriage that Richard put it on. "Now," ordered Garrick, "throw those rags out the window."

"They're all I have," Richard cried as the actor stooped and sent Richard's old breeches flying out into the stormy night.

"If the Duke believes you and I warrant you he will, you'll never need for these wretched things again," Garrick said, calmly tossing out Richard's coat, waistcoat and shirt. "And if he needs persuading, I'll persuade him, never fear, my lad. You are fortunate that David Garrick arrived early to check that faulty wire and those pulleys that failed at last night's performance. I have the ear of the Pelham brothers. Now hurry and finish dressing. The street where the Duke lives is not far."

Richard threw on the clothes Garrick had given him while the carriage jolted down a narrow street and around a sharp corner. I've never been so tired or so hungry in all of my life, Richard thought. I can barely keep going and here I am in an elegant carriage going to see two of the greatest men in England, and I don't even own the clothes on my own back. All I have in the world is what's in this leather purse, inside David Garrick's borrowed shirt, and by now I may have lost Betsy and Abby, too. The whole world ought to be in Bedlam. They're all loonies and I'm the biggest one of all.

Richard had barely finished fixing the lace neckband when the carriage pulled up smoothly before a tall brick house with the usual white door and black ironwork. Here again, a fine carriage with a coat of arms on the door waited outside. "The First Lord of the Treasury is here," said Garrick with great satisfaction. "Just as I said he would be. Hop out, boy, and make it up to the steps as fast as you can. Damn! Why didn't I have the good sense to remember to get cloaks from the wardrobe? Rain can be ruinous to velvet and satin." Garrick looked down ruefully at his elegant yellow suit. It made him look like a sprightly yellow bird. "Well, I didn't think of it and I have already spotted my satin leaving the theater. There's no help for it," Garrick sighed, and nimbly flung open the carriage door, leaped down, and fled to the sanctuary of the Duke of Newcastle's doorway. He was pounding with the knocker before Richard was halfway up the steps.

A tall footman in blue livery opened the door and stood eyeing David Garrick with disdain. Garrick reached into his pockets and put a golden guinea into the man's outstretched hand. The footman stood aside, bowing and smiling, while Garrick and Richard stepped indoors.

"Tell his Grace that David Garrick is calling on a matter of the greatest urgency and importance and begs for an immediate interview with him and the First Lord of the Treasury," Garrick ordered.

The servant bowed once more and hurried importantly down a black and white tiled hall, throwing open double doors at one side. Garrick looked critically at Richard's attire and began fussing with the neckband and the lace, pulling at the azure waistcoat and telling Richard to shake down the ruffles at his wrist. "You'll do," he said without enthusiasm. "Gray is not your color though. I should have put you all in azure, but the fit of the coat is not bad. Look at yourself in the glass and see what you think."

The Duke of Newcastle's hall was lined with gold and silver framed mirrors that reflected white marble busts of Roman statesmen and emperors. Richard walked over and stood in front of a full-length glass, a marble bust on each side of him. He gasped at what he saw. The gray velvet suit fit him beautifully. There was not a wrinkle or ill-fitting spot. Richard shrugged his shoulders and shot out his arms; even his sleeves were the proper length. Only his scuffed muddy shoes betrayed the image of a man of fashion. At least I'm not a complete popinjay, Richard thought. He turned to speak to David Garrick about the suit, but Garrick was smiling and pointed behind him. Richard swung about to face two elderly men who had come quietly out into the hall.

They were obviously brothers and were close to the same age. Both had heavy faces, tired eyes beneath slanting gray brows, firm sad mouths, pink complexions and full-length powdered wigs. One of them was dressed in black satin with diamond buttons and white silk stockings, and the other wore violet velvet with a purple and silver thread waistcoat.

The man in violet pulled at his ear and smiled at Garrick. "Well, Davy, what brings you to honor my house this thundering night? And who, sirrah, is this handsome young coxcomb, who preens himself before my mirror? He's too old to be a new Cupid at the Drury Lane. Is he another of your actors newly come from Ireland?"

Garrick bowed with great elegance to both gentlemen and spoke to the man in violet. "Your Grace, allow me to present Richard Larkin from the American Colonies. He has news of great importance for you and the First Lord of the Treasury."

The Duke of Newcastle raised his eyebrows in fright and whipped out a handkerchief clapping it over his nose. "From the Colonies?" he snorted through it. "Does he bring any strange fevers with him?"

Garrick looked at Richard warningly and Richard bowed, imitating the actor as well as he could. "No, your Grace," he said. "I have been inoculated against smallpox. And I don't preen myself, really. I've never had such fine clothes before. Master Garrick loaned them to me."

The Duke of Newcastle sniffed into his handkerchief. "Come now, this is highly irregular, Garrick? What has this lad to do with the Pelhams?"

"Take us into your closet, your Grace, and permit the boy to tell you. It is of the gravest importance, believe me."

Newcastle coughed delicately. "You have always diverted me on the stage, Davy, but tonight I am in no great humor for amusement. I do not like this storm. I believe it releases dangerous vapors."

"You will not be amused, I guarantee you," stated Garrick almost angrily. Richard was impressed to see how easily he treated such great lords.

The younger brother, Henry Pelham, came slowly forward, his mournful eyes intent on Richard. He turned to his brother. "It will not delay our chess game long," he said. "Let us hear the boy. He has a good face, and I believe he is intelligent." He turned about and led the way back to the double doors.

Garrick took Richard's arm and whispered in his ear. "Listen to me, Larkin. Henry Pelham is partial to boys who stand up straight and tell the truth. He has no sons of his own left to him. He lost both of his boys in one year to a throat malady. He will treat you fairly. Address yourself largely to him. And tell your story just as you told it to me and call them 'my lords.' "

Richard nodded as they went into the room behind the double doors. Henry Pelham carefully closed them himself, shutting out the liveried footman.

"This is a secret matter?" the First Lord of the Treasury asked Garrick and Richard with a faint smile. "Won't you and the boy be seated?"

Garrick motioned for Richard to find himself a chair and Richard looked about hastily for something more substantial than the spindly gold and velvet chairs he'd seen in Vega's salon. Although the blue and gray room of the Duke of Newcastle was as ornate as Vega's, it contained more practical furniture. Blue armchairs had been placed about the room. Two were set on each side of a small table where an ivory and ebony chess set lay. Henry Pelham and the Duke of Newcastle seated themselves at the table and Richard sat down nearby. Garrick, perched canarylike on the arm of a fourth chair. The three men looked expectantly at Richard. The Duke of Newcastle peered over his handkerchief.

"Pray tell us now, boy," he urged in a high muffled voice.

"My lords, there is a Jacobite plot, set for November tenth, to kidnap or kill King George," stated Richard. "The chief people in this plot are Prince Charles Edward Stuart, the kings of France, Sweden, and Prussia, and in this country Lady Primrose, Alastair Ruadh Macdonnell and Alexander Murray, who was killed in a duel with Macdonnell last night in France."

The Pelham brothers looked significantly at each other, but neither looked as surprised or horrified as Richard had expected. Henry Pelham spoke gently to the boy, "You are well informed, lad. What is your part in this? Continue."

Richard was so shocked that for a moment he was speechless. But he went on, prompted by a sharp cough from Garrick. "I learned about the plot, my lords, when I was a potboy at a London tavern. I overheard the plotters, who called themselves the Society of the Stars, and I saw one of them kill a merchant named Carlton."

Newcastle nodded slightly. "Then you are the potboy at the Seven Stars tavern that the Jacobites were hunting? Where did you go when you ran away?"

Richard was aghast. So they knew this already. Who had told them?

"Go on, boy," squeaked Newcastle.

"I went to Chiswick where I worked for William Hogarth, the painter." Henry Pelham looked disgusted at the mention of Hogarth's name and grunted, "Painter Pug." But Richard went on. "I met your agent, William Craig, there and I know who murdered him."

Now the Duke did seem startled. He leaned forward, taking away his handkerchief. "Who was it?"

"Alastair Ruadh Macdonnell, better known as Antares the Red, your Grace."

Henry Pelham sighed deeply and folded his hands over his stomach. "Go on, please," he echoed.

"I said I'd give Craig the letter I had hidden away, the letter that Macdonnell dropped the night of Carlton's murder, but Craig was killed before I got the chance to give it to him. I worked at Chiswick House, trying to contact another Hanoverian agent that William Craig had said might be there. But Valentine Elliott, the Earl of Burlington's steward, who is a Jacobite, found me out and I was kidnapped and taken to Lady Primrose's house, where I was questioned. Then I was taken to France so the Prince could decide what to do with me. They decided I was a Hanoverian spy as well as witness to the murder, and Alexander Murray wanted to have me killed, but the Prince wouldn't let him do it."

Newcastle giggled. "How tender of Charles Edward Stuart! He is a soft-hearted fool. Very interesting, indeed. But how did you get away?"

Richard was offended at the Duke's manner and at his laughter. The Pelhams certainly acted strangely. "Alastair Ruadh Macdonnell helped me escape, as he wanted his letter so badly. It had great personal value to him, he said. When we arrived in London, I ran away from him and went straight to Master Garrick at the Drury Lane. Macdonnell is still in London, for he has an appointment to keep here, he told me. You probably could find him, my lords."

"Forget Macdonnell, and for your information, we needed no agent at Chiswick House." Henry Pelham said and swung about to face Garrick. "What do you know of this boy?"

"I saw him at the Earl of Burlington's villa at Chiswick," Garrick said, not mentioning Richard's visit to Samuel Johnson.

"Have you spoken of this to anyone else, boy?" Newcastle sniffed.

"Only to Master Garrick and to Betsy Lewes, a kitchen maid at Hogarth's house."

"Does she babble?" asked the Duke angrily.

"No," cried Richard. "I don't even know if she's still alive, my lords. Alexander Murray sent an agent of his called Spica to find Betsy and learn if I told her anything."

"Peter McNeil, no doubt," Henry Pelham said to his brother.

"Yes, of course," agreed the Duke, reaching into a tiny drawer on the side of the chess table, and pulling out a sheet of paper to study it carefully.

"Does anyone else know? It is of the greatest importance to us that no one knows," Henry Pelham's face darkened with concern.

"No," Richard lied, thinking fleetingly of Samuel Johnson. Johnson would never speak of his conversation with Richard.

"Tell us of the duel between Macdonnell and Alexander Murray," commanded the Duke.

"Murray tried to stop Macdonnell from taking me away from St. Omer," Richard explained. "Macdonnell had to kill Murray before Murray killed him and me, my lords, and he wanted his letter badly enough to do this."

"Alexander Murray is wounded and at the point of death but still alive, alas," Henry Pelham said dryly. "We've had word from one of our swiftest couriers earlier this night."

"He was Sirius, the leader of the Society of the Stars, my lords. They may postpone the plot until he's well enough to lead them. He was to raise the Westminster mob."

Henry Pelham shook his head. "Nothing will happen on November tenth. Nothing at all. They will postpone the plot, but not because of Alexander Murray."

The Duke of Newcastle chimed in. "The Society of the Stars is a muddleheaded lot and the members talk too much to boot. Would you like to know more about the plot?" Highly taken with the surprise he'd given the boy, Newcastle continued before Richard could answer. "The Highlands of Scotland are to rise up again once London and the Tower of London have been taken. The men of the Prince's Ogilvy Regiment are to capture St. James's Palace and the royal family. The Jacobites feel that the British army will join them."

Henry Pelham grunted, picking up a pawn from the chess board and setting it down again. "The army and the navy do not like my administration, it seems. I do not favor a large body of troops nor do I think England needs them." He smiled wearily. "For the first time in some years England is on a good financial footing, but I cannot please everyone, no matter how . . ."

"Tell me of Macdonnell," Newcastle interrupted almost rudely. "What of this letter? Did you read it? What did it say?"

Richard was bewildered. The Pelhams knew more of the plot than he did. "I looked at the letter, your Grace. It was signed Alec Guthry and addressed to Grandpapa. There wasn't much to it except that it mentioned a Mr. Kenady and a Miss Philips and November tenth. I think it must have been in code, and Macdonnell was very eager to have it back, so it must have said something important. It wasn't in his handwriting though, and I don't know who the people in the letter are. Their names never came up in anything that the Society of the Stars talked about when I was around."

Henry Pelham barked loudly, and tears ran down his cheeks. To Richard's amazement he realized that the sober First Lord of the Treasury was roaring with laughter. Now the Duke joined him, his high-pitched giggle rising above his brother's mirth. "Did they ever refer to us, my boy?" asked Henry Pelham breathlessly.

"Only once or twice to you, my lord," said Richard nervously. "They spoke of the Duke of Newcastle and his agents several times, but they sometimes called him something else."

Garrick hissed at Richard in warning but under Henry Pelham's amused gaze, Richard went on. "They called the Duke, 'Hubble Bubble.' "

Newcastle was suddenly silent, his handkerchief plastered to his mouth, his forehead reddening above it. The paper shook in his hands, and Henry Pelham howled even more with laughter.

"They'll pay for that!" Newcastle vowed, his voice trembling with rage.

Henry Pelham spoke again, wiping the tears from his eyes.

"I haven't been so entertained in years. Let the boy know who is involved in the conspiracy. He already knows much of what there is to know. First of all, what people in the Society of Stars do you know by name, Richard Larkin?"

Richard looked thoughtfully at Henry Pelham and then spoke slowly. "Sirius is Alexander Murray; Antares is Alastair Ruadh Macdonnell; Vega is Lady Primrose, my lords. The real names for Betelgeuse and Rigel are Seagraves and Goring, but they're still in France. Prince Charles Edward Stuart is Regulus and Spica must be Peter McNeil, as you just told me, but I don't know who Capella and Arcturus are. There are other names, too, that I heard Macdonnell say once, but I have never met them. I think that Mars is Frederick of Prussia, and the Sun is King James. Polaris, who is to go to Scotland to muster the clans for the Prince, is a Doctor Archibald Cameron, and someone called Deneb goes with him."

"Deneb would be MacDonald of Lochgarry. These are the men we want—the last two the boy mentioned. We'll take these two up. They can be trapped." Newcastle leaned across the chess table to speak to his brother.

"Oh, enlighten the boy," said Henry Pelham. "Read from your list."

"Capella is Swymmer, a member of King George's Parliament and a prime traitor, and Arcturus is Alderman Heathcote, one of the most powerful of the London merchants," Newcastle read delicately and with precision. "Mercury is Lord Elibank or Patrick Murray and Alexander Murray's brother, a man who sympathizes with the plot and who is a staunch Jacobite. Altair, Castor and Pollux are Jacobite agents in Prussia, but their names do not concern us here. Aldebaran and Fomalhaut are Englishmen of high degree, but they do not concern us either at the moment. They are not vital members of the Society of the Stars and are even less dangerous than that pack of Barbary apes, who consider trying to take London."

"But the plot!" gasped Richard. "You know all about it, and you just sit here doing nothing! Shouldn't you call out the army, my lords?"

David Garrick burst into a spell of coughing and choking at Richard's words. But the Pelham brothers ignored his interruption.

"The plot will not come to fruition," said Henry Pelham comfortably. "It would not succeed even if the Jacobites tried their November tenth attempt. The conspirators are chapfallen and disheartened and the kings of Sweden, France, and Prussia will not keep their pledges. They only play with the Prince. The people who plot against King George are constantly watched even though they do not suspect it. We know their every move, and we can take them up at any moment. Because we know everything, we need do nothing."

"But William Craig and Carlton were murdered! William Craig saved my life!" Richard exclaimed, ignoring Garrick's warning glances.

"So they were, indeed, my sentimental colonial, but in order to make an omelet, one must break eggs, as the French say," Newcastle crooked an eyebrow at Richard.

"What are you going to do?" cried Richard, forgetting himself and where he was. "They could have murdered Betsy and everyone else in Hogarth's house."

"I doubt if they murdered that wretch of a painter. More's the pity if they didn't, considering those low and vulgar cartoons he does of the King and of our government." The Duke sneezed violently into his handkerchief.

Richard sat silent for a moment. So these gentle-seeming elderly men are the greatest lords in England. It seemed hard to believe. If he understood what the Duke of Newcastle had said, they weren't going to do a thing about the plot or the murderers. These men were no better than the Jacobites. Neither of them is half the man the Prince is. The Prince had been angry when he heard of Carlton's murder; he valued his old companions. The Pelhams don't care a thing about Betsy or Abby or me. They don't even care about William Craig, their own agent. A loud knocking and scuffling at the door broke the silence.

"What in the name of the devil is that?" asked Henry Pelham, getting up from his chair.

"Treason! Treason!" shouted a loud voice outside. The next moment the doors burst open and the footman and a short man in a rain-spattered cloak came tumbling into the room.

"It's Master Hogarth," Richard shouted, leaping out of his chair.

The footman had his hand on Hogarth's collar and held the little man firm. "Shall I eject him, my lord?" he asked the Duke of Newcastle.

"My God, no," said Henry Pelham, speaking for the Duke. "I detest you, sirrah, as much as I know you abominate me, but I'd just as soon not have one of your vile cartoons about the Pelhams all over London tomorrow. Furthermore, our meeting here concerns you somewhat. Footman, release this man and go back to your post. If my brother's other caller arrives early, take him to the Red Room but do not show him in here."

William Hogarth was angry and wet and resembled nothing so much as his little dog Trump. He shook himself and rearranged his clothing. He glared at the Pelhams and David Garrick and then bared his teeth at Richard. "There's that wretched lying boy," he bellowed. "He involved my household in a murder and with the magistrate in Chiswick. He used my home as a refuge for himself, a spy, and he enlisted my silly jill-flirt of a kitchen girl as an accomplice. He has even hidden the letter of a Jacobite plotter in my grounds somewhere, not that the girl or I know where it is. I'll have you transported back to your Colonies, my boy. I know everything about you."

"Betsy!" cried Richard. "Is Betsy all right? How are Abby and Matt?"

"Betsy Lewes is at my house in Leicester Fields and so are Abby and Matt!" shouted the painter. "Betsy is as well as can be expected, seeing that she shot and killed a man who broke in on her last night."

"Betsy killed Spica?" asked Richard.

"Ah, I must remove Peter McNeil," said the Duke of Newcastle happily, looking at his list. "Now where did I leave that confounded quill of mine?"

"I was at Windsor working on a portrait," Hogarth hopped up and down in his fury. "I came back to London in this accursed downpour only an hour ago to find the Chiswick magistrate, the girl Betsy Lewes, and the child Abby and my old fool Matt at my Leicester Fields house waiting for me. They had all been there since morning. The Lewes girl had told the magistrate the man was a robber, but he came back to see me to verify her story. I am a prominent man in Chiswick. And now that the magistrate is finally satisfied and gone, Betsy Lewes tells me the wild tale that this boy had fed her. That the Jacobites plan to take London on the tenth of this month! She insisted I come here to save England and this

Larkin boy." Here Hogarth shook his fist at Richard. "And here I find you, Larkin, alive and well, hobnobbing with the Pelhams after deserting me to work for the Earl of Burlington, my mortal enemy. I've been bubbled over and over by you, my lad. There's no plot. You lied to the girl, and you made a fool of me by my coming here."

"It is the truth, William. Calm yourself," said David Garrick, speaking for the first time.

Hogarth looked at them in frank disbelief. The Pelhams smiled. "You really do mean that this is all true?" the painter sounded deflated. "The Lewes girl and Larkin tell the truth?"

"It is true, sirrah," Henry Pelham said calmly. "And there is a letter secreted somewhere about your house, but it will remain where it is and never be found, if you are wise. Now, sit down and keep your silence. We've seen enough tonight of your famous temper. Our business is not with you, but with the boy." He turned quickly to face Richard, and the bewildered painter found a chair and sat down heavily.

"You know too much, lad. We cannot let you be free in London any longer. The Jacobites will be hunting you, if they aren't already seeking you here. They must not take you up again. It would be disastrous to our purposes. Take your choice, boy. Will you go to the Tower of London to be kept as our guest until we can find a suitable ship to send you back to the Colonies? Or must we do away with you and clap you into Bedlam hospital with the madmen where no one will believe you and where we can have you muzzled if the need arises?"

"I have never wanted anything except to go back to the Colonies. I promise I won't say anything." Richard stared hard at the kindly seeming Henry Pelham and asked, "Will the murderers be punished, my lord?"

"Spica is already dead, and Macdonnell shall be dealt with as he deserves," the Duke of Newcastle answered for his brother, with a slight twisted smile.

"That's not enough," Richard cried out. "There's something strange about Macdonnell, my lords. He's more dangerous than all the others put together. He isn't what he pretends to be. Don't forget about the letter he wants. That letter means something. You know who everyone else is, but you don't know who Grandpapa and Mr. Kenady and Miss Philips are."

"Do sit down, Larkin," Henry Pelham quietly commanded. "I am Grandpapa," he said simply, "and the Duke of Newcastle is Mr. Kenady."

Richard could not quite believe his ears. "You are Grandpapa, my lord," he said slowly, "but who is Miss Philips and who is Alec Guthry?"

"Miss Philips is 'Bonnie Prince Charlie,' as the Jacobites call him, and Alec Guthry is a very important agent of ours."

"But why would a Jacobite like Macdonnell want the letter?" Richard asked.

Both of the Pelhams smiled faintly. Finally, after a long silence Newcastle spoke up, "You know enough of our affairs now, Richard Larkin, to be a danger to King George and England. Will you go back to the Colonies or will you lie in the Tower of London forever? Believe me, we have ways of dealing with those who threaten the King and the throne."

"I won't go anywhere until the murderer of William Craig is found and punished," Richard said, folding his arms. "This hasn't been easy for me, my lords. You owe me that much. Macdonnell tried to kill me, too. At least I can avenge Craig, who saved my life at the Seven Stars."

"Young fool," hissed Pelham, "you don't know how deep

the game is, do you? Take a bag of gold from us and go home to your backward Colonies. I'll not make the offer again. And inasmuch as you don't know what is happening, what has happened and what could happen if news of this latest Jacobite plot leaked out in England, I'll tell you now. We have sources of information that must not be betrayed. The Jacobite attempts may not yet be at an end, and we must keep these informants secret, but there are reasons even more significant. I spoke to you before of the firmness of the financial position of England. Whether you know it or not England's finances were profoundly shaken by the Jacobite uprising of 1745, and I cannot permit this to happen again. It could ruin England if there were a panic. And as everyone knows, we are once more on the verge of war with France. Last year I consolidated many of the debts owed by the government to its various lenders at a lower rate of interest. These so-called Consols have been selling very well and have put our finances on a very good base. I will have nothing disturb that. If it means permitting a murderer to go free, I will permit it. If it means hiding treason, I will hide it. I will permit nothing to interfere. William Craig knew very well the dangers he ran."

Richard's face blanched. Politics which could use murder and treason as its instruments were completely beyond his understanding. It was impossible for him to believe that Henry Pelham put the success of his financial scheme before the death of William Craig.

Richard began to protest again but David Garrick cut him off, "My boy, have you ever seen a riot or a panic? Have you ever seen the mobs rise? London would be steeped in blood, I tell you. I saw the Westminster mob rise for Alexander Murray. It was a terrible thing, believe me. A mob is like a wild beast."

The Pelham brothers nodded agreement. William Hogarth turned to Richard, "Well, what are you going to do, Larkin?" he asked.

"Will you pay for three passages to the Colonies?" Richard eyed the Duke of Newcastle.

"For whom?" the Duke snapped suspiciously.

"For Betsy Lewes and for Abby, who is only three years old, my lords."

"It would be a wise move to ship the Lewes wench away, too," said Newcastle thoughtfully to his brother. "She knows too much."

"Agreed, then," was Henry Pelham's comment. "We'll arrange three passages on the first ship that goes to Philadelphia and in the meantime Larkin and the Lewes girl will be lodged in the Tower. Not as prisoners, but, let us say, as guests of the King. And a bag of gold will go with them to guarantee their silence. It will be sent to you as you embark and leave England forever. You are fortunate, boy," he said. "You could have come off far worse than this in these great matters."

The Duke of Newcastle removed his handkerchief and looked full face at Richard. "You will never speak of this, lad, if you want no harm to come to Jeremy Belcher and your friends at the Seven Stars. Ah, yes, we know all about them and their Jacobite leanings, but we shall not pick them up unless you babble. For that matter, Master Garrick and Master Hogarth here could incur our displeasure if you ever spoke of the Society of the Stars again."

"I won't say anything," said Richard angrily, noticing how Garrick and Hogarth stiffened at the Duke's words.

"Well said," stated Newcastle, "now I need not tell Master Hogarth and Master Garrick to keep their tongues from wagging. They are wise enough men to know that, without being ordered to do so." The Duke swung about to stare at a tall clock over his shoulder. "Now I shall bid you all good night. I have another caller to see yet."

Richard, Hogarth and Garrick rose, bowed deeply and went out through the door and into the long hallway. As the double doors closed behind them, another door opened at the other end of the hall. Richard looked up and to his amazement Antares the Red, elegant in a sea-green brocade suit and gold-flowered waistcoat, stepped out into the hall. For a second he gaped at Richard, then he regained his composure and walked toward them.

"So this is your appointment?" Richard asked furiously, as everything suddenly became clear to him. "You spy for both sides! You're Alec Guthry, as well as Alastair Macdonnell, aren't you? You disguised your handwriting to write that letter. You were going to send it to the Duke of Newcastle."

"Aye, you have the right of it," was the lofty and unconcerned reply.

"If you're a Hanoverian spy, why did you kill their agent at Chiswick?" Richard cried out.

"We were competitors for Pelham gold," Antares grinned. "I could not let him get ahead of me. I had better uses for King George's pay. But it is no large matter. The man was old and had lived his life."

"Well, you failed to kill Alexander Murray!" Richard shouted at the blond man as Hogarth and Garrick stood speechless.

"Ah, now that is sad news," agreed Antares, shaking his fair head slightly. "Macdonnell must try again, it seems. I am truly sorry."

"Murray will tell the Prince all about you. I think he

knows you're a traitor to your Prince—and to everyone else."

Antares bowed ceremoniously to Hogarth and Garrick. "The Prince will not believe Alexander Murray, and he will welcome me back with open arms to serve the Jacobite cause. The boy judges me too harshly, good sirs. I may be called a traitor to many, but I am ever true to myself, Antares the Red." He moved elegantly toward the double doors.

Richard jumped in front of him. "Those dragoons on the clifftop this morning! They were sent by the Duke to see that you got here safely, weren't they? That's why they didn't bother us and that's why you weren't worried about them. You expected them."

Antares bared his teeth in a snarl, "Aye, that's true, devil's brat. Now get out of my way," and he hit Richard a backhand blow that sent him sprawling against one of the Duke's mirrors. Then he opened the doors and disappeared inside.

Richard was heartsick. It was plain now how the Pelham brothers had known everything that occurred among the supporters of the Prince. Antares was the source of information they chose to keep secret. And it was clear, too, why Antares wanted the missing letter. He was Alec Guthry. It was vital to him that no loyal Jacobite found that letter and connected it with Antares, who in so many words offered to deliver the Prince, or Miss Philips, to the Hanoverians. Richard felt sorry for the Prince, who trusted the traitorous Antares. He walked slowly up to David Garrick. "Next time you see Samuel Johnson, please tell him that I liked Bonnie Prince Charlie better than I liked the Pelham brothers. The Prince wouldn't have wanted murder to go unpunished." Richard hesitated for a moment, then went on, "Could you tell Samuel Johnson too that I really met his Prince and liked him? You wouldn't have to tell him what happened here tonight, for the Pelhams wouldn't allow that. Tell him, that I thank him for what he did for me when I first came to England and that I won't forget him and that I said goodbye."

"I'll tell him," promised Garrick. "He'll be pleased to know that you liked Prince Charles Edward."

"I think that if things had worked out differently I could have followed the Prince too. He's a better man than either of the Pelhams."

David Garrick's face wore an odd, sad smile as he listened.

William Hogarth moved toward the front door and called to them. "Come along now. The Duke's carriage is ready, Larkin, to take you to the Tower of London. I'll bring Betsy there myself. Look at the sky. Let's get away while we can. The storm's over."

And it was true. Richard paused on the top step and looked up at the ebony sky. The air was fresh and pure, and oddly enough there was not a single star to be seen in the heavens.

On the morning of November 12, before most Londoners were awake, a black closed carriage clattered swiftly across the drawbridge of the great grim Tower of London and came to a stop at the docks where the tall ships lay at anchor.

A boy and a girl got down from the carriage and stood for a moment on the wintry docks waiting while a man in blue livery walked briskly toward them. He carried a small leather bag in his hand and this he gave to the boy in the gray velvet suit. The girl in the plain gray dress and old cloak looked away toward the ship and the man turned on his heel and left. They waited until a second carriage came into sight. This time a short man in a bright green coat alighted and held up his arms for a little fairhaired child, wrapped in a coverlet against the cold. He put her down on the street.

The two young people came forward and the girl knelt to embrace the child, lifting her up again, while the man and the boy clasped hands.

"They gave you the bag of gold?" William Hogarth asked. "They kept their promise?"

Richard nodded. "Yes, sir. It's in my pocket, and I've learned enough in London to take good care of it. I want to thank you for everything, and I hope you'll forgive me for all the trouble I caused you."

"Tush, it was nothing," Hogarth declared. "Have you made plans about what you'll do in Pennsylvania? You'll be a rich man there with the Pelham gold."

"I don't know," said Richard. "Maybe I'll go out and farm or maybe I'll go into a trade. I haven't made up my mind. There's one thing I won't do, sir. I won't be a spy."

Hogarth smiled. "The Latin poets will do you little good as a farmer or a merchant, boy. And I doubt if they even aided you as a spy." He fished into his pocket and pulled out a letter, stamped with his seal. "This is a letter to a man I correspond with. He can tell you what would be best for you. I doubt if you'll have trouble finding him in Philadelphia. Now, you'd best get on that ship and leave England. I hope the Colonies will be a happier place for you than England has been. November 10th has come and gone without a murmur. Perhaps England will change some day. There are quite a few of us working for that right now. They say there's hope that the grandson of German George could be a real king. It seems he may turn out to be more Englishman than German."

"I hope so, and thank you, sir, for the letter." Richard turned and touched Betsy's shoulder. "Go down to the women's quarters, Betsy," he said, "and see that you and Abby have a good place for yourselves, then meet me on the deck when we sail. If you don't like your cabin, let me know. I'll get you a better one."

"Yes, Dick. Goodbye, Master Hogarth." Betsy curtsied, smiled sadly at the painter, and headed toward the ship.

"You take good care of Betsy Lewes and Abby," Hogarth commented to Richard. "Have you any plans for them?"

"I'll adopt Abby and she and Betsy can board with some friends of mine in Philadelphia," Richard said, "and when we think it's time and we're old enough, I think I'll marry Betsy if she'll have me. We'll raise Abby ourselves then. Don't worry, sir, we'll all three stick together."

Hogarth laughed. "Goodbye and good luck, then, Richard Larkin. You haven't done so badly in old England after all, have you? Now don't you forget the letter I gave you." He clapped Richard on the back and bounced jauntily into his carriage.

Richard stood watching the painter depart. He'd met some of the greatest men in England, and he'd learned a great deal about how the old world wags. But it was good to be going back to the new world where he belonged. Hogarth's carriage rattled off, and Richard looked down at the painter's letter of introduction. In Hogarth's strong handwriting were the words: For Benjamin Franklin, Esquire, Philadelphia. Richard smiled with surprise and walked toward the ship. Benjamin Franklin! The greatest man in the Colonies. That was a good enough beginning for anyone. He whistled a gay tune, a tune he did not even recognize now—it was the melody he'd heard the Jacobites sing.

O Vanity of youthfull Blood,
So by Misuse to poison Good:
Reason awakes, & views unbarr'd
The sacred Gates he watch'd to guard;

Approaching views the Harpy, Law;
And Poverty with icy Paw

Ready to
That Vice

Invented Painted & Engrav'd by Wm. Hogarth, &

poor Remains | Cold Penitence, lame After-Thought, | Call back his guilty Pleasures dead,
all his Gains. | With Fears, Despair, & Horrors fraught, | Whom he hath wrong'd, & whom betray'd

June ye 25 . 1735. According to Act of Parliament. Plate. 4.

Notes

LONDON

London in mid-eighteenth century was even more crowded, callous, unsanitary, dangerous and licentious than we have pictured it. Murder was commonplace, as were robbery and assault. The prison system was barbaric. Men and women were imprisoned for debt, hanged for stealing a scrap of food and flogged for many trivial offenses. Over two hundred crimes were punishable by death. Gaol fever was common. The hapless prisoners in Newgate, the Fleet or Bridewell usually found their relief only in death. Executions were held in public; it was considered holiday fun for men and women to witness a hanging or a beheading. Mere boys were hanged along with hardened and vicious criminals.

A fashionable pastime of the day was to tour Bedlam, or Bethlehem Hospital, to see the chained and beaten madmen. Brutal sports were popular with many Londoners. Fights were staged between a bear and dogs or between a bull and dogs. Even a match between a badger and dogs was considered good sport.

Women and girls of loose character strolled the city and criminals waited in dark alleys to rob and murder for a few pennies. The roads leading into London were infested with highwaymen, who stopped travelers and coaches.

Sanitation was in its infancy in the eighteenth century. The upper classes were only beginning to consider bathing as the mark of anything but eccentricity. It was considered no social disgrace to have lice. Plumbing was almost unknown. Naturally, disease was rampant. Tuberculosis raged among all classes. Smallpox was still the curse of England in 1752, for the English did not readily adopt the practice of inoculation, although it was known. A woman who had no pock marks on her face, no matter what her features or her figure, would be considered a great beauty for this single reason. The doctors of the day knew little. They relied on bleeding and purging as their chief remedies and thereby killed many of their patients. Infant mortality rates were, by twentieth-century standards, incredibly high. The eighteenth century did not know refrigeration. Tainted milk and meat killed many Englishmen.

The plight of orphans, or parish children, was a scandal. Attempts were made by many public-spirited Londoners (among them William Hogarth) to help these children and stop the terrible mortality among them. Results were not particularly satisfactory, however. In any event, parish children who survived under the system then current could look forward to a miserable life of hard manual work or a wretched existence in a workhouse.

Yet, given all of these horrors, the England of that day was considered something of a model on the continent, where conditions were far worse.

Excellent accounts of eighteenth-century England are to be found in Dorothy Marshall's *English People in the Eighteenth Century* or E. B. Chancellor's *London in the Eighteenth Century*. There are also many good contemporary sources. The novel *Roderick Random*, written by Tobias Smollett and published in 1748, presents an interesting contemporary picture of England by a sharp and satirical critic. Henry Fielding's *Tom Jones* is another good novel of the time. The sentimental *Amelia* by the same author was very popular in eighteenth-century England, and although long and dull to modern readers, it does depict something of the life of a middle-class woman and her family.

CHISWICK

Naturally, in two hundred years Chiswick has changed a great deal. Many rows of newer houses stand now where Richard

Larkin, Abby and Betsy Lewes walked across the open fields. However, many of the fine old seventeenth- and eighteenth-century houses still stand on Chiswick Mall. Chiswick House itself has recently been restored by the government, to bring it as much as possible to what it was in the Earl of Burlington's time.

William Hogarth's house was severely damaged by bombs in World War II, but it has also been restored, and to this day the old mulberry tree bears fruit every summer.

Both Chiswick House and Hogarth House are open to the public for a small maintenance fee today, and in the spring the magnificent grounds of Chiswick House are a lovely sight.

Old St. Nicholas Church has not changed much. Services are held there today just as they were, long before Hogarth's time.

THE SEVEN STARS

The real Seven Stars tavern was demolished long ago; however, some of the older taverns are still preserved in London and elsewhere in England. Just off Fleet Street in Wine Office Court, only a few steps from Gough Square, where Samuel Johnson's house still stands, a hungry and thirsty man can find a restaurant and tavern called the Olde Cheshire Cheese. It is claimed that this inn is well over four hundred years old, and that the great Samuel Johnson was a frequent customer there. We have based Jeremy Belcher's Seven Stars on the Olde Cheshire Cheese.

JACOBITISM AND THE JACOBITES

The Elibank Plot actually existed, and just as the Pelhams predicted, it never did come to fruition. Early in 1753 Doctor Archibald Camron, a Jacobite physician (the Polaris of this book), was caught in Scotland trying to raise the clans. He was brought to London on an old sentence of treason, his participation in the '45, and hanged in the summer of 1753. Modern historians believe that he was really executed to show plotters, like Alexander Murray, that their scheme could not succeed, for Archibald Cameron was the only person who paid for his part in the Elibank Plot. Deneb, or MacDonald of Lochgarry, was never caught by the Hanoverians although he, too, was in Scotland with Archibald Cameron on the same errand to the clans. None of the other conspirators was ever apprehended. As a matter of fact, the existence of the Elibank Plot was kept a state secret for many years. The documents pertaining to it were found in the Windsor Castle archives early in the twentieth century.

After 1752 the Stuarts never again seriously tried to regain the throne of England. Charles Edward Stuart, or "Bonnie Prince Charlie," ended his days in Italy in 1788, a bitter disillusioned old man, who found his only comfort in the wine bottle. In fact, King George III granted a pension to the last Stuart, Charles Edward's younger brother, Henry, Cardinal York. The Stuart brothers left no direct descendants.

Dr. Samuel Johnson was always something of a Jacobite, but he finally mellowed enough to accept a pension from the Hanoverian King of Great Britain.

Alexander Murray (our Sirius) lived until 1777, always involved in one European conspiracy or another, The account of the duel between him and Antares is purely fictional.

Nothing more is known of Lady Primrose (Vega), Alderman Heathcote (Arcturus), or Mr. Swymmer (our Capella). Henry Goring (the Rigel of our story) finally broke with Bonnie Prince Charlie, and little more is known of Seagraves (our Betelgeuse).

As for Antares, there is still a very great deal of mystery and controversy surrounding him. Most historians believe that Alastair Ruadh Macdonnell did sell the Stuart secrets to the Duke of Newcastle and his brother, Henry Pelham. Certainly, some of Macdonnell's contemporaries suspected him. It is clear that there was a Hanoverian spy in the Prince's confidence, but some say that it was not Macdonnell at all. Alastair Ruadh Macdonnell died, unhonored and unmourned, on his family estates in Scotland in 1761. If the story of the spy, whom we have called Antares, interests you, we recommend Andrew Lang's *Pickle, the Spy*.

The chief authority on Jacobitism and its melancholy history is Sir Charles Petrie, whose latest one-volume edition, *The Jacobite Movement,* covers the subject concisely and without the usual sentimentality.

THE HOUSE OF HANOVER

George II, or "German George," as he was nicknamed, was an extremely unpopular king. Not one of the Hanoverians ever became well liked until Victoria took the throne in mid-nineteenth century, a hundred years after George II. German George was greedy, vulgar, selfish and thoughtless. The charges that he cared nothing for England are probably true. He considered himself first and foremost a Hanoverian German, and thought of his subjects in England as "king-murderers" because Parliament had beheaded the seventeenth-century Stuart king, Charles I. George II despised music, art, poetry and the members of his own family, who reciprocated his dislike. The first two Hanoverian kings barely knew the country they ruled, and the country hated them, rejoicing when George II died in 1760.

(The House of Windsor, the present ruling house of England, is actually Hanoverian. Elizabeth II is a descendant of the Protestant princes who come from Hanover, Germany, 1714.)

The Duke of Cumberland, or "Billy the Butcher," was even more detested than his father, George II. There were constant Jacobite schemes afoot to assassinate him for his vicious and cruel repression of the 1745 uprising, yet the Duke lived until 1765, dying then of natural causes.

THE STUARTS

James III, the "Old Pretender" died in Europe in 1766, but the princes of Europe refused to recognize his son, Prince Charles Edward Stuart, as King Charles of England. The Duke of York, the younger brother of Bonnie Prince Charlie, became a Cardinal in the Roman Catholic Church. This was another mortal blow to Stuart hopes.

Charles Edward had offered himself once as a Protestant to the English people, but by the end of the 1750's the English no longer cared much about him, although the Stuarts have always held a special place in Scottish hearts. Today he is thought of in England, Ireland and particularly in Scotland, as a glamorous and sadly romantic figure, forever young, dashing, charming, handsome and ill-fated.

Many people have written exciting books about the Stuarts. Bonnie Prince Charlie is a character in Sir Walter Scott's *Redgauntlet.* The modern novelist, John Buchan, deals with the '45 in his *Midwinter,* and Samuel Johnson is one of the main characters.

LONDONERS OF RENOWN

In 1755 Samuel Johnson finally published the dictionary which made him famous. For many years he was one of the greatest literary figures in England, and today he remains one of the greatest men England has ever produced. Johnson despised the American Colonists and the Scots, and his pronounced views on many things are amusing and interesting to read about today. His temper was actually as fierce as we have depicted it, and it is true that he roamed the streets of London at night putting pennies in the hands of sleeping homeless children. Too, he was famed for his ugliness and for his strange and terrible periodic melancholy. Several current biographies give a good picture of his life, although James Boswell's classic, *Life of Johnson,* is the best known by far, and most others are drawn from this. Vastly honored and admired, Samuel Johnson died in 1784.

William Hogarth died in 1764, stricken by a fatal illness (which was probably apoplexy). He died while reading a letter from his friend in the American Colonies, Benjamin Franklin. His tomb and that of his family can be seen today in St. Nicholas churchyard in Chiswick. A poem honoring Hogarth and written by David Garrick is inscribed on it. Reproductions of William Hogarth's satirical paintings can be seen in any book dealing with the history of English art, although his "Shrimp Girl" is considered by many to be his finest work, if not one of the finest paintings any English artist has ever produced. If anyone is to learn about eighteenth-century England, he must study Hogarth's paintings and etchings. In this book the two Hogarth prints, "The Times" and "Vanity of Youthful Blood—1735," as well as the decorative spot illustrations are reproduced from original strikes of Hogarth engravings.

It is quite true that the painter and his wife were patrons of the Foundling Hospital and that they took orphans into their houses at Leicester Fields and Chiswick. The parish records at Old St. Nicholas Church testify to this.

Richard Boyle, the Earl of Burlington of our story, died in 1753. A patron of men like the poet Alexander Pope and of the arts in general, he cannot be forgotten. The jewel-like Chiswick House stands as his best monument.

For many years "the great Garrick," who actually was a pupil of Samuel Johnson at Lichfield and who did come to London with Johnson to find his fortune, was the leading actor of the English theater. To this day his name is one that every theater lover knows and reveres. Although David Garrick tampered with Shakespeare and so enraged many people, his great performances at the Drury Lane Theatre remain a part of the theatrical tradition and history. His pretty Italian wife was the ward of the Earl and Countess of Burlington, and for some years they bitterly resisted her marrying the famous actor.

David Garrick died in 1779. His wife survived him many years, dying at Twickenham in 1799.

Henry Pelham, Chancellor of the Exchequer and First Lord of the Treasury, died in 1754. It is true that he did keep the Elibank Plot secret in order not to betray the identity of his informant and, most importantly, to keep his financial scheme of the Consols on a firm basis. Henry Pelham was a wise, tolerant and rather timid man. Historians are in agreement that he was easily one of the most capable men in English political life in the eighteenth century.

Thomas Pelham-Holles, Duke of Newcastle, was the often underestimated head of a vast and remarkable spy system. His peculiar physical mannerisms and his horror of disease made him a laughingstock in his own time. Few realized how far-reaching and clever a politician he actually was. Today historians evaluate him more accurately. The mass of Newcastle papers and documents in the British Museum is supposedly so great that no one wants to try to sort them out, and much information is still to be discovered about the Duke's administration of foreign affairs. The unpopular George II owed much of the security of his throne to the watchfulness and constant machinations of the tireless and efficient Newcastle. The Duke survived his brother, dying in 1768. With his death England lost one of her most able men.

Wherever possible, we have consulted portraits of the characters in *At the Seven Stars*. Naturally men so renowned in their own times as were Samuel Johnson and David Garrick had their portraits painted. William Hogarth actually did paint David Garrick and his wife, and Garrick was displeased with the portrait. Hogarth sometimes painted himself and his family and servants. One of his most famous paintings is of himself and his dog Trump.

There are paintings of Henry Pelham and the Duke of Newcastle, as well as of the Earl of Burlington. As for the Jacobites, Prince Charles Edward Stuart was often painted throughout his life, and there are portraits of both Alexander Murray and Alastair Ruadh Macdonnell.

We would like to acknowledge our debts to the British Museum, the National Portrait Gallery (England), and the National Gallery of Scotland. Credit is also due the American Philosophical Society, whose financial assistance helped support this research.

We have tried to make our historical personages as real as it is possible to make them in every way—in speech, personality, views, action and in their physical appearance in 1752.

John and Patricia Beatty

JOHN AND PATRICIA BEATTY

Both John and Patricia Beatty were born in Portland, Oregon and were graduated from Reed College, Portland.

John Beatty earned his M.A. from Stanford University, and his Ph.D. from the University of Washington. He has taught at Reed College, the University of Washington, and at the University of Delaware. Presently, he and his wife Patricia, and their five-year-old daughter Ann, reside in Riverside, California. He is Associate Professor of History and Humanities at the University of California, Riverside, specializing in 17th and 18th Century History.

The Beattys lived in London in 1959-1960, during which time they collected little-known facts about London and the political ferment of 1752. At the Seven Stars *is the outcome of their combined talents and interests.*

Patricia Beatty, a former teacher of high school English and history, has published two other children's books. John Beatty is the co-author of a college humanities text.